sweet disaster

CERI GRENELLE

BOOK 1 IN THE STUPID AWESOME LOVE SERIES

For the city of my heart.

1

SOPHIE

MOVES INTO A NEW BUILDING. THERE ARE SEXY ASSHOLES.

The first time we argue, I feel alive. I'm sweating, my blood's pumping, and my hair is sticking to my face in the stinking New York City humidity. I don't know what life really is until some asshole starts screaming at me to move my van from *his* spot, because it feels so damn good to yell right back at him.

"Get your U-Haul out of my parking spot!"

This guy's hollering at me from across the street.

"Excuse me?" I call back, convinced he isn't speaking to me. No one ever yells at me. I'm unassuming and introverted. I'm a wallpaper ninja, blending so well people can't even find me to yell at me.

But the guy across the street sees me, clear as day.

"Are you deaf?" he yells with slow and exaggerated articulation. "Get your damn moving van out of my spot."

I'm not the type of person to engage in a verbal fight. I'm quiet—even when someone pisses me off. I roll with the chaotic nature of my beautifully harsh city: a strand of seaweed in the

1

ocean, riding the tides. But after surviving the day from hell, only to be accosted by this bear of a man? I fight back, like I never have before.

"Last time I checked there are no spots assigned to people on this block, or anywhere else in Brooklyn."

"It's an unwritten rule."

I mimic his earlier tone, hitting every consonant and unleashing my New York accent to embellish the attitude. "If you couldn't tell, I'm moving into the building and there's an *actual* written rule that if I double-park the U-Haul, I'll get a ticket."

"That's not my problem, baby." He steps into the street, waiting for a break in traffic to cross. "Find a new spot."

I nearly drop the moving box in outrage before remembering it has wine glasses mom sent from Napa. Breaking them would be a crime. I'll need them before this shit day is over, especially after getting a look at the man charging at me like a bull chasing red.

As he crosses the street I expect to see a guido with a beer gut, and while I imagine he's got a decent percentage of Italian heritage, there sure as hell ain't no beer gut. Instead I'm greeted by a fit and trim physique, tanned skin, and biceps I could drool over. The muscles in his arms tense and roll with every word, every wild gesticulation. He levels with me on the sidewalk and removes his sunglasses, revealing dark eyes flecked with gold. He's shockingly handsome—like runway model handsome—combined with the grittiness of a rock star and the best parts of a native New Yorker. I'm wearing the tank top I slept in last night, a ratty old sports bra, and shorts I haven't washed for two weeks.

This day is the pits.

"Because of your stupid van, I had to circle the surrounding blocks for twenty minutes to find a spot for my pickup truck. A paid, limited-parking, spot."

"How is your poor car choice my fault? Who in their right mind has a pickup truck and lives in Brooklyn? You're just asking for endless nights searching for parking. What do you do when it snows?"

The challenge in his eyes is like a book I have to devour. One flexed bicep, an arched eyebrow, and I'm hooked.

He shoots a disparaging glance at my van before asking, "You're moving into this building?" He points at my new place.

I've propped the outer foyer door open and there are boxes preloaded onto a dolly at the top of the stoop.

"No." I lay the sarcasm on thick. "I've come here to unload this van with the sole purpose of pissing you off. I thought, 'who in all of New York can I make the most miserable today?' " I raise one arm in a fist pump. "I won!"

His eyes widen like he can't believe I'm not backing down, and I might be hallucinating from the heat, but I swear I catch a smile before he starts laying into me again, our voices getting louder and louder.

"I don't care what you're doing; I need this spot for my truck, and you need to move."

"I will move my truck when I'm good and ready."

"You'll move now."

"No."

"No? That's it?"

"That's it?" I repeat, dumbfounded. As if the world revolves around this asshole's giant ego. "I'll tell you what's it. *It's* ninety-eight degrees outside. I had to take a day off work to move because the management company of this stupid new building insists I move one week after signing the lease, much to the dismay of my boss, who was kinda pissed I didn't come in today."

He opens his mouth to speak and I cover it with my hand, unwilling to break my stride. I haven't unloaded like this in years.

"And then the rental company loses my reservation for the van, and proceeds to send me to two consecutive branches 'till I found one that has the size I reserved. *Two branches.*"

His eyes narrow as he crosses his arms, but he doesn't stop me. I'm on a damn roll, releasing pressure built by an awful day, and years of containing my opinion to the written word. I keep my hand on his lips, not because it feels nice or anything, but because I need to get this off my chest and he's the unlucky bastard who's gonna hear it. Not even an introvert of my level can keep it cool after the shit storm of my day.

"The Task Rabbit guys I hired to load the truck were an hour late and on the drive over no less than three cabbies—*three*—cut me off on the bridge, and I'm pretty sure I heard one of my boxes fall over and break as I swerved to get out of the way. And now, to put the icing on a great big turd of a cake, a loudmouth jackass is ordering me to move my van after getting a spot directly in front of my new building. He wants to shit on the one good thing that's happened to me today. You want to know what's *it?*" I'm panting it's so hard to get the last words out.

"That's fucking it."

I've lived in various spots around New York City my entire life but until this moment I've never adhered to the loud-mouthed-I-don't-need-a-filter culture. With this guy and his amber-streaked hair and gold cross around his neck—I let go of all my insecurities and worry over what people will think and just let it fly. Over a parking spot, of all things.

A freakin' parking spot.

When he takes my hand away from his mouth, cradling my wrist with an almost shocking tenderness, making my skin itch, I ask, "Who the fuck do you think you are?"

My yelling draws the attention of passing pedestrians. I think I see a smartphone or two recording us. He sees them too, a frown pulling his features into severity. It transforms his smooth edges into a creature of rougher origins, a true piece of him I find both unnerving and intriguing.

"I think I'm the guy who needs you to move your van, so I can park my pickup truck here, in the only spot on this block that fits it." His voice is low, but there's a definite heat behind it. Whether it's the same annoyed tone from before or something new I can't tell, and after the scene I just made, I don't think I want to know.

He's still holding my hand, swiping his thumb back and forth across my wrist.

"Do you verbally attack every unsuspecting person who parks in *your spot*, or am I just lucky?"

"Baby, you don't know what lucky is, but I'd be more than happy to show you."

That might be a warning or a come on…or both.

I advance on him, my bravado knowing no ends today. "Don't call me baby, asshole."

He matches me step for step. "Till you move out of my spot, I'll call you what I want, *baby*."

I want to kick him, but the way he says baby flashes through my body like a heat wave. A deliciously sexy heat wave.

Actually, I should kick myself to get my good sense back.

His hand is still holding my wrist. I'm starting to think I don't want him to let go.

"Why don't you go cool off with a walk around the block, go pump some iron, take some steroids, or do whatever it is you guido types do."

"You say guido like it's a bad thing. Where are you from that you can cast aspersions on my character?" He laughs when my eyebrows shoot up, casually leaning toward me as if I didn't just spit my entire day up on him.

He finally lets go of my wrist, and I feel the loss of his heat, even in the humid air.

"Guidos know big words too, baby."

God, why does fighting with him feel so good? I should want to smack him, and I do, but having his lips so close to mine makes me want different things. Sinful, sexy, and dirty things.

"You perpetuate that stereotype yourself. You're doing it now, yelling at me like an Italian thug."

His hand clutches his heart. "You wound me, baby. I should take you inside, throw you over my knee and teach you a lesson."

His immodest threat makes me blush, but not because I'm scandalized, but because now I know I kinda want it. And God, he sees it. He sees the shift from anger to lust. He sees my skin flush in color from something other than fury, and he grabs hold.

"You can't tell me to move the van," I say before he can interject with another *baby*.

"I can tell you whatever I want; it's up to you to behave and actually do it."

"Who says I need to behave?"

"The laws of decency."

"You're screaming at an innocent woman like a madman, and you have the balls to call me indecent?"

"I have balls for many different scenarios. I keep them in a velvet-lined drawer and take them out when such occasions arise."

Don't laugh. Don't fucking laugh.

I open my mouth to start another round, but before I can get a word in His Almighty Dickishness turns on a dime and flashes a roguish grin, the asshole gone in a flash. The result is devastating. His body is all fully-grown man, but his smile is whimsical and childlike, more open than what I'm prepared for. I was raised on cynicism and sarcasm. Pure honesty is alarming.

"Listen, the longer we stand here, the hotter and crankier I get. I'm gonna speed this up for us. What floor you movin' into?"

"Why?"

He runs his hands through his hair, seeking an outlet. I know the feeling; I'm as jittery as kid with A.D.D. "I'm gonna help you move so you can get your ugly van out of my way."

His offer, combined with the sudden change in his demeanor, throws me so far off balance I answer without thinking, "Third floor."

"What a coincidence. I'm on the fourth. Welcome to the building. C'mon, baby, show me what you need moved."

"You live here?"

"Yes." He peers into the van, seeing all the boxes and furniture pieces I could cram into it. "Were you gonna move that loveseat by yourself?"

"You live here." I point at my new address, making it obviously clear which building I mean because I need to know absolutely, without any doubt, that the man I've just screamed at, like a an unashamed weirdo, like I'm never gonna see him again, lives one floor above me. "At *this* building."

"Yes. This building." He grins, his teeth accompanied by a sparkle.

It is singularly unfair that a man so annoying can be so profoundly attractive. He's checking all my boxes. Which only makes me angrier.

"I don't need your help." What I don't need is this big gulp of man in my apartment. "I'm stronger than I look."

He sighs, leans against the hated van with his arms in his pockets. Unassuming. Harmless. Ha!

"I'm sorry I yelled at you earlier."

I dip my chin and stare at him with an eyebrow arched in sarcastic doubt.

"Okay, I am sorry I made your day harder. Let me make it up to you. Let me help you move in."

He doesn't wait for me to accept, of course, just turns back to the open van, eyeing it like a mountain to be climbed.

"What do you want moved first?"

He's genuine. He's actually offering to help me, after spending a good twenty minutes making an ass of himself by demanding I move for his benefit. And all of sudden he's helping me, like this is who he was all along. Like I'm not the only one who's had a shit day.

"How about the ones labeled kitchen? That's the best room in my apartment," he chuckles to himself. I figure it must be an inside joke until he proves he's gotta have the single most massive ego in all of Brooklyn. "It's only the best due to my superb cooking. Do you like linguine?"

"Yes," I mumble automatically, unable to deal with the shift in his demeanor. I'm practically out of breath from hollering at him, and my body is on a knife's edge, tempted by this hunk of man, and he's talking about fucking linguine.

"Baby." There's that word again. "You haven't had linguine till you've had my linguine."

Oh, I want his linguine.

Without another word he gathers two boxes, one on each shoulder. He looks like a textbook illustration of an ancient Roman hauling cement blocks to build a great structure.

He catches me staring and winks.

I will not let Lord Linguine show me up. I will prove I can do this by myself, and maybe that will make him go away. I grab a box, then another, and another, balancing them and forcing myself to smile. These boxes weigh nothing. I'm not killing myself in the heat to prove anything. I perform heavy lifting on a regular basis.

"You got—"

"I'm fine," I grunt, hobbling up the steps to the building, the weight of the boxes turning me slower than molasses.

The elevator is out of order—don't cry, don't cry—so it's pointless to use the dolly. We're forced to take the stairs.

"Are you sure?" he asks.

"Stop asking me," I grunt.

Christ, this hurts so much. I'm going to die. My knees will break, and I'll crumble in on myself, forced to listen to Lord Linguine laugh as he steps over me.

My foot catches on the top step, and the boxes start to tumble. Before I can even cry out, he's there, deftly placing his boxes down to help me, making sure I don't fall. One hand on my waist, the other supporting the three boxes.

"Thanks." The adrenaline from the near fall pulses through my veins as I look up at him. We're close, barely a breath apart, and I can't catch my breath. I can't stop looking into his eyes.

Is it possible for a man's gaze to smolder and shine at the same time?

"You're welcome."

He sounds normal, no longer filled with false bravado, almost kind.

"What would my Ma say if I let you land ass up?"

There's the idiot I've come to know.

We make it to the third floor, and I almost collapse when we reach my door.

"Is it unlocked?" Linguine asks, shuffling in front of me.

"Yes."

He slides the door open, sets the boxes in the kitchen where I direct him to, as if they're light as a feather, then comes over and takes all three of my boxes away. He doesn't so much as grimace from the weight, and I hate him more than ever.

"Let's take a break"

"Shut up, there's still more."

I ignore his deep chuckles as we go back to the van.

I don't repeat my earlier folly, but I make him carry the heavier stuff to pay him back for being so smug. He doesn't complain, just lugs another two boxes onto his shoulders and places them where I tell him.

I trail behind him each time we go back down the stairs to the first floor. His back muscles flex with every step, on display through the thin, white tank top. It's a nice view, and I don't stop myself from raking my gaze down his waist to what I can only describe as the most delicious bubble butt ensconced in pants tailor-made for his ass.

He faces me once he hits the sidewalk, a self-satisfied smirk highlighting a mouth and cheekbones I'm slowly starting to obsess over in my head, and I think he knows I've been looking. I don't care. I'm taking full advantage of the view while I can, except when he calls me on it.

"You looking at my ass, baby?"

"No," I say too quickly, cursing my lack of finesse.

"I can feel your eyes on me."

"You're hallucinating." We get to the van, and I'm surprised by how little is left to move.

"Don't worry, I've been looking at yours too."

"You son of a——"

"I've got time for one more trip," he says, his arm brushing mine as he reaches for more boxes.

Electricity shoots through my body. Our eyes meet. He licks his lips. I can't have him in my apartment anymore, filling it up with

CERI GRENELLE

his raw energy and body so beautiful I've come to appreciate it for the work of art it is.

"You can stop right now, I didn't need your help when I started, and I don't need it now."

He ignores me, grabbing another two boxes.

"I said I don't need your—" He grabs two more boxes and runs up to the building, like a puppy stealing a shoe, trying to instigate a play session. Except this is a grown man who I can barely look at without thinking dirty thoughts. "—what a freaking asshole..."

We're in my apartment again, the space getting smaller and smaller with every second I'm near him. We're so close to each other, yet a million miles away.

He sets the boxes by the entrance and runs his fingers through his hair as he straightens from a crouch, his slacks stretched taut over muscular thighs.

His hair looks soft. Does he highlight it to get that color? Beautiful amber streaks piercing through pitch black.

I push my hands through my curly, pixie-length haircut, mussing it up to distract myself. I gnaw at my bottom lip and press down till I feel a pinch, a reminder not to stare at him. It's just so damn hard.

He catches me looking again, and I glance away, coming down from the high of strong emotions and physical exertion. But it's not enough. I feel anxious and incomplete, like I'm missing something.

Like whatever is passing between us isn't over.

"I'd say thank you, but I don't think you helping me makes up for your dickishness earlier." I shrug, unrepentant.

He doesn't move, just keeps looking at me as his hands slowly lower. No other response. My heart beats a little faster when he licks his lips, and wet heat that has nothing to do with summer humidity blooms between my legs.

"You can go now." I don't really want him to go. I want him to stand in the middle of my apartment, so I can stare at him a while longer. The last time I was near a man so beautiful was for an article I wrote on the trials of the male model life. Those guys are paid to be gorgeous, but they've got nothing on Lord Linguine.

He nods, as though he hears and understands, but makes no moves to leave. He just keeps looking at me, and now he's touching his bottom lip with his thumb. Dear Lord, his mouth is sumptuous. No, not just sumptuous. It's fat and thick, made more tantalizing by the way it plumps whenever he bites down.

Who is this guy?

He's been carrying my heaviest boxes up and down the stairs without a drop of perspiration, like some Greek god. I'm sweating worse than a roasted pig and am most likely still flushed and red after our argument—thanks, Irish coloring. My clothes are wrinkled and gross, and I can't recall if I brushed my teeth this morning.

But I know the look he's giving me, like there's nothing in the world he wants more. It should scare me. I don't know him at all, and yet…and yet…that itch in my skin is all from him. One argumentative word from my new neighbor and I've unleashed more personality on the world than in the past five years.

Male desire emanates from his gaze like the sun at high noon; no doubt I'll get burned if I don't protect myself. I would usually feel uncomfortable, wary even, if someone I don't know keeps staring at me like he does, but after spending the last hour with him—feeling his hand on my back when I nearly missed a step on one of our ascents, staring at his ass, watching his muscles tense and roll with every step, watching his lips like my favorite TV show—all I feel is an intense need.

The realization slaps me in the face so hard I nearly take a step back.

I want Lord Linguine. I want his beautiful body covering mine. I want his lips on places that haven't felt the touch of a man in longer than I care to admit. I want him inside me. I want him to use my body till I'm wrung out and this awful day is erased.

But all I say is, "See you around the building."

Again, no response, just staring, with the occasional lip licks or flickers of his gaze. He's looking at my body the same way I'm looking at his. Seeing him want me only makes me want him more.

Proof of his humanity shows as moisture drips down the side of his tanned face, tripping over a thin layer of manicured stubble. Shit, he's beautiful, in a brutal, New York City way. And considering the way he shifts, his tight-fitting trousers stretching taut, a long hard line now highlighted at the front of his pants, I'm pretty sure he's thinking the same thing about me.

I bite my bottom lip deliberately to see what he does. He watches the move then finally speaks. His voice is as far from the riotous nature of our initial encounter as it can get.

"I could stay, help you unpack some stuff."

I nearly prevaricate, but decide to stick to honesty. We both know what's happening here.

"That's not what would happen if you stayed."

"It's your choice. If you don't want me to stay, I'll leave. We'll nod at each other as we pass in the hallway, like this was an unremarkable encounter. We'll go back to being strangers. I don't want that, but I promise I'll leave if you do."

"Oh, now you care what I think?" Stalling. Stalling, I am so stalling.

"I've been hanging on your every word for the past hour, and in no world would I ever want to make a woman uncomfortable, so yeah, I care a whole fucking lot." His body is tense, practically vibrating, yet he stays put. Waiting for me.

"Tell me what you want, baby."

Do I want what he's offering?

"I'll make you feel so good."

Uninhibited sex between strangers?

After the day I've had?

He takes a step forward. We're nearly on top of each other now. My hands itch to touch him. "Say yes."

Fuck yes, I do.

"Yes."

2

SOPHIE

DOES A CRAZY, SEXY, THING. AND IT'S OH, SO GOOD.

The tension snaps and within a hot second, I've got him against the wall in my soon-to-be new bedroom. His lips are on mine for a brief, harsh moment—and they're even more delightful than I could have ever imagined—then he spins and lifts me all in one move. I wrap my legs around his waist, sighing into the sensation of a thick erection rubbing against me through our clothes.

"Door is still open," he grunts. Before I can say I don't care, he sets me down and runs into the main living area to kick the offensive thing closed. I watch as he stalks back to me, intent on what he wants. His intense focus should make me nervous— before today this much attention from a stranger would have— but I revel in it.

Knowing this beast of a man wants me is the greatest aphrodisiac of my short, quiet life.

And the sexiest part of all this is I know I can stop it right here, come to my senses and kick him out, and he'll go. Without a word or complaint. Lord Linguine may have an ego the size of Manhattan, but he asked what I wanted. What I needed. What he can do for me.

I could come to my senses and act ashamed, but there's no reasoning away what I want. I have no sense to return to. He's something other than Lord Linguine now. He's a release. A way to expel the buzzing in my head and stress that comes from living in a crowded, beehive of a city.

He returns to pressing his body along mine, hikes my legs into the exact position they were before, and kisses me. The buzzing melts away entirely, and all that's left is the bliss of his arms holding me up and his lips on mine, his tongue teasing the seam of my mouth.

I moan into him, gripping the darker, slightly wavy hair at his nape. He's Italian—no doubt about it with that white tank top and gold cross—but there's something else there, an ancestry that brings his golden tone to a darker hue. It's sexy and tantalizing and I do everything I can to touch all the bits of skin I can reach. And oh, thank the Lord for iron-pumping, New York Italians because the muscles under his skin are tight and undulating, and I can't stop squeezing them. I'm addicted to the sensation of his arms tensing and flexing as his sexy lips do delectable things to me.

He sets me down on the floor, my legs like jelly. All we've done is kiss, and I'm a mess.

"I'm not sorry I yelled at you," he says, a sexy asshole smirk on his face, confirming my earlier doubts. His eyebrows are thick, and he looks like a bruiser. How can such a trim man have so many muscles? "If I hadn't called you out, I don't think we would have gotten to this point. And it *is* my parking spot." His New York accent is ridiculously thick—spot sounds like *spawt*.

"But I'm gonna try to make it up to you, ya know, since I hurt your feelings."

I want to smack him for the hurt feelings line, but then he sinks to his knees, pulls my shorts and underwear down, and goes to town on my pussy.

Fuck yes, I am here for this.

I push him away briefly to step out of my shorts then unabashedly lift one leg to rest my foot on his shoulder. He groans, mutters how sexy I am, how fucking beautiful my pussy is. He doesn't even complain that I still have my flip-flops on, sandals that have walked the sidewalks of New York City and are probably disgustingly dirty.

But he's dirty too, in his own way.

"I can lick your clit all day."

Oh shit, he's a talker, and it's freaking awesome.

"You're so slippery," he says between sloppy kisses. His tongue dips inside me, and I put my fist in my mouth to keep the neighbors from hearing my screams and calling the cops. "Did you get hot from our fight? Were you this wet before it?"

I can't say a word. My mind is in hurricane mode, tossing thoughts and fantasies around like trash bags blowing in the wind.

He pinches my clit, waking me from my sex-crazed bewilderment. "Tell me."

"Your voice," I moan. When I begin to talk, he pushes his face so far between my legs I can only see his hair. It takes everything I have to keep standing. "Your voice. The second you called me baby, I creamed my underwear. Even though you're an asshole."

The man is sucking on my clit, and I just had to call him an asshole. Who is this new woman I've become in the past hour? I don't know her. Why would she berate someone who is so expertly fucking her clit?

He licks me from cunt to slit before speaking again, the flat of his tongue rubbing deliciously hard, like he's savoring his favorite ice cream. "Does the sound of my voice make you want to argue more?" He delves back in, his tongue doing this weird swirly thing around my nub.

I must look so swollen.

"Yes. Yes. Yes." My fist pounds the wall with each word.

He looks up at me with a stupid smirk. "Do you admit that's my parking spot?"

I actually go to smack him this time, exasperated by his arrogance. He catches my hand and kisses the inside of my wrist. I would call it tender, except he licks from my wrist to my palm, doing the swirly thing to my skin there. There's liquid dripping down my thighs now. He sees it, of course he sees it. He lets my hand go then licks up the long drop, groaning as he goes.

"You taste so good, baby."

I hate endearments like honey and sweetheart and *baby*. They're sexist and demeaning. But this guy could call me his little slut and I would. Not. Fucking. Care. Especially if he keeps licking me like that. *Please, please don't stop doing that crazy thing with your tongue.*

He takes my foot off his wide shoulder, and I fight to hold a whimper of disappointment back. His tongue was so gorgeous, why would he keep it from me? I need it back there. I need him to make me come. I was so close.

"I know what you need, baby, don't worry."

Fuck, did I say that out loud? I think I did. Either that or he reads minds. Or I'm panting so hard for him to fuck me that I'm making it completely obvious what it is I want. He doesn't have to be a mind reader to see how turned on I am, or how much I want him.

He puts his finger against my clit and begins to rub, so lightly and so fast, but it's like he knows exactly what I need, just like he said. He *is* a damn mind reader. The coiling in my womb spins tighter and faster until I'm right there.

"Almost. Almost. Don't stop."

"Gonna stop for a second."

"No, you bastard" His tongue replaces the quick movements of his finger. "Oh, fuck yes, keep doing that. I'm coming, I'm coming."

The coil unwinds then falls off a cliff and explodes. My sex pulses, seeking something to squeeze. He provides it, with two fingers easing into me as the walls of my pussy throb. I whimper and whine as the orgasm comes in waves, subsiding into little beats. I love that part.

"There's nothing more beautiful than feeling a woman come apart." He's stroking my hip with one hand while his fingers remain inside me, looking up at me with something close to awe on his face. "You're beautiful." There's no doubt he believes what he's saying.

This untainted honesty makes my stomach flip. His sincerity is too intense, too raw for what this is. A quick fuck, nothing more. I need to bring us back to basics.

I shove him away and say in no uncertain terms, "Fuck me. Now."

His grin turns devilish, and he pulls me to the floor, laying me on my back. Of all the ways I imagined we would do this—and many, many ways have crossed my mind over the last ten minutes as he's been licking me like a lollipop—this was the last position I thought he'd go for.

He's sitting back on his heels, undoing his belt and zipper. I look away, so wound up inside from such a chaotic day. I went from excitement about moving into my new place, misery at the hot mess the whole process turned out to be, fury at the presumptuous egotism of my new neighbor, then incendiary lust for that same man. All in a matter of hours. No one could blame me for lying on the floor, trying not to stare at the beautiful man crawling over me.

But…why shouldn't I look?

He is the outlet to let those churning emotions go, to take my release with someone who won't expect anything from me tomorrow. And yet, the two different people he's presented throw me off balance. It's a dichotomy: the guido top half and the put-together businessman on bottom. He's even wearing dress shoes. What would this whole thing have looked like if he'd been in a suit top to bottom?

Oh Christ, I don't know if I would have lasted even five seconds.

He's right on top of me now, but I can't feel his length against me. I hope that's not a bad sign.

"Hey," he says gently, grasping my chin and turning me to face him, his eyes practically glowing in the low light of my apartment, the sunset covering our city in an amber radiance. "You with me?"

This concern isn't how rough and ready one-night stands are supposed to go. Time to move things along.

I wrap my leg around his waist and pull him flat against me.

"What are you waiting for?"

"For you. We can stop if you want."

He's gritting his teeth when he says it—he'd probably have blue balls for a year if we did.

"I don't want to stop. This is what I want."

I grab him by the hair and kiss him, trying to get him to focus on sex and not concern himself with me. I make the kiss rough, biting and snapping at each other. It's a kiss crafted to drain the blood from his brain and make him think with his dick, a kiss for taking over. But he doesn't let me.

He cradles my face and slows the furious pace, sipping at my lips and sweeping me up in the moment, brushing gentle fingers through my hair. It's so—so…fuck, I love it. It might be the best kiss I've ever had. I wrap my arms around him, holding on tight as he sucks on my tongue and rubs his thumb back and forth against my cheek.

This man would never let me look away, and the thought is radical and terrifying.

"Come inside me," I say as he pulls away.

"There you are, baby." He kisses the corner of my mouth before working on his pants again.

"I'm not your baby." I've got to argue with him on principle now.

His cock pops out, and I can't help my eyes going wide. It's…it's big. I think it's bigger than anything I've taken before…and really, really thick. He could split me in two. I look up, and the playful smiles are gone. The plush lips are pursed in a tight line, and his brow crinkles with what I can only identify as anxiety, contradicting his kind confidence of a moment ago.

Where's the smarmy asshole I've grown to hate-lust after so quickly? He's waiting for me to say something, make a disparaging comment about the size and how there's no way in hell I'd get that massive thing inside me. This is a problem for him. I don't like this unsure, worried look. I don't like thinking of women in his past giving him shit for something he was born with.

Something beautiful, that's a part of him. Something I am going to get inside me even if it takes all night.

I wrap my hand around the shaft, my fingers barely long enough to circle his girth. He grunts and rests his head against my shoulder as I spread the liquid at his slit along the delicious length of him.

"I need you inside me. Condom?"

He nods, relief and anticipation painting his expression. "I got you."

He pulls a condom wrapper from his pocket, and I *have* to tease him for it.

"You just keep those things handy? Fuck a lot of random women? I bet the grannies in this neighborhood are primed for the taking. A stud like you would do real well with that crowd."

He grins, not the smarmy smirk from before, but something that tells me he's having fun. A lot of fun. Should I be surprised that I am too?

"Never know when a stunning woman I can't keep my hands off of is gonna park in my spot. Gotta be ready."

I kick him in the chest a little, not hard enough to hurt but with enough force that it pushes him on his ass. His eyes light with the fire from our earlier fight.

"You gonna stare at me till I come again? You started this, now finish it." I lay back, opening my legs wide for him to come between them. "Fuck me."

I embrace him with my thighs and watch as he rolls the condom on. It's mesmerizing, seeing a condom stretch over the fattest cock I've ever seen. I'm worried it will snap and hurt something. He does it slow, like he knows it's driving me crazy. I smack his arm, restless and pissed, knowing he's making me wait.

Maybe I should apologize for all the brutish ways I've treated him, but he groans the instant my hand meets his skin and pushes my legs wider. I grin up at him and bite my lip. He watches the movement, the veins in his neck popping and his face turning red. There's nothing better than watching intense, physical responses on a man brought on by his lust for me. This is the best kind of sex. We didn't have to chat over a few drinks, talk about the same things I talk about on every new first date. We saw each other and formed a kinship over equal parts frustration, anger, and exhaustion, and fuck, it is so good and full of release. My body is still vibrating from the aftershocks of one orgasm and from the delicious thought of orgasms I haven't had yet.

He supports one of my legs with a hand under my knee and grips my waist with the other. I clutch the wrist he has at my waist, squeezing, both scared and excited at the thought of having him inside me. It's a good scared, one that gets my adrenaline pumping and makes my cunt so slippery I feel the liquid with every shift of my legs or tensing of my muscles.

His cock is at my entrance. He pushes lightly, looking down at our joining with such penetrating concentration it feels like he's treating this moment as the most important thing he'll ever do.

"I got you," he says again, but this time his voice is threadbare. The arrogance from a moment ago gone.

"Give me more, then."

He does, and it's slow—which is okay because the whale-like size of his cock burns—and he takes his time, never looking away from the spot. He moves in fits and starts, pressing further inside me with teeny thrusts, stretching me.

Once he's in to the hilt, he lets my leg go and comes down over me, our clothed chests meeting. I'm so full I think I might burst from the pleasure and pain. It takes a while to adjust to his size, but I can feel him rub against my clit as he shifts position slightly, adjusting his hips to get a better angle. Little fireworks go off in my pussy, making me jerk and shiver every time his movements hit the right place.

I can't hold the moan back. I clench the sides of his neck. It's thick, probably grew strong from holding up that big ego of his.

His parking spot, what a jerk.

A jerk I've lost my mind over after meeting an hour ago.

He doesn't move yet. He frames my face, his forearms supporting his body on the floor. We watch each other. My mouth is open, breathing hard to keep up with the pace of things despite our bodies remaining stationary. He smiles, and it churns my gut, makes me nauseous, and adds to the one ulcer I've already got. Then he kisses me. His stubble itches, but at the same time his jaw feels smooth and perfect against my skin.

The kiss is beautiful. It's slow and sweet, and his lips are so full I could bite down on them like gripping a pillow. So, I do it. I bite his bottom lip. Hard.

He growls at me. *Growls.* I feel a new gush of liquid between my thighs, and his response is to just let go. Finally.

His hips begin to roll. He's not shoving inside me like a battering ram—he's dancing with me, grinding and swaying and moving my hips to his rhythm. I'm panting from the joyful hedonism of it. Then he starts talking, and I lose my fucking mind.

26

"You were kind of a bitch earlier." The words are harsh, but I am grinning through the whole litany of insults he unleashes on me. I'm just as mean to him.

"And you *are* an asshole. You arrogant piece of shit—ah!" He rubs my clit. When did he move his hand?

He knows I like it, keeps rubbing me and fucking me and talking at me. It's the best sex I've ever had. "You just need my big cock, don't you, baby?"

I crawl my hands up into his dark curls again and tug so hard he yells in pain.

"Shut your mouth and just fuck me already."

Don't know why I say it, but I'm sure as shit glad I do.

He really starts to move now. No more sensual rolls of his hips, now he's thrusting. We're sliding along the hardwood floor with each shove.

"Your pussy is so tight." He bites my shoulder, grunting every time his cock pushes into me, stretches me. "But you're taking me." He sounds like he can't believe it. "You okay?" he asks without stopping the maddening force of his undulation.

I want to laugh, but I'm in such a state of twisted-up mess that I can't. It's too good to laugh at, too painful and too euphoric. "Don't stop," is all I can say.

He doesn't. But he does switch up the angle a bit, and his pace picks up. His face is all concentration; he's biting his bottom lip alongside dents from my own teeth marks.

He's getting close, and so am I. I lick the column of his gloriously corded neck and grip his massive shoulders. His body is formidable, how would he even get the damn limbs into a suit jacket? I can't imagine it. He'd look like a 1940s gangster playing at sophistication.

27

We're both crooning and grunting, so loud, and I don't care. I would scream his name if I knew it, and that thought does make me laugh. I move to a new apartment, and I've become a completely different woman. I like this new person; she's daring and grabs at opportunities when they present themselves. Sexy opportunities. I want to be her all the time.

With this man—this stranger who thinks he owns a public parking spot. I am her.

"You think this is funny?" His hips are meeting mine in a rhythmic drumming, and the sound is loud as a slap. "What about this is funny, baby?" He's playing, so I play with him, telling him what I'm thinking.

"I don't know your name."

His eyes widen, the thought clearly never crossing his mind. He obviously doesn't know my name. Who needs names when there are bodies in need of fucking? Then he grins, and I know I'm gonna take issue with what he says next, when puts his lips against mine and says, "Call me Lord and Master."

I punch his shoulder, and when I go to do it again, he catches both my hands and puts them over my head. I struggle, trying to kick him, but the shifting embeds his prick even deeper in me. He holds my wrists in one meaty hand and brings his free hand down to my clit. He rubs at it lightly but quickly, using the pads of two fingers, just as his thrusting continues.

"Fighting with you makes me hotter. I need to come—I'm gonna come—but I want you with me. What do you need? Tell me how to make you come."

"Keep doing that to my clit." I shift my hips slightly, getting his cock's movement inside me where I need it. "There. Fuck me there. Oh, fuck, right there, right there. Right there. Right there."

I come, and there's no doubt in my mind the neighbors will call emergency services once they hear me screaming.

"Oh shit, you're squeezing me. I'm with you."

He kisses me, swallowing my crazy loud moans. But I also think he does it to hide his voice. He's grunting so hard into me, his hips shuddering with each burst of cum filling the condom. He slows down until his hips are pressing so hard against me, like he can't separate from my body without losing himself.

We lie there for a long while, his face in my neck, my hands stroking his hair and over his back. We're both filthy and sweaty, and not just from the sex. My apartment is hot; I never turned the air conditioning on, and it's over ninety degrees outside.

It's only May. What will the rest of the summer bring?

"So," he says. I'm relieved when I hear him. If he'd fallen asleep on top of me I might have been mortified…and slightly okay with keeping his heat inside me, a thought I'll take to my grave. He rolls off, gripping the condom base as he starts to pull out. I wince from the pain of a too-quick shift. This was no slow and easy fuck, and it's been a long time for me. I'm stretched to my limits.

He sees my expression and stops. Instead of moving, he kisses my cheek a little, rubbing his nose against me. He's affectionate after sex, and I can't decide whether I like this sweet side or want him to remain an asshole.

Pulling out all the way, slowly this time, watching me, then getting rid of the condom, he ties it up and puts it in his pants pocket. I appreciate him not throwing it on the floor. This is a new apartment, after all.

He reaches back and grabs my shorts. I'm still lying on my back, enjoying watching him as I recover from the crazy, bonkers sex. It will take days for my pussy to revert to its usual size.

29

He lifts my legs and gently slides my shorts back on, sans underwear, zipping and buttoning, tying the fabric belt. It's intimate and soothing and gives me a moment of peace, allowing my heart to return to a normal pace. He rubs my legs, touching and stroking me, looking over my body like it's the first time he's seeing me, as though he wasn't inside me moments ago.

He meets my gaze. His eyes look dark brown splashed with gold, but there is a hint of hazel, a shot of yellowish green near his irises, hiding a side of his personality that's only starting to peek out now. I can't reconcile this tenderness to the bum who screamed at me out on the street.

"How much stuff do you have left to move in?"

"You helped carry most of the boxes before we—you know—so I just have the furniture left. My sister and friend are gonna come over tonight to help with the rest."

He nods, not taking his eyes off me. "Okay then."

"Okay then."

I don't move. I'm very doubtful I can stand. He crawls over me, just as he did before we fucked, and settles his body over mine. We kiss, and it's slow and different from the wild sex. I wrap my arms around him and give in to the need to hold him as tight as I can.

When it's over, we're both smiling.

"You're not allowed to be like this."

"Like what?" He quirks his head.

"Nice. Involved."

"What should I be like?" He nuzzles against my neck, leaving a trail of kisses up to my lips.

"Distant. Aloof." I sigh into another kiss. "Scrambling to put your pants on and high tail it out of here before I ask you for a coffee or a date."

"Oh, well… I was going to ask you for a coffee. Does that make you the one scrabbling for your pants?"

"No." Yes? Maybe?

"Would you say yes to coffee?"

"Not tonight."

"Maybe another time…baby?" He says baby like a lascivious player, all deep and clichéd.

I snort, delighted by his sense of play. He kisses me again, lingering over my lips like he doesn't want this perfect time in space to end. I feel it, too. Earlier I wanted a quickie to help me burn off the frustration of the day, but now I don't know what I want.

He helps me stand. I duck into the restroom to pee and only realize after I start that the toilet paper hasn't been stocked yet. I huff, prepared to just wipe off with my hands then run hot water over them—because there's also no soap—when there's a knock. He opens the door wide enough to toss a roll inside.

"Thought you might need this." A packaged bar of soap follows the toilet paper. "And that. Found it in one of your boxes."

My rude, sweet neighbor is full of surprises. I reach for the toilet paper and soap. Once finished, I catch my reflection in the mirror and am a little stunned by what I see. How I look isn't new; the novelty comes from my eyes: bright green and more invigorated than I've seen them in a long time, renewed with energy and unashamed by what I just shared with a stranger.

He doesn't feel like a stranger anymore, despite still not knowing his name.

We don't say a word as he walks me to the U-Haul, but we're anything but silent. The backs of his fingers brush my knuckles. I straighten the twisted strap of his shirt, dragging my fingers along his bare shoulder. He places his hand low and steadying on my back as we exit the building. I don't need him to guide me, but the pressure of his touch on my skin is a brand of memory. Every caress and kiss of the past hour blankets me as if I were reliving it.

We reach the van, and I'm relieved to see it's locked. I couldn't remember whether I hit the fob before storming up to the apartment.

We turn to each other, and before either of us can say a word a cab pulls up a few buildings down. I recognize my sister and Adele in the car.

Perfect timing, and yet I want them to go away.

"My friends are here." I nod over to the car, idling while they pay.

"Okay then," he says again, and it makes me want to smack him.

My expression must be hilarious because he laughs, which only pisses me off more.

"Okay then," I say with a thick layer of sarcasm, petulantly crossing my arms.

He softens my edges with a kiss on my cheek, his tongue darting out to taste my skin. "I'm in 407B, come visit."

"You just barged into my apartment and had your way with me, the least you can do is make the effort to come see me."

He opens his mouth to argue then thinks better of it. "Okay. I can do that."

Wow, progress.

"Promise?" I ask, slowly stepping forward, enjoying flirting.

"Cross my heart." He shortens the gap between us. "Come to dinner with me. I can't leave you thinking my brand of seduction is nothing but that mess up there." He waves up at the building.

"So, insulting a woman till she mauls you isn't your usual technique?"

"Surprisingly, no. Though with this success rate maybe it should be."

We're so close now the lengths of our bodies are touching, restarting the molten heat in my belly with a slow, languid ache. The passion and lust from earlier remains, suspended at a low simmer.

"I didn't think it was so bad."

"No?"

I look back at the street, make sure Gemma and Adele haven't exited the cab yet, and then lean forward to give him a deep, hard kiss. I want to linger over his lips, drink him in deep, but I don't want anyone seeing us. Not yet. It will take me a while to process this frenetic rendezvous.

My stomach spins like a dreidel when we move apart, his smile open and pleasured. He leans down and whispers, "Move the van when you're done. My truck is parked in a four-hour parking zone. *Baby.*"

With that he walks across the street, no doubt making the sojourn back to wherever he parked his truck. I watch his ass the entire time. His cell rings as he reaches the curb, and he answers with a wink in my direction.

"*Pronto? Ciao* Vincent, *come stai?*"

Ha! He's speaking Italian. Totally called that.

3

SOPHIE

TURNS A PAGE IN HER BOOK.

"Sophie!"

Ugh. How am I going to spend the rest of the evening with Gemma and Adele after this crazy thing? I don't want to be around anyone right now. I'm still tender inside and in my psyche. I want to bask in the afterglow, take a shower and then a nap. I want to stay up all night eating ice cream and watching *Moonstruck*.

"Earth to Sophie!" My big sister, Gemma, yells from the street, holding the largest bottle of champagne I've ever seen. Our childhood friend, Adele, is right behind her with the flutes.

"You brought champagne glasses?"

Gemma kisses me on the cheek. "We knew you only had wine glasses, so consider these a housewarming present."

Her long, red hair is swept up in a stylish twist. Her eyes are large and green, but a lighter shade than mine, making her look a tad severe. Unlike my freckle-explosion skin, the only marks covering her face are a splash of delicate spots along her nose and cheeks, and the polo shirt and cargo shorts are crisp and perfectly put together.

I have to tease her a bit, because she looks so composed, and it just doesn't suit who I know her to really be.

"Wow, Gemma, drinks on a work night? I'm shocked."

"I know right?" Adele says—picking up my teasing—her blonde hair pulled into a fun topknot that in no way detracts from her style. A simple shorts and tank top ensemble can't diminish the sensual sway of her hips or the raw femininity she exudes. "She's been so stuffed up lately I'm worried she'll start shitting perfectly formed cubes."

Gemma whacks Adele on her arm. "You're disgusting."

My big sister and her best friend were always the envy of all the girls, myself included. Everyone wanted to date them or be them, yet they never let the attention go to their heads, despite nasty rumors to the contrary.

I know who these women are beyond those superficial stereotypes, and as we joke and tease, it turns out now more than ever, on a night my world has been turned upside down, I'm so thankful to have them.

I'm glad they're here.

"Can we drink first then lug heavy furniture?" Adele asks, eyeing the moving van with dread.

"Actually, we don't need to move much. Just the largish furniture pieces, but we can probably get it done quickly."

"Did you hire movers?" Adele sounds thrilled.

"No…a friendly neighbor offered to help me." So friendly he made me come twice. Impeccable service.

"Oh, Sophie," Gemma says, ruffling my hair, making it stick out at odd angles. "Do not let some sleazy guy into your life. He's nice to you, does stuff for you, and then the next thing you know he expects lurid and depraved acts."

I almost laugh when I realize that's sort of what happened, except I was a willing participant of all the lurid and depraved acts. More than willing. So willing I can't wait to do them again.

Come to dinner with me.

What will dinner with the mystery neighbor be like? I'm tempted to look at the mailboxes to find out his name, but also want to hold onto the clandestine quality of our meeting a bit longer.

After putting the champagne and glasses safely in the apartment, we move my coffee table, couch, bed frame and mattress up the stairs and get them placed. It takes some stumbles and a few bruised knees, but we manage. The rest of my furniture I ordered from Bob's, with a delivery date later in the week.

Despite Adele and Gemma begging to do it in the morning, I drive the van back to a local U-Haul drop-off a few blocks away. I smile as I walk back, my mind flooded with his insults and the way he held me.

The girls have the champagne popped and are filling the glasses by the time I return.

"A toast," Gemma says after pouring the champagne. "To my baby sister finally escaping creepy Craigslist roommates and moving into her own place. You're gonna take the world by storm. I'll bet my reputation you'll be writing for the *New York Times* or *The New Yorker* in the next year."

"Here's to that." Our glasses clink and we drink.

"Oh," Adele jumps in. "And for having the balls to persuade a guy into helping you unload all those boxes. Very well done."

She winks, and I can't help but blush. They know my experience in seduction is minimal at best. I've had one dud of a long-term relationship and the rest of my encounters with men have been one-night stands, most of those fueled by more than a little alcohol. Relationships just aren't my thing. But neither is jumping a guy's bones a mere hour after meeting him...then coaxing him to come see me again.

God, who have I become? I've turned into the old Gemma, wild and carefree. I watch her sip her champagne, laugh when she teases Adele for the large bun on top of her head. Gemma is quiet and reserved, all the abrasive bravery I always loved about her tucked away in a box. It makes me sad to see her this way, but as she said to me the one time I brought it up, *everyone needs to grow up sometime, Sophie.*

I was the quiet, serious one. I was the introvert, spending hours inside reading periodicals and dreaming of having my own articles published. I never really pursued anyone, or took chances. Even with my work and the delicate topics I'm occasionally allowed to focus on, I've never been brave enough to go out on a limb and take a stand, to fight and tell the stories I'm yearning to tell. To fight for anything.

But why can't I? There are so many stories I want to tell...why should I keep them contained and inside? Maybe there's something to be said for the tell-it-like-it-is New Yorker way of life. If I can stand up for myself to a stranger, scream at him in the middle of the street without a care in the world what people are thinking of me, why can't I take more chances in life? Look what the chance I took today got me.

"What's with you?" Gemma asks later in the evening. "You're more spaced out than usual."

I consider telling Gemma and Adele about the very, very, *very* friendly neighbor but decide to keep it to myself. The giddiness has yet to abate, and my body is still recovering. It's too dear to share. In fact, I don't know if I'll tell anyone about it. I want to keep it for myself and see where things might lead with Mr. 407B.

"Thinking about an article." It's not exactly a lie; I'm always thinking about the next topic, the next evolution in social justice.

"I don't know" Adele says, sitting cross-legged on the coffee table, playing with the edge of her champagne glass. "You have a glow."

Adele is far too perceptive for her own good, having a knack at reading people I've never encountered in anyone else.

I give them something to put them off the scent.

"The nice neighbor was pretty hot; I may be thinking of him."

"Oooh." Adele places her glass on the coffee table and leans forward. "Tell us more. Is he the sexy, bookish, nerdy type? You always go for those."

"No, actually…he's as far from my type as anyone could be."

"Maybe this is a positive step in your dating evolution," Gemma offers.

"Her dating evolution?" Adele snorts. "What the hell is that?"

"We all stick to a certain type, what we think we want, then as we mature it evolves into what we need."

"And Murray is what you need?" Adele asks, her opinion of Gemma's boyfriend not far from mine.

"Yes," Gemma says in a familiar grumble. "He is what I need, and what I want, and if you ask me again I'm going to have you sent to a psych ward. I'll tell them you've developed an

39

obsessive compulsion for asking the same question over and over."

"No need to get huffy with me again. I get it. Your type has changed."

Adele and I exchange suspicious looks as Gemma glances at her phone. Murray is fine if what you're looking for is a Wall Street lawyer who cares more about image than substance.

Gemma deserves better.

"All right, girlies," Adele says, standing to give us both a kiss on the forehead. "It's late, and I have to meet with a client at the ass crack of dawn. They want to see what the apartment I'm showing will look like during a sunrise."

Adele points to me when she reaches my door. "Change these locks, and let me know if things progress with the sexy neighbor. Maybe he'll ask you out for coffee. Good night, loves."

"Bye."

"Good night."

Oh, if only she knew how far past coffee we've already gone.

"Seriously, Sophie," Gemma says. "Be careful. You've never lived alone before."

I walk Gemma to the door, and we hug tightly. She may have changed, but she's still my sister, and I love her dearly for her concern. She always made me feel supported when our parents weren't there to fill that need.

"Don't worry about me."

"You're my baby sister, who else am I supposed to worry about?"

You. Your happiness.

"Worry how to keep Murray under heel; I don't trust him."

"Murray has a facade he presents to the world. He's not so bad once you get to know him. I wish you'd try harder."

"I will. I'm sorry; I promise I will."

We say goodnight, promising to meet up for traditional afternoon sangrias soon.

Despite my worry for Gemma, I'm distracted by thoughts of Mr. 407B the rest of the evening. My body aches to feel him inside me again, and though I loathe admitting it, I'd be happy just to see him smile at me in the hallway, learn his name… maybe even spend time with him. The whole encounter has turned me into an embarrassingly hot mess.

"It's turned me into something, all right," I mutter to myself after pulling clothes from a box and dressing for bed.

I open my window and stretch my legs onto the fire escape, watching the evening pedestrians speed walk despite the late hour. They don't have anywhere to go with such urgency at this time of night—their speed and insistence are simply ingrained into their DNA.

You either move fast in this city, or you get trampled, and for the first time in a long while, I feel desired and confident enough to push my way through, and rise above the foot traffic.

The next day that confidence is flying high. But after forty-eight hours with no contact from Mr. 407B, I start to doubt. A full fucking week of radio silence passes. Five days of zero sexy Italians barging into my apartment to sex me up; six days of zero invitations to coffee or linguine dinners. On the seventh night I find myself in front of his apartment door, leaning against the wood, trying to hear if he's home, and I know I've officially lost it.

It was a one-time thing, apparently—everything he said afterward just air. I knew better to get my hopes up.

I won't make the same mistake twice.

4

TONY

BANGS ON A SEXY NEIGHBOR'S DOOR.

Seven days after the hot sex.

My entire body aches as I step outta the cab. Not from any hard, physical labor, but from staying in one position for so long. A nine-hour trip in a metal flying deathtrap, followed by bumper-to-bumper traffic on the drive from LaGuardia, is not the way I wanted to end an already stressful emergency business trip.

A full week in Italy trying to fix the massive fuck-up my boss created—*former* boss, I should say—and I didn't get to step out of the hotel once. When they called me last week, I let myself get excited by the prospect of spending all that time in Rome. The firm trusts me enough to deal with the mess, and they're finally considering me for higher positions. But even better, I'd be in my favorite place in the world, the center of a million pieces of art I studied in school. I could've spent a whole day with the frescos at Villa Farnesina. Heaven. Except it didn't work out like that. I was in meeting rooms the whole time. I

43

might as well have been back in New York, in close proximity to a sexy, curly-haired, freckle-covered blonde I've been craving since leaving the States.

I drag my suitcase up the stairs, avoiding the old elevator. Knowing my luck, I'll get stuck in it, and then it will take me even longer to get into bed. When I reach the third floor I pause, wondering if she's home. I shake my head at my obsessive lunacy. What would she do if I knocked on her door, pushed my way in, and fucked her on the floor again? Thinking back on that day, as I have a thousand times over the past week, I have no idea who that guy was. I'm not like that. But when I yelled at her to get out of my spot, stressed and at my wit's end after a crap day, she turned to me with a burning fire in her eyes, nearly dropped the box she was holding and just ripped into me.

I've never been more turned on in my life.

She was a storm of shameless rage and passion. Short, bleached blonde hair, a petite yet sensuously curvy body—Christ, I need to see those breasts next time—but what truly captivated me was the freckles. Millions and millions of freckles covering her face and body like a Jackson Pollock painting. I've never seen anything like it, and the way her cheeks heated as she yelled at me highlighted their delicate beauty even more.

I'm going to lick and kiss every single one of those freckles.

"It's late. I'll see her tomorrow," I promise myself with regret, continuing up to the fourth floor and into my one-bedroom apartment. I thought about her more times than I cared to admit this past week, kicking myself for not getting her number before leaving so I could text, maybe even have some more fights or phone sex. It would have been a nice stress reliever.

I shower, my cock half hard from thinking of her, but I don't have the energy to do anything about it, and by the time I step out of the glass enclosure, wet and naked, I collapse on my bed and fall asleep.

Pounding. Loud, intense pounding rattles my brain.

I open my eyes, the corners feeling gritty and dry. I catch the time from the clock on the nightstand. Two in the morning. I've barely slept three hours.

It takes me a second to realize the pounding isn't in my head— it's a loud bass beat coming from below my apartment.

Who the fuck is playing music this loud? Our building has noise ordinances, and nobody breaks them because the landlord is a hard-ass. Sometimes new tenants don't know any better. They eventually cut it out after someone complains. But there are no new tenants—

My brain stops. There is a new tenant. She just moved in a week ago, and her smart mouth and hot body stirs something in me like I never felt before. She might not know the finer points of the noise rules.

Maybe someone should teach her.

Feeling revived by the prospect of seeing her, I jump out of bed. I put on a pair of jeans and nothing else, keeping the button undone, knowing what effect I want to have on her, and slip out of my apartment. I pad down to her floor and listen to the loud music, trying to hear if there is anyone in there with her. Maybe she's having a party, or maybe she has a guy in there and she doesn't want her neighbors to hear the loud moaning.

I'm not crazy about the thought of another man being in there with her. Has she been with anyone since we were together? I don't know, and ultimately it doesn't matter, because I sure as hell know how to make her forget any man that came before me.

I bang on the door, as loud as I can.

Is this how a rational adult man would or should act? I don't know, but then again nothing about what we had that first day was rational, so why should we try something different now?

I keep banging, not giving her a break to stop whatever it is she's doing. I'm relentless until the music turns off, then the faint sound of footsteps approaching filters through the door. Locks and chains come undone and the door flies open.

Holy shit, she's the most beautifully arresting woman I've ever seen. Skin burnished by the sun, with freckles covering every inch of her face and stretching down onto her neck. I've never seen this many freckles on a person in my life, and every single one is sexier than the last. Bright, clear green eyes turn dark in anger as she stares at me, recognizes me. Her body is lush, her breasts large and prominent through the tight tank top she's wearing. I can see her nipples through the thin shirt, and my semi surges into a full hard-on.

"What?" she asks, sounding pissed. She crosses her arms over her chest, waiting for my answer. It's a crime to cover those breasts.

I could try to be suave in response to her accusatory tone, try to be nice and coaxing…but it's not our style.

"Your music is too fucking loud. Turn it down." I head toward the stairs, leaving it there. If she's feeling anything like I'm feeling, she won't let me abandon the conversation with a short order. I get a thrill when I hear her step out of her apartment, following me.

"Who the fuck do you think you are? You can't ask me nicely like a normal human being? You have to bang on my door like an asshole, like you have a right to, and then you tell me—no— you *order* me to turn my music down? Go fuck yourself."

She gives me the finger then turns on her heel.

My balls start to ache, I want her so badly.

It's my turn to follow, and she makes it easy by storming back into her apartment without closing the door behind her.

When she turns to face me, her cheeks are red, her short, blonde hair frizzing. It sticks out at odd ends, making her appear wild. The crazier she looks, the harder my dick gets. I cup her cheek, intending to apologize for disappearing this week.

"Get off." She kicks out at me, hitting my shin. I grin back at her, the kick nothing more than a pinprick. She's fighting, but she's not aiming to truly hurt. Where would the fun be in that?

"Get out." She shoves at my chest then steps back, circling the edge of her apartment. "I did not invite you in here."

I keep moving, slamming her door closed behind me.

"Is this how it's gonna be? You show up and push your way into my place whenever you want? You gonna fuck me and not talk to me for another week? Because I gotta tell you, dickhead, I'm not interested in being the convenient piece of ass in your building whenever you don't have some other woman to bring home." She's panting with rage, and I'm so hard I have to fight to form words; there's no blood left in my brain.

I need to be careful here, because despite her fury, I think there's real hurt in her eyes. We shared something special, and then I had to leave for work and was too stupid to tell her. I messed up, but I can make this right again, get us back on track.

When I finally speak my words are forced and mangled through gritted teeth.

"I left the country on an emergency business trip. I planned to come see you the next day, I promised you I would, but I had to fly out that night. We never exchanged numbers, and I didn't

47

realize until I arrived at the airport that I'd forgotten to leave a note."

"Yeah, right. Whatever. Fine."

Oh, no. The feminine word of death. *Fine.*

I grip her arms, careful not to squeeze too tightly. The fighting thing we've got going is fun, but I never want to take it to a point where I scare her. There's no fun in fear. "You don't believe me? Come up to my place, I'll show you the suitcase I haven't unpacked yet, and boarding passes, and my passport stamped by Italians. You need some proof? I got it."

"I'm not coming up to your apartment."

"Why not?"

"Because you're just trying to get laid."

That's true, but that's not the only thing happening here.

"You're lying."

Okay, that pisses me off.

"You don't know me. Why would I lie?"

"Exactly. I don't know you, so why would I trust you?"

I shrug. "I guess you'll just have to see it to believe it."

And without waiting for another word from Miss Smart Mouth, I pick her up and throw her over my shoulder.

"What the holy fuck—"

I grab the keys hanging on a hook near the door and exit the apartment. She kicks and smacks my back as I whip around, throwing her off balance.

"You're clearly upset," I say in a low, rational tone against her yelling. "I understand. If I had the best sex of my life with someone who then disappeared, I would be pretty mad, too."

"You're an egomaniac!" She decks me hard on my shoulder blade. I feel it in my teeth and know I'll have a bruise. It's worth it, especially since she never asks me to put her down. Never says no. And I'm listening for it, for any hint she's not into this.

It takes me forever to get all her locks closed.

"Jesus, woman, how many locks did you install on this door?"

The moment strikes me at how different it is for a single man to live in the city than it is for a single woman. I didn't install extra locks or even change the old ones when I moved in. It sucks she has to live like that. I want her to bring that fierceness up to my place without worrying some creep might be waiting for her in her apartment when we're done.

The irony of worrying about her safety while carting her out of her apartment does not escape me.

"Not enough locks to keep the building's resident lunatics out."

For that I hitch her up higher onto my shoulder. She's airborne for a second then lands with a prominent *oof*.

"Come on, crazy." I smack her ass then walk the flight of stairs up to my floor.

"You are such a dick." She says 'dick' really loud. It bounces off the hallway walls. There's no way the neighbors aren't hearing this.

"I can't wait to see this proof, Mr. World Traveler." She emphasizes her statement with a fist on my kidney. It's like she can't help herself.

"Mr. Rodriguez? It's so late, what's this noise about?"

I turn toward the small voice coming from the apartment across from mine.

"Sorry to disturb you, Mrs. Goldstein. We'll try to be quieter."

The frail yet spunky older woman's eyes light up as she sees Sophie. "Oh, is this a new friend? How romantic."

Sophie tries to turn to the tiny woman. "This man has dragged me out of my apartment. He is a lunatic."

"Oh, to be young again. Have fun, you kids." Mrs. Goldstein winks at me then quietly returns to her apartment.

"Is everyone in this building insane?" Sophie yells.

I walk through my unlocked door. "Baby, you're gonna eat your words."

"Keep dreaming."

I switch the light on.

I can feel her arms spreading out in question.

"I'm not seein' anything. Where's this proof, Lord Linguine?"

Lord Linguine? She has got some pair of balls on her.

"In the bedroom." I turn us in that direction.

"No fucking way. Put me down right this second."

She thinks I'm only trying to get her into my bed. I am. I have every intention of fucking her tonight, but my suitcase and passport are in there as well. The bedroom is a practical need.

"Trust me"

"I don't trust you," she says too quickly, squirming to get away. "I don't know you."

I put her down. I understood what was happening the first

time. Two people needing a release, no explanations necessary. I don't usually do the crazy, one-night-stand thing, and my eagerness to see her and have her in my apartment affirms it turned into something more than a stress reliever toward the end.

But what about now?

She doesn't trust me. Is she scared of me? By all rights I shouldn't trust her either—that sexy, sometimes timid facade could be hiding a facet of her personality that will only turn into a complication later. I've done complicated and have no desire to get into a relationship laden with layers of rules.

But here she is, and here I am. I want her, and her saying she doesn't trust me feels like a challenge. This is more than a one-night stand—I can feel it—and I'll earn her trust if it takes all year to do it.

I storm into the bedroom, ignoring all the names she calls me as she follows of her own volition. I'll weaken, maybe even back down, if I look at her gorgeous green eyes.

I reach for my passport and chuck it at her.

"Here, you freak."

She catches it deftly and tosses it right back, hitting me square in the chest. Her eyes turn emerald with fury, and she's practically spitting fire. This woman is no princess waiting in a tower. She's the fucking dragon.

"You think I give a fuck? You!" She grabs a hairbrush and hauls it at me. "You just threw me over your shoulder like some asshole Viking."

The toiletry bag on my dresser comes flying at me. I duck, shielding my head in case I left it open and my razor comes flying out.

"I only wanted to prove I was away. I didn't mean to leave you hanging—"

"You think you're some god bestowing your magical cock on me, and I've been drooling and waiting for it to return? You are a narcissist. You're an—"

I almost think she's serious. I almost think I crossed the line, went too far when I lugged her from her apartment. This is part of the game, and the game never involves real fear or anger. But then I see a small smile she's trying to hide. It peeks out at the corners of her mouth whenever she turns to look for something to throw at me.

Christ, that smile could do me in for good. I love that she's willing to play rough with me. I love this brand of crazy she's showing off, so brazen and wild. I was always careful and deliberate in every aspect of my past relationships, whether purely sexual or otherwise. I made sure to do everything right, say all the perfect things, and put my needs last.

At work, every decision is a calculated risk. What steps will get me further up the ladder? How do I appease my superiors and make it so I'm absolutely necessary to the company? What move do I need to play to win the board? How do I accomplish it all and stay true to who I am?

There's no rest, no letting go. There's only the goal and the tension permanently embedded in my spine by working toward that goal.

But this bonkers woman? She plays with me. Teases me. Lets herself go and allows me to do the same. I never felt so free to be me. She's throwing shit as if her life depended on it, her rage more steeped in feminine fury than any *femme fatale*. But none of it is one-sided. The weapons I throw might only be verbal, but they're just as sharp and aimed with the purpose of seeking mutual pleasure.

It's definitely the craziest foreplay I ever participated in. And the hottest.

But I will not be unsure about her. I will not let this go any further without knowing she wants me.

"Tell me this isn't sex. Tell me you're actually pissed at me. Tell me you don't want this. We can stop, and you can walk back to your place, and I'll never bother you again."

She crosses her arms around her midsection, her fingers digging into the thin fabric of her shirt.

"Tell me one thing."

"Yes."

"Prove to me you had an emergency business meeting. That you didn't ghost me for a week until you got the itch to fuck me again."

Fuck yes, I can do that. I grab my cell and play the voicemail that prompted my trip.

"Antonio Rodriguez. This is Gabriel, Mr. Petrov's personal assistant. He needs you to catch the next flight to Rome. The idiots running the office have destroyed a contract we need to keep shipping costs down. If you save this contract, or come up with a superior alternate solution, we will schedule a meeting to discuss your future. Don't fuck this up."

"Look at the date." I hand her the phone.

"The night we met."

"I was on my way to the airport before you even moved the U-Haul. I called the Super asking him to leave you my number or tell you where I went."

"Seriously? What did he say?"

"He told me to fuck off."

She tilts her head, considering me for a moment.

"Where were you really?"

"I told you where I was"

"Prove it." Her eyebrows wiggle for half a second, and all the blood is rerouted back to my cock.

She's playing again.

Thank God. I play along.

"The proof of where I've been is on the floor. You can pick that passport up and see I'm not lying, or you can get out now." I emphasize my meaning by pointing at the front door. "Don't forget to do what I said and keep the music down."

She can't hide the outraged smile now. She's even laughing.

"You're such a—"

"Asshole? Dick? Heard all those before. C'mon baby, I'm sure you've got something original in there."

This time she doesn't use words, she just grabs the nearest thing to throw at me. It's a cell phone charger. Followed by a plastic bottle of hair product. I keep on taunting her. A wireless mouse flies past my head. When she grabs my bottle of cologne I run to stop her, but I'm too late. It shatters against the wall behind me. We both watch in stunned silence as the pungent liquid drips down the wall. I'm never gonna get that smell out. I'll probably lose my deposit.

My hand is holding hers—the hand that threw the bottle. While we stare at the splash mark on my wall I bring it down to rest on my abdomen. She spreads her fingers, the digits tripping over my muscles.

I look down at her. Her chest is heaving, and her hard nipples peek through the fabric. She's not wearing a bra. All she has on is a thin, strappy tank top and black, skin-tight cotton shorts, so short they could be panties...in fact, I think they might be.

"What are you wearing?" I ask, my voice deep and quiet.

She looks down at herself, startled. "Um, oh—shit." She's blushing now. "I'm in my underwear." Then she does something more surprising than breaking my cologne bottle: she pulls the zipper on my jeans down and my dick pops out, the tip shiny with precum.

"You're not wearing underwear." Her voice is husky.

I act just as outrageously and cup her between her legs. Her panties are soaked. I couldn't see the wet stain through the dark fabric. I rub her through it. She closes her eyes and moans, biting her bottom lip.

"We're both wearing too much." I push the cotton between her pussy lips, pulsing my fingers up and down, simulating exactly what I wanted to do to her.

"Yes," she cries, dipping her hand into my pants and gripping the base of my cock. "Oh, God. I forgot how big it is." She's staring at it like it's her new favorite toy. I kind of hope it is. "I want to suck it."

"Oh, you did not just say that. Fuck, no."

She looks at me like I'm crazy. "You don't want me to suck your cock?"

"I do. I want that more than anything. But if you do, I might come the second your lips are within an inch of it. Not even touching it. If your lips touch me there, it will explode, and I'll never have sex again."

She grins. "I don't think that'll happen. Unless you're a newbie at this whole sex thing, then I could understand having a short fuse. Was I your first? Have you been working up the courage to make sweet and tender love to me again?"

She's rubbing my shaft, jerking me off as she heckles me.

"You're a bitch."

"Oh c'mon, *baby*. Heard that one before. I'm sure you've got something original in there." She mimics my accent as she uses my words against me. I deserve all of it, and I *love* it.

I'm crazy about the way she matches me, how she doesn't back down. She's strong. So fucking gorgeous. I push my jeans down till they're around my knees. I really am worried I'll go off if her lips touch me, but I'm not gonna deny myself this pleasure.

She looks me over, licking her lips as her perusal stops on her hand, still wrapped around my cock. "You're just gonna have to prove something else to me now." She goes on her knees, but before she can take my cock in her mouth, I crouch down to kiss her. I grip the bottom of her thin-as-paper tank top and lift it off her when I stand. She grins up at me, her heavy breasts resting against her chest, the pink nipples hard as pebbles. There are freckles covering her chest and abdomen. Not one inch of her is free of freckles.

"I bet it would feel so good to oil your tits and rub my cock between them. I want to come all over those sexy freckles. Would you want that?"

She doesn't answer, but she's got this crazed look on her now. Not the one she has when we fight—this one is stretched, pained and confused, like the sexual tension is twisting her up inside. Without wasting another second, she takes me by the base, points the tip at her mouth and engulfs me in one swallow.

I cry out, resting my hands in her hair. I don't tug. If I tug, I'll fuck her mouth like an animal. I feel like an animal, but I remember all the locks on her door that weren't there the day she moved in, and I don't want to scare her. There's a balance to our crazed rendezvous, and I won't ruin it.

She sucks me, her head bobbing on my cock like she's racing, like she's eating me up because she's starving. Then she stops her mouth at my tip and moves her tongue around the slit, playing with it. A hand cups my balls, and I go breathless when she squeezes.

"Aw," she says, looking up at me. There's a devilish glint in her eyes. "You're doing so well."

I stare down at her for a second before I start to laugh. That's it. She's getting fucked. I pull her up from under her arms—she's laughing too—and I kiss her, making sure to press her bare chest against mine. Her plush breasts feel so good, her nipples poking at my skin like little diamonds.

We undress, trying to keep kissing through it all, though we both need to pull away when we step out of our bottoms. We laugh at how absurd we look, then I pick her up and throw her on the bed.

Seeing her there in my space ignites a protective and primitive response. She's in my apartment, naked in my bed, legs spread, her arms gripping the bars of the headboard above her. I pull out a condom from the bedside table and throw it on the sheets next to her hip before prowling over her. Her breasts are rising and falling in a steady but heavy rhythm.

I take a nipple into my mouth and suck on it. She sighs, her hands sliding into my hair, pushing me harder against her breast. Her hips are rolling, simulating what she wants. I want it too, but she's so naked underneath me, and I want it a different way than before. I want to hear her scream, and the animal part of me is twisting my fuse, as she called it, making it tighter and shorter with each second I touch her.

I slick a finger into her cunt, making sure she's as wet as we need to get me inside her. She squirms at my touch, but I hold her down with a hand on her womb. I fuck her a little bit there; play with her clit until she's panting. My fingers come out shiny and coated in her juices. I lick them, savoring the heady taste, and her eyes widen, watching me suck on them.

She shakes her head and without a word flips herself over onto her hands and knees. She looks back at me, commanding me to fuck her without saying a damn word. It's the hottest thing I've ever seen, and now I'm doubly unsure that I'll last for half a second.

"Oh, shit, yes." I struggle to put the condom on without breaking it. My dick is so hard it hurts, my stomach a mess of knots. "Look at me," I almost growl at her. She stares back at me over her shoulder. "Keep looking at me."

I push inside her before she can say another word. I watch her face, making sure she's not in pain. It's why I don't usually fuck from behind. A woman can hide a lot from a man in this position, and there is no universe where I want her to hide anything from me, pleasure or pain. If this isn't working for her, we'll find another way. Just the fact that she's willing to try my abnormally large cock out is a balm. I will do whatever she wants, whatever she needs.

"Okay?" I ask, starting to pull in and out of her, keeping the pulsing shallow.

She nods, her mouth hanging open and her face scrunched. "You're deep this way."

"Good or bad?" My brain won't let me form real sentences anymore. All that smooth dirty talk we had before is gone. I'm a base creature now.

"Yeah, good. Real good." She turns away but reaches back and pats my hand on her waist. "I got you," she says, reminding me of our first night together.

I bend over and bite her shoulder, needing to feel her smooth, freckle-covered back against my chest. I wrap an arm around her waist, and she holds me there.

We fuck hard now. I don't hold anything back, but I check in with her every few minutes, every time I change the angle, needing a new way to get deeper and deeper, making sure she's okay and enjoying it. We end up on our sides, and this has to be her favorite position because she goes insane. She squirms and moans as I take her from behind. My hand is playing with her nub, and I'm rolling my hips in a pace even I didn't think I could achieve.

"Please don't stop." She's never said please to me before, but I think she's so far gone she can't help it now. "Ah, don't stop fucking me. Right there. It's amazing."

"You're amazing," I grunt, rubbing her fast until she comes around my cock, the ripples pulling my own orgasm right to the edge. I squeeze the base of my cock to hold myself off, trying to make this last a little longer. I never want it to end.

After she cools down I turn her onto her stomach, lying flat, her legs pressed together making her sheathe even tighter. I push into the tight channel, grunting and panting as her ass and pussy squeeze the life out of me. Her hands grip my pillows, and she eggs me on, taunting me to fucking do it and come inside her. My pace is uneven, my rhythm all over the place.

"I need your come inside me."

I come less than thirty seconds later, laughing in amazement. I shut my eyes, trying to feel it all at once: her ass cushioning my body, her pussy squeezing my cock with aftershocks, her skin erupting in goosebumps as I bite down on her shoulder. My balls almost hurt as they push the hot cum into the condom, my body taut and stretched to its limits. I wish we were bare, but that can come later, after we know each other better.

After there's trust.

Not wanting to squish her, I tug us onto our sides again once my orgasm subsides. I pull out slowly, remembering how she didn't like the fast movement last time, then chuck the condom into the waste bin. She sighs in contentment when I come back, cuddling behind her. I am not ashamed of the word cuddling—I want to cuddle and snuggle and bury deep into her. Of course, it also gives me access to her bare breasts, so I take one in hand and squeeze, playing with the nipple. She chuckles.

"Like those, huh?"

"What did you expect? This was only my second time making sweet and tender love, after all." I slap her ass for accusing me of being a virgin.

She yelps, then takes my hand and returns it to her breast. "I like it too."

She smells sweaty and like the cologne that's probably dripping onto my sheets. "Will you stay with me tonight?" I ask, praying she'll say yes.

She turns around, resting her head on my arm. "Yes, Mr. Rodriguez. What was your full name? It was muffled on the recording."

"Antonio Rodriguez. Call me Tony."

"Rodriguez?"

"My ma's family is from Sicily, but my pop is Colombian." I kiss her nose.

"I want to see your passport."

"Christ, woman." I lean over the side of the bed and retrieve the passport, dropping it on her stomach, and then snuggling back up to her warm body. I'm overheated, could probably benefit from some space, but I don't want to stop touching her.

She flips through it, her eyebrows rising. "You travel a lot, huh?" She ends on the latest page. "Rome, Italy." Her sigh is dramatic and overwrought. "I suppose you were telling the truth."

"Do I get an apology for trashing my apartment?"

Her eyes narrow, but her smile never disappears. "You tossed me over your shoulder as if I were some wench you intended to sully. I trashed your apartment. We're even."

I chuckle, letting the matter go. We close our eyes for a moment, living in the quiet space we've created, the aftermath of a storm.

"I was so focused on catching the last flight out of LaGuardia that night I barely had time to remember to pack my underwear."

"Gasp. Were you commando in your pristine suits? Naughty."

"No," I say quickly, not wanting her to think I'm some man child. "I grabbed some before running out the door. It wasn't until I was on the plane that everything came rushing back to me."

"It was only sex. I understood the deal." She shrugs a little, trying to be all nonchalant, as if that insane first day meant nothing.

"I know this is a radical thought, but maybe we can do this 'just sex' on a regular basis?"

"But that might lead to more than just sex. I might actually come to expect things from you." Her tone is sarcastic, but I think it's vital she understands I'm okay with that. I want her to trust me with more than her mockery and her barbs. Yes, it sweeps the road and paves the way for us to play and indulge, but there's a better, deeper side to being so easy with another person, one I haven't explored in a long time.

I want so many things with her, and I don't know if I'd be willing to give them up now that I've had a taste.

I open up a bit, beyond the teasing, and let her see the gravity tugging at my thoughts. "I think I could handle that."

I could more than handle it; I want it. I never want this decadent feeling to end.

She smiles indulgently at me, trailing her hand down my abdomen until she touches my cock. It wouldn't take much more of that to revive it.

I kiss her, rub myself into her hand. "You're the most beautiful woman."

"Uh-huh." her voice drips with that ever-present sarcasm, but there's a new, vulnerable edge there that surprises me. I chase it down, not wanting her to doubt what she does to me.

"The moment I saw you on the street I thought you were gorgeous. Then you screamed at me, and my cock got so hard I'm surprised I was able to say one coherent word to you." When she laughs, her freckles bunch into a darker mass of skin. I keep going. "Your body drives me crazy, but it's that mouth— that dirty, mean, smart mouth—that turns me into the asshole you've come to know. I'm not like this with anyone else."

My length is hard in her hand again, but she's not doing anything too seriously. She's playing, stroking the tip, just touching. I don't mind. I like it, this sexy, rude, and sweet affection.

"What's your name?" I ask.

She pushes me, gets on top, straddling me. She's still dewy; I can feel it and the short hairs of her cunt against my stomach. My cock is behind her, nudging her ass. I don't do anything…I don't think she's on top of me to fuck me just yet. We're playing, feeling each other out as we take a breather.

"Sophie," she says quietly, her hands tracing my muscles.

"You like my body, Sophie?" I ask, loving the attention. At her honest and enthusiastic nod, I give her a secret part of me. "I like that you do. It makes me feel good." I run my hands up and down her sides before saying, "Some women think I'm too big all over, not just my…you know…"

She grins. She probably thinks it's funny I can't say it now. But the words cock and dick seem out of place in this moment. I feel like we're in a quiet corner of the city, where it's just us.

"I think your body is perfection." She's giving me a greater gift than she'll ever know, saying these things. "I go crazy over how big you are. I love how you can cradle or cuddle or fuck or surround me, and I never feel exposed. You're there for my body and…" She shrugs, embarrassment making her go quiet. "And you got me."

I hug her down to my chest, and we lay together in silence for a while, maybe we can even fall asleep like this. Eventually she shivers in the air-conditioned room, and we crawl under the sheet, knowing anything more will be too warm with our combined body heat.

"Sophie short for Sophia? My Ma will like me dating an Italian girl."

I've got my arm around her as her head uses my chest as a pillow, playing with the short blonde curls on her head. They're so cute and airy, like they can fly in the wind, nudged by the slightest breeze.

"Just Sophie…Sophie Flanagan."

"Oh no," I cover my eyes in anguish. "Not an Irish."

I pear down at her to see her reaction, and she lifts her head, appropriately appalled by my comment. "*An* Irish?"

"This is gonna be like *West Side Story*, honey." I sigh dramatically. "We can't tell anyone. Our affair is doomed."

"Well, it's appropriate your name is Tony, then." She pats my chest. "It was nice knowing you. Thanks for the sex."

"Whaddya mean?"

"Spoiler alert—Tony's the one who dies in West Side Story. Maria lives. Women always outlast the men." She snuggles close to me, her voice drifting as sleep starts to claim her. "We're smarter."

Can't argue with that. Well, I can, but it sounds like she really needs sleep, and I know where arguments take us. I shake her a bit, waking her for a brief second.

"You doing anything tomorrow?" It will be Saturday, but I don't know if she works on weekends. "Can I take you to brunch?"

She bites her lip, hesitates before answering. "Yes."

I don't want to read too much into the moment, but as I hold her in my arms, listening to her steady breathing, the tight feeling in my chest strengthens, and the sweet moment makes way for panic.

She couldn't have come into my life at a worse time.

5

SOPHIE

LIKES CHICKEN AND WAFFLES. A LOT.

Tony takes me to a kitschy little restaurant in Hell's Kitchen for brunch the next morning. It looks like a 1950s diner with a music theme. Each of the gender-neutral bathrooms is modeled after a musical artist. I use the Cher bathroom and am greeted by "Believe" blasting in my ears and a Cher doll vibrating by some sort of defunct machine. I think it's supposed to be shaking its hips...it looks like it's having a seizure.

I love the place instantly, but before we get there, we need to traverse the subway system.

Hell's Kitchen is close to Times Square and a long way from our building in Brooklyn, especially for a very hungry woman who had her door broken down by a sex maniac the night before. I tell him this as we're waiting for the train, and he doesn't fight me on my exaggeration like I want him to. He simply pulls me to him with that stupid, knowing smirk, and kisses me.

The kiss is deliciously uncomfortable. It's so hot on the subway platform, and we're already sweating. It's not even ten in the morning, and the weatherman on NY1 is saying it's gonna be another scorcher. I chuckled as I drank my coffee in Tony's apartment that morning, watching the local news. *It was definitely a scorcher last night, Bill.*

"Temperatures reached peak hotness," Tony chimes in from the bedroom doorway, his voice mimicking the weatherman's.

I'd unknowingly said it out loud, but Tony's willingness to play along lures me into the silly exchange.

"Local conditions are breaking records, among other things."

"Hard and dangerous weather fronts are on the way."

"The humidity has climates turning exceedingly wet."

Tony's laugh is so loud it could be a bark.

My stomach flips, knowing I made him laugh…then it flips for a whole 'nother reason as he takes my hand when we walk toward the subway, the intimacy of the morning giving me chills and making me nervous.

Too much too soon, my heart shouts a warning.

We board the C train at High Street, and I groan in relief as the air conditioning hits me. It's always a crapshoot whether the air will be working on a subway car. I've traveled full lengths of trains in the past just to find one with working A/C.

"Oh, heaven," he sighs in response to my groan. I think he might be teasing my love of air conditioning, but I'm not sure. It would be so easy for me to pick a fight with him over it, but I've been in a state of relaxed pleasure since the kiss on the subway platform, the imprint of his hands on my waist still hot.

Such a little gesture, yet so big in so many ways.

It makes me nervous, this new and large thing I feel for a man I just met. I don't know what scares me more, that I'm not sure what kind of man he is yet, or the idea that he might feel the same way about me.

But worst of all, I'm worried what will happen to me if I let myself feel these big things.

I want to tell him how I'm thirty and have only had one long-term relationship, and it was back in college. I want to explain how Brian was a sweet guy at first, but after a while his teasing jokes turned into hurtful barbs and judgments. I became so focused on pleasing him I forgot who I was and turned into a puppy trailing its master. I lost so many friends after falling in love for the first time. I'm terrified of losing myself in a man and trading in everything I've worked for to gratify him.

I've labored like a madwoman since breaking up with Brian, trying to find my place in the world, and finally, after years of confusion and soul searching, I'm happy with who I've become and what my life is.

I was okay with a life absent of a dedicated relationship. I figured it wasn't in my story. Adding a man into an equation I so carefully constructed these past few years would only upset the balance.

But then an asshole yells at me on the street and says *he's got me*, and I'm tangled up again, thrown back into my early twenties, where happy endings are still a possibility.

This connection can't be that.

I'm just feeling flighty and princess-like because he treats me so well. I mean, of course he's being a gentleman. I sucked the life out of his cock last night, and he knows he'll get more if he keeps behaving.

It's just sex. I need to keep reminding myself. Nothing more.

There aren't enough seats on the train for us to sit next to each other, so he gestures for me to take one near the door. I shake my head, not needing it. He rolls his eyes and sits down, then pulls me onto his lap. There's nothing rude about how we're sitting. My legs are to one side of his, trying to be as unobtrusive to the other passengers as possible, and he's got his arms around my waist to steady me.

I'm usually in awe of couples and how they can easily show affection in public like this. Aren't they hyperaware of people staring at them? Aren't they worried someone will get pissed and tell them to get a room? With Tony, I start to understand.

Together like this, we're the only ones on the train.

"Are you going to have breakfast or lunch?" I play with the edge of his shirt. He's got on this short-sleeved V-neck in a dark blue, and jeans that fit his body so perfectly I didn't think I'd ever get out of the building after seeing the fabric hug his ass for the first time.

I made him twirl on the landing to my floor as I salivated over his body. The wolf whistle I responded with earned me a laughing, bubbly kiss. I've never been kissed in a bubbly way before. I think I like it. Of course, his gold chain and cross are nestled in a thatch of chest hair, and I'm sure he only mussed his hair around with his fingers to get that delightfully tossed and casual look.

It takes me an hour just to shower and get my frizzy little curls under control and arranged in some sort of presentable fashion, then another ten minutes to find a bra that won't show too much under my tank top. I checked the mirror a million times to make sure my shorts aren't too short or cutting into my thighs from the two pieces of cake I had the night before. Those fudgy, chocolate slices are sitting inside my body, tossing calories at me and laughing.

"Both. That's what's great about brunch." He's got one hand on my bare thigh to stop me from sliding off his lap when the train comes to a sudden stop in the tunnel. His thumb rubs up and down my skin, and all of a sudden, the A/C just isn't cutting it. "But really what makes it brunch are the alcohol and meat options on the menu."

"You can have bacon and sausage at breakfast. Those are pretty meaty." I want to kick myself right after I say the word meaty.

"Mmm," he whispers in my ear, biting the shell. "Tell me all about your intimate knowledge of meat."

I smack his arm; it's becoming routine now. "Shuddup."

He sits back, and we continue our very important conversation as the train starts to move again. It will take us thirty minutes to travel to midtown, but if this train doesn't start running consistently we'll never get there, and I'll starve. I'm getting hangry just thinking about the journey.

"Okay, bacon and sausage, yes—standard breakfast fare. But what about fried chicken?"

"Who do you think you are, eating fried chicken for breakfast?" I shake my head, my tone full of mock disdain. "No, that's gotta wait till lunch."

He gestures like a professor shouting *eureka*. "Hence, brunch. It was made for those who want chicken for breakfast."

"What kind of monster are you? That's like wearing white after Labor Day."

"I've never understood that rule. And when that fried chicken is paired with waffles, I fucking *love* eating it for breakfast."

I place my hands on his chest in excitement. I'm so hungry I can already taste the crispy, buttery, syrupy goodness.

"*Oh*. Oh, I love fried chicken and waffles. I didn't get where you were going before, but now I see it. Oh, that shit is good. Are we going somewhere with chicken and waffles? Tell me yes—and don't tease me, or I might murder you. I'm so hungry."

"I would never tease a hungry woman about food. What kind of man do you think I am?"

The kind that fucks me on my floor after arguing with me but wakes up in the middle of the night to cover me with the sheet because it's fallen off, and I'm shivering so hard I shake the bed. He didn't know the shaking woke me, too. He tucked it around me, making sure it was snug, then gave me the sweetest, most unbearable little kiss to the back of my neck.

He's that kind of man.

All I say is, "I don't really know you."

"No, we don't know each other," he admits. Something catches his eye, and he nods across the train. I follow his gaze to see an old lady picking her teeth…with a chopstick.

Delightful.

We grin at each other, equally enchanted and horrified by the people of New York.

"Where did you go to college?" he asks.

"Why?"

"This is me getting to know you."

"Can't we just stick to fighting and fucking?"

He shakes me a bit. "C'mon. Please?"

Who can say no that face?

"NYU. You?"

"Pratt."

"Nice. What did you study?"

"Art History."

I nearly do a double take. "What? Is that what you do for work? Did you rush off to Rome to debate the origin of some newly discovered painting?"

"No. I wish...not that that's what art historians actually do. When I went for my masters I switched to business."

"Why?"

"Art history wasn't practical. I wanted to make my mark on the world, and I knew business was the way to go. Make a lotta money, live the good life. That's what I want."

I don't believe that for a second, but he notices me dubious staring and gives me a smarmy wink.

"I have a certain lifestyle I like to live. I wasn't going to be able to afford all my pristine suits, as you call them, on an art historian's salary."

He sounds wistful yet determined, almost like he gladly sacrificed something he loves to become anyone but who he is. I don't like it, but I figure we've all got our hang-ups, and I don't know him well enough to push him on it.

"So, what were you doing in Rome?"

"I work for a firm that preserves dying businesses. I ascertain the weaknesses and the strengths, determine what aspects can be salvaged and are worth investing time and money. It's challenging, especially when there's no chance at saving jobs, but I try to focus on disposing of the rot, work to scrape away burned bits, redeeming what's still fresh underneath. Some people in this business just fire everyone and start over. But it's not right to blame employees for the failings of their inept superiors."

"Hhmm"

"What?"

"I don't think someone who cares about the livelihoods of the little guys is only focused on money and living a particular life-style. You're not as shallow as you want people to think."

"I'm not that deep, baby. I'm actually crazy shallow. But just because I like climbing the corporate ladder doesn't mean I trample those on my way up."

I lean forward, our noses touching, our eyes meeting. "I don't believe you."

He kisses me quickly then changes the subject. "What about you? What do you do?"

"Oh, I'm boring."

"Tell me."

"Stop, my life is a dull slog. You don't want to hear about it."

His gaze softens, the playfulness not completely gone. He twirls one of my short curls around his fingers. "But I want to know you. I want to fight with you more. I want to spend time with you."

Too much, too soon.

"That can't be good for our health."

"Spending time together?"

"The fighting." I wrap my arms around his neck.

"Baby, you know you love it when we fight. Your face gets all flushed, and I can only imagine you being hot and bothered in other places—"

"I am not listening to this on the subway." I cover my ears. "Nopety-nope."

"Nopety-nope?" His barking laugh bounces off the walls. "Did you just say nopety?"

"What if I did?" I am thoroughly embarrassed by my childish phrase but there is no way in hell I'm ever backing down where Tony is concerned. That's what's great about arguing with him.

A week ago, I would have called a propensity for staving off conflict to be one of my defining traits. Years of listening to my parents fight until our home life crumbled instilled a deep disinclination to argue with anyone. After a fight, my Dad would disappear, which only led to more fights, which in the end resulted in Mom going away and never coming back to New York.

I hate fighting, with anyone.

But with Tony, arguing isn't a vehicle for wounding someone. It's a clean and pure way to express emotion and passion. It's the method in which I can be the person I was always too timid to become, and I know he'd never use his sharp words against me.

The best part is that I don't think either of us will ever admit defeat, which means there's only one, delicious way to expend our energy.

"Nothing," he shrugs, still smirking. Oof! That smirk pisses me off and turns me on at the same time. "It's just that you, Irish, are crazy sexy." I intend to fight him on that, but he quickly asks me another question. "Tell me more about you, Miss Irish Flanagan. What are your hopes? Dreams? Sleeping habits? What kind of food do you like? What kind of food do you hate, so I know never to cook it for you?"

"You cook more than linguine?"

"My ma is the greatest home cook in all New York City! Of course I cook more than linguine."

"What will you cook for me?"

"Nopety-nope." He wiggles his eyebrows when he says it. "We're not getting off track here. I would very much like it if you answered my questions."

"What is this, a job interview?"

He jiggles his legs, making me bounce on his lap. "C'mon, pretty please?"

Again, with that face.

"I hate pickles and cucumbers, and don't ever feed me raw tomatoes. Cooked are fine but not raw. I'm not into super spicy, but I'll try anything once. I love sushi with an intensity that sometimes scares me, and I'm a morning person."

"What were you doing last night blasting that music?"

I will never, ever tell him that. Not ever.

"I came home late from my sister's engagement party."

"Okay, so it's compulsive for you to blast music when returning from parties?"

"Yes, that's exactly it."

"What aren't you saying?"

"Nothing."

"Tell me." He bites my bottom lip, admonishing me.

"No."

"I'm gonna tickle you if you don't tell me."

"You wouldn't dare." I dig my hands into his shoulders.

"Oh, yes. I'm gonna tickle you, on the C train. And you will most likely squirm and become that obnoxious person who can't control herself on a crowded train. And everyone around you will judge, because that's what New Yorkers do best." He leans in to whisper, sounding scandalized. "Someone might even make a rude comment to us about it, or post a picture of us on Twitter with a disparaging tweet."

"I hate you."

"Funny enough, baby, I think that might be a little bit true. And I'm cool with it."

I give him my best stink eye. "You'd be okay with me hating you a little?"

"It'll make things interesting."

God, his accent is so thick he says it like *intrestin*.

I. Love. It.

I grip his chin a little hard, showing him that edge he means when he says *intrestin*. He thinks I'll argue with him—he's got a gleefully expectant look in his eyes, like a kid knowing what he's getting for Christmas.

I'm almost sorry to disappoint him with a simple kiss. But I make it good. I don't use my tongue. I don't bite. It's purely a meeting of lips, mine pressed to his. I keep my hand on his chin and my eyes wide open. I show him everything I'm feeling right then: the confusion, the giddiness, the contentment. I'm scared of what he's doing to me, what he could make me forget about myself, but I would be an idiot to turn away from this.

I'm terrified this might be considered a date, and I'm putting everything out into the open like a hopeless romantic or a stalker. I only want him to see me. To know me.

I pull away slowly, anticipating a rude or sarcastic comment.

"Maybe you don't hate me a little." I know there's more, so I wait. "You must hate me a lot because only someone who despises me would give me the most amazing kiss I've ever had on the fucking C train where I can't do anything about the hard-on I'm now sporting." His accent disappears to adopt a bland and exaggerated tone. "Be careful on the roads, folks, this heat wave is sure to turn into one long, hard weekend."

I laugh because I'm stupid happy and kiss him again. He takes his phone out and snaps a selfie of us. We become that couple on the train that sees only each other.

6

TONY

REFUSES TO GIVE UP. TIME TO MAKE A PLAN.

"Excuse me?" Sophie waves the waitress down. "Can we have more of this syrup? It's might be the best thing I've ever eaten."

The waitress laughs, moved by Sophie's infectious smile. I don't blame her; who wouldn't get hypnotized by the way her millions of freckles bunch up when she grins? I wanna play connect-the-dots with them so badly I have to restrain myself. She's even got freckles on her lips, like a cat with spots.

"Sure thing." The waitress walks off, and Sophie dips a piece of fried chicken into whatever syrup is left on the plate. She's completely forgotten what silverware is at this point and is devouring her food like an animal.

"Are you always like this?" I ask, mesmerized.

"Starving? Yes." She chews the chicken with her eyes closed and her mouth open. It's sort of disgusting and hilarious, which just combines to amplify her unique charm.

"No, I mean so..." I gesture to her, unable to find the words. "Unashamed."

Her chewing slows. She's focusing on her plate now. There's always so much happening inside her head—I want to turn her pages and read the lines in her story. She's a puzzle. Every time we talk, I learn something brilliant about her. Like how she may be brash and brazen with me when we're in the middle of an argument or in bed, but she's not impervious to insecurities. There's a history there I want to learn, if she'll let me.

She drops her chicken onto her plate.

"You must think I'm this crazy chick—and I hate that word— who fucks any guy who walks past me. Like, who does that, right? What person in their right mind, unless they're a sex addict, would just—"

"Wait, no!" She can't think I have that impression of her. "There's nothing wrong with casual sex—I mean, you already know how much *I* approve of it. By shameless I meant how you embrace who you are and don't seem to give a shit. Don't ever be afraid to take what you want, especially concerning sex. Sex with me. I'll always be down."

She nods, looking chagrined. "You should know I'm not like this. I don't make a habit of screaming my opinions at people. Or screwing them five minutes after meeting them."

"I guess I bring out the best in you."

She snorts. "You definitely bring out something in me."

I can't tell whether that's good or bad, so I stay silent and listen. I talk enough; it's time to learn who Sophie is.

"My mom sort of developed a who-gives-a-shit-attitude after moving to California, so I guess I get that from her." Her voice is thoughtful, tentative. "But I'm usually way more self-conscious than this. Lots more, actually."

I grasp her hand and squeeze, uncaring that it's covered in

syrup. My Lord, she's the messiest eater I've ever dined with. "I like you like this."

Sticky hands and all.

"I think I like me like this, too. If that makes any sense." We eat in silence for a bit, smiling over our drinks and waffles. I ordered a mint julep because it's brunch, and I'm allowed to get a fun cocktail every now and then, despite my Y chromosome, and she gets a mimosa with pineapple juice instead of orange juice. She doesn't like orange juice.

Would it be weird if I rid my apartment of all orange juice products?

"So, whose business were you saving in Rome?" she asks, after taking a sip of her drink. I try not to focus on her neck as she swallows or how her tongue licks away the taste of the fizzy champagne on her lips.

"Mine. We were just bought by Petrov Incorporated."

"Wow, isn't he like the richest guy in New York?"

"Tell me about it. For some reason that intense bastard likes the way we assess failing businesses. He saw potential for us to go global, so we set up some offices in Europe and Asia. But the VPs keep firing the people they hire to run the Rome office. They originally wanted someone from Italy, who's familiar with the locals and that area, but now I think they'd settle for someone competent."

I hesitate, wondering if it's too early to tell her this, if I'm implying too much by mentioning it. But I try to put myself in her shoes, and if she were the one facing a monumental shift in her life, one that would definitely affect any type of relationship, I'd want to know.

"I did really well this past week—salvaged an account we

thought was almost ruined. It helps that my maternal grand-mother emigrated from Italy; they see me as one of their lost children."

"That's sounds very Italian."

"Petrov called me the day I returned to the States, said he was impressed." I take a deep breath, hoping this doesn't destroy everything. Now that I'm about to say it, I realize I've been avoiding it.

"He hinted he's gonna offer me the VP position in Italy. I'd get to live in Rome."

The clinking of her silverware pauses for a moment.

"Wow," she says staring down at her plate. "Rome is cool, not that I've ever been. That would be quite the adventure."

Look at me. Why aren't you looking at me? Don't pull away.

"It's a lot like New York except way older. I feel at home there, at least my Italian side does."

"Sounds awesome." Her voice is strained. "When would you move?"

"They need someone established by the end of next month."

"So, you're here for two months, essentially, then that's it."

"Yeah, that's it. But—"

"So, this." She points back and forth between us, finally looking at me, challenging me. "This is what to you?"

"This is good. Actually, this is fucking fantastic." I reach for her hand, but she pulls away, crossing her arms. "We are good together. You see that, don't you?"

"Of course I do, which is why we need to stop this now before it goes any further. I can't risk myself with you when you're moving away in two months." She scrubs her hair, her eyes wide in alarm. The confident and playful woman I've come to know disappearing before my eyes.

"Tony, this was great." She pastes on a fake-ass smile. "You're great. Last night and last week were amazing. But it needs to end here."

"You running away, baby?"

"Don't do that. Don't think you understand what's going on inside my head."

"Maybe if you told me anything about you, I would."

"You basically interviewed me on the train."

"I know you went to NYU, and you hate pickles, and I'm pretty sure you mentioned having a sister last week, but that's it. You gave me nothing else. Tell me, if I weren't moving away, if I was gonna live in New York till my dying breath, would you give this a chance?"

"There is no this. '*Thises*' don't happen between two people who scream at each other like it's a game. I mean, that's fucked up when you think about it." Her laugh is hollow.

"That's just how we let our freak flags fly."

"I didn't have a freak flag before you."

"Everybody's got a freak flag, baby, you're just in denial about the irrefutably sexy and argumentative colors you're waving. You're the first woman I've ever felt comfortable enough to wave mine with. It's freeing. You've gotta feel that too."

"That's not me." She shakes her head, fighting more with herself then with me.

Her denial isn't something I'm going to solve over brunch. It runs deep.

"I should go," she says abruptly, at her limits. "Thank you for last night. It was a lot of fun. I'll see you around the building."

"I could chase you."

"See, you think I'm running," she says reasonably, like it's the logical conclusion. "But I'm being practical. We're good in bed, there's no denying that, and if you were staying in the country it might become more. But you're not, so I won't put myself on the line. I won't take that chance."

"I never pinned you for a coward." I regret the words the second they're out of my mouth. Being cantankerous isn't going to help my cause, but she only exacerbates my anger when she pulls out some cash, like I'd be so callous to think she'd owe me something if I paid for her meal.

"If you put one fucking dollar on the table, I will sweep these plates away and fuck you in front of every diner here," I growl at her.

She glares at me with reddening cheeks and throws a couple twenties on the table before getting up, grabbing her purse and walking out.

I curse at myself. Great job, asshole. You had to be a dick. You had to let your loud mouth run away from you. You know better than that. You know to tread lightly or else it always ends this way.

No, that's not what drew me to Sophie. She didn't shy away from the force of my loud personality—she embraced it. Embraced me.

I don't wanna let that go.

I pull out my phone and check to see how long it will take for her to get home from the closest train station. There are a lot of delays so at least an hour. I can work with an hour. I pay the check, taking her money with every intention of giving it back, and start to form a plan.

She's afraid of being hurt, of getting in too deep before I leave. I'm afraid of losing her completely without giving us at least a small chance. I can work with this. It's another challenge, like at work. A problem to solve.

What's the first step to take when considering taking on a project?

"Research."

I hail a cab and duck inside, giving the cabbie the address of my favorite Italian deli then unlock my phone to do a search for Sophie Flanagan.

"What the—"

Not only do I get one hit, but I get hundreds. I click the first link. It takes me to a popular website known for its simple yet funny lists. It's pure entertainment. But every now and then there's a larger, more in-depth think piece, and that's what I'm looking at now. I start reading, flicking through her articles, one by one.

Deep equity. Social justice. Intersectionality. Gender equality. So many current and vital topics and she covers them all with wit and the necessary gravitas to get her message across.

She's brilliant, utterly brilliant, but with every deep and emotional piece comes a lighter, fluffier post. Cat memes. Deconstructions of online videos, written with proper sarcasm. Popular TV show recaps, though I kinda like those and get swept up by her glowing review of last season's favored super-hero show.

She likes superheroes. She's kind of a nerd. It's hot.

There are a million sides to Sophie that fascinate, and capture, and she called herself boring? Dull? Fuck that.

Man, I'll never know what possessed me to offer her help moving in. She was shrieking at me, calling me an arrogant dickhead, gesturing at the U-Haul like a crazy person, and all I could think was she's so tiny yet fearless—a mini hurricane, right on the edge of Brooklyn, threatening to tear the place down. I couldn't keep my eyes off her, and I didn't wanna stop.

I've never met a person less boring than Miss Irish Sophie Flanagan.

I click over to her social media profiles. She's not present on Tumblr or snapchat, but she posts on Twitter. I look through her tweets and see political commentary, live tweeting of the shows she recaps, and a worrying obsession with a British baking show. But two tweets catch my eye. One from the night we first met, then another the day before I returned from Italy.

LIFE IS UNEXPECTED AND BEAUTIFUL. NEW APARTMENT, NEW LIFE, NEW ADVENTURE? #WHATADAY #ILOVENYC

The next one makes my heart sink, reinforcing the damage I made by leaving without a word.

CONGRATS GEMMA AND MURRAY ON YOUR ENGAGEMENT. WHAT A CATCH, SIS. NOT ALL GUYS ARE ASSHOLES. #TRUTH #GEMMANDMURRAYENGAGEMENT

I switch to her Facebook, surprised to see it isn't private. I flick through her photo albums. There are a lot of pics with a red-haired woman. Must be her sister. But a blonde pops up a lot with comments on Sophie's posts. I'll bet my ass these were the two women coming over to help her move that night. My assumption is proved correct when I come across a selfie posted by her sister.

Three women holding champagne glasses in Sophie's apartment. She's wearing the wrinkled clothes she had on when we met, her hair a disheveled mess, and a glisten on her skin from the hot day. But damn, she is glowing as bright as the sun.

Yeah, I felt that searing luminosity for a while after that day too.

I finally come across a picture of an older woman, with Gemma and Sophie on either side of her. They're standing in front of the Golden Gate Bridge. The woman looks like Sophie's sister: tall, with long, frizzy hair, a graying auburn. She's smiling, her arms around the two girls, clearly enjoying their time together. But Sophie looks...sad.

Sophie's head rests on the woman's shoulder, her smile small and forced. She said her mother lives in California. Maybe they don't see each other often. When did she move there? Why aren't there any pictures of her father in these albums?

On a whim I switch over to my pictures, searching through the images of my family. We're all there, the five of us plus mine and my brothers' friends. Our house is always packed, always full to bursting with love and affection.

Well, lately it's been rough.

But compared to my hectic and present family, Sophie's life feels almost bare of love, save for her sister and the blonde woman. Has she always been alone? It makes me feel almost guilty I grew up with so much love and she...I don't know what she had from her parents.

I turn the phone off and lean my elbow on the window, watching but unseeing as the city streaks past.

Sophie doesn't want to risk her heart on me. I'm leaving in a couple months, so what's the point, right? But maybe I can convince her to start something she can't get hurt by—an arrangement that won't leave her emotionally attached.

I'll offer a fling, and it will be hot and dirty and satisfying as fuck. She'll never notice I'm playing the long game, making her fall in love with me, inch by inch, day by day.

She doesn't need to know I'm playing for keeps.

And when I play, I always win.

7

SOPHIE

DOESN'T DO RELATIONSHIPS, BUT CAN'T TURN DOWN ITALIAN FOOD. OR SEXY ITALIANS.

When I get to my building there's a delectable smell wafting from an open window that has me salivating. Garlic and basil and warm bread. So comforting and familiar. I sit on the stoop, relishing the scent, not wanting to head inside just yet. The trains were backed up so badly it's almost five o'clock by the time I get home. I didn't mind the delays, though; it gave me time to reassess what happened today, Tony's words rumbling in my brain like thunder.

You're the first woman I've ever felt comfortable enough to wave mine with. It's freeing.

He looked so full of regret after calling me a coward. And, oh God, the expression on his face when I pulled my hand away? It guts me to even remember. It was like I slapped him, insulted his mother, and then spit in his face, all at once.

He acts like I'm the first woman to ever embrace his wild brand of loving. But it's not all wild—it's tender and sweet, too. He looks after me the whole time.

Stop thinking about that.

I don't do relationships. Haven't I learned my lesson after all this time?

What's the point of even trying?

This is what's called emotional baggage, and I just dumped a shit-ton of it on Tony.

He called me a coward, and it made me so mad…because it's true. I run to avoid getting hurt. I ghost men with the potential to claim a place in my heart and avoid conflict so as not to get embroiled in pain.

The fact that he's moving is just a convenient excuse to get the hell out of Dodge.

God, why can't I be a normal human being with normal relationships?

Didn't I promise myself I'd stop making these spineless decisions? Embrace the new and improved Sophie? What happened to that epiphany?

I won't let it end like this. Tony and I can't be together, his impending move to Italy a clear and present barrier, but I can at least be friendly. I didn't need to run out of the restaurant like a perpetually single woman running from the diapers aisle in a drug store.

First, I need to make it up to him.

I call Murray, knowing he has hookups with all kinds of companies and organizations. I ask for a favor, and he surprisingly gives it to me without a word about owing him.

"We're gonna be family soon, Phie. No paybacks necessary. I'll email the tickets once I've got them."

"Thanks, Murray," I say before hanging up, pleased by his willingness to help. Maybe Gemma is right, and I haven't been giving him enough of a chance.

It's weird to think of all the guys I've dated since Brian, my one actual relationship. They all read like great husbands on paper. Good jobs, nice apartments, funny, good-looking, talented. I ran from each one. I find something wrong with them, a flaw I can't fix or don't want to try, and then give up.

I'm a coward when it comes to relationships.

Have you always been this stupid, Sophie?

Brian's words attack my thoughts like a blade, the hurtful exchanges lying in wait in the corners of my mind, keeping me from forgetting how painful that last year with him was. It doesn't matter whether I keep seeing Tony, I don't think I'll ever trust a man enough not to run.

What's the point of even trying?

What's the point? Seems to be the theme of my life. What do I get?

The door to the building opens, and as if summoned straight from my mind he's there, in an apron claiming in proud letters he is the one and only Master Italian Chef. Underneath the apron he's wearing…nothing but skin.

"What the fuck are you doing?" I want to stand and push him back into the building, but I must be in shock from seeing all his muscles peeking out of the apron because my body won't move. "Someone is going to call the cops on you for public indecency."

"Well, I was completely naked before and thought I should put something on before coming out to get you."

"So, you chose an apron?" This asshole has confidence leaking out his pores. "Is this like a fetish or something?"

"No, I like to cook naked."

"You're screwing with me right now."

"I'm not."

"This can't be real. You are not a real person." My statement is only proved true by the spatula he's waving around as he talks. How did I not see that until now?

"I swear it's true. I mean, what other kind of guy would cook a three-course meal, the best meal he's ever cooked, with the full intention of carrying it down to a beautiful woman's apartment in the hopes he could prove to her he's not an insensitive idiot who says things before thinking them through?"

"You were cooking me dinner?" I point to the building. "Those smells are coming from your apartment?"

He sits on the stoop next to me. His bare butt is on the cement. He's gonna need to disinfect his ass for a month.

"I made my favorite meal for you. Garlic bread, gnocchi, a little antipasto, vodka sauce." He kisses his fingers in approval and sends it to God.

"You made all that? When did you have the time?" His bare leg rubs against mine. He's doing it on purpose, and though this whole vision is somewhat tempting, I'm not about to give in and forgive him instantly.

Where would the fun in that be?

"Okay, so I didn't make it all from scratch, you're right. I'd need to invent a time machine for that. But I did make the vodka sauce. I had it frozen from the last batch I made a few weeks ago. I promise it's even better now. The bread, the gnocchi, and the antipasti came from my favorite Italian deli. I swear, you've never had meat sauce until you've had their meat sauce."

He swears. He keeps swearing. Keeps promising me things. How do I trust those promises?

"I'd like to take you there sometime. Maybe we can go tomorrow and get a couple of sandwiches?"

My God, does this man even listen? I can't do this with him. He's sitting on our building stoop, naked, risking imprisonment after cooking me a meal. What man cooks naked? One, that can't be completely sanitary. Two, he is risking some very tender bits and pieces, putting them so close to boiling water and hot oil.

And he's doing it for me. To apologize. To make me happy.

"We're messed up," I blurt out, so confused by how much I want him.

He nods. "We should be observed and analyzed."

"*The X-Files* has got nothing on our strange truths."

I take a deep breath and try to look at him directly. Be serious and convince him I've drawn a line. Which is pretty much impossible to do when he's dressed like a lunatic.

"I can't be in a relationship with you. I need to know what's happening a month from now. Two months from now. I don't like uncertainty. If I let myself get caught up in you just for you to leave…"

His eyes glint as he says, "You wouldn't know what's happening a month from now, even if we did start a traditional relationship. We could end up hating each other and break up like a million other couples."

"All the more reason not to start anything."

His lips thin as he thinks for a minute, his leg bouncing on the stoop, making other things bounce, but I am not thinking about those other things.

"I'm liking what's happening here. I don't want it to end. But I respect your boundaries. So, I'm proposing a fling." His voice is steadier now, lower pitch. The joke seems to be over. "You and me, hot and heavy for a month or two. Then we go our separate ways. No hurt feelings. No misunderstandings."

"And if you don't get the job in Rome?"

"Then we part amicably. Nod to each other in the hallway like good neighbors."

No one gets hurt. Fun, sexy times and a lot of Italian food for a couple months and then he's gone, or we become friends. No strings attached. I think I can do that. I feel his leg pressing against mine, and the little hairs scraping along my skin start to turn me on. I want him so badly leg hair is controlling my libido.

"Deal," I say. "Just a fling."

"Deal." We shake on it, his smooth grip sparking my excitement.

"But I have a couple strings to add."

Of course he does.

"Like what?"

"First, we're exclusive."

"Done." I give that one up easily, no problem. "I couldn't handle all of you" I wave my hands around his general direction. "plus someone else."

"I'll take that as a compliment."

My hand pats his in encouragement. "Good for you."

He rolls his eyes with a groan but kisses me, short and sweet. It leaves me breathless and all the more aware of what he isn't wearing under that apron.

We seriously need to get inside before someone calls the cops.

Yup, that is the only reason I want to be back in the apartment with him. Naked. Alone.

"We go on dates, you meet my friends, maybe my family, and I meet yours."

My dirty thoughts come to a screeching halt.

"That's relationship shit."

"What can it hurt? You have it in your mind that I'm leaving, that there's no chance for us, why not live this thing to the fullest?"

I snort. "That is such a weak argument—I almost feel sorry for you."

"Think of it like my final goodbye. I want to spend as much time with you as I can, but I'll also have to see my family."

He is unbearably charming. It's almost annoying. Almost.

"I'll do the dates, *maybe* meet some friends, but I can't do the family thing. It's too personal, and you agreed, fling. Only fling."

"It's okay; I know it sounds like a lot. You can sit with it for a bit, mull it over."

"There will be no mulling. I made up my mind."

"Naw, it's all good. Take it under consideration, weigh the pros and cons. You got this, baby!" He claps like he's cheering me on at a sports game.

"There are only cons," I yell, but I can't stop smiling too, laughing at his absurdity.

"You only say that because you haven't had my ma and pop's cooking."

He keeps making concessions, little adjustments to suit my weirdness. Hell, he is sitting here, bare-assed naked on a filthy stoop, attempting to coax me into a meal with him, seducing me with laughter. He's apologizing, in his own peculiar way—and Tony has many peculiarities, most of which I have yet to discover, but there's one I know intimately.

Tony likes the fighting. In fact, I think he enjoys it so much he came out here wearing nothing but an apron to cajole me into a fight. He knew I'd be outraged, shocked into an argument like an electric charge to a failing heart.

He understands what kick-starts my lust, my passion…because it's the same for him. He teases me when we're in public, but nothing so outrageous as this. He keeps it hidden, like he's afraid to show his true unruly colors, to be himself.

Maybe I'm not the only one who relinquished their inhibitions the day we met. Maybe, with me, Tony can be himself.

And sitting on a dirty stoop, with his junk blowing in the wind under a thin apron, Tony is taking the step to be himself… except not completely. This conciliatory and understanding conversation is not how we make up.

Tony needs something else from me. My silence hurt him, and that doesn't sit right with me. Tony loves the fighting, as long as we each say our piece, something I'll have to remember in the future.

I make a choice. I might regret it. But my pulse beats harder every time he looks at me with his big eyes, or smiles, or jokes. Hell, even Tony breathing turns me on. Look what his leg has hair done to my sanity! There really is no choice at all.

"You were gonna carry the dinner down to me?"

"Only if I couldn't convince you to come up to my place and see how I've set it all up."

I lean forward and whisper, "Is it laid out in a pretty table setting?"

"Baby, it's the most beautiful table setting you've ever seen."

"Show me."

I make him walk in front of me when he takes me to his apartment.

"I knew you liked my ass," he says, bounding up the stairs then stopping at the first landing to pose.

It's true, I love watching his perfect bubble butt flex. I'm flushed and lightheaded by the time we get to his apartment, eager to get him into bed. But he's oblivious and adorably intent on showing me all the work he put into the place setting.

Tony's right, the dishes are arranged beautifully. The plates are a good quality, not purchased from Ikea like mine. They have a delicate design tracing the edges, gold against white. Actual cloth napkins wrapped in gold-filigreed napkin rings hug the settings, and everything matches. Two bottles of wine sit next to mammoth glasses, ready for pouring. There are even candles. Not cheap little candles bought at the corner bodega—these are tall and white and wouldn't be out of place in a grand ballroom on some estate in the Hamptons.

I look up at him. He's watching carefully, wary. He's put himself out on the line for me, and I hope I'm not taking a misstep when I shrug and say, "It's okay, I guess."

His mouth hangs open for about two seconds before his ego predictably takes over. "It's *okay*? I looked up on Pinterest how to set a table for you. Hell, I went on Pinterest for you. The least you can do is show some gratitude."

"Oh, so I'm supposed to be grateful that you made me a meal? A meal mostly bought at a *store*." I emphasize the word store like it's dirty.

He looks like I've murdered his whole family, or worse, insulted the Mets.

"A store? Delphino's is not just a store. It's the most authentic Italian deli you will find in the whole damn city. The olive oil there? They have it shipped straight from Italy."

"Yeah, well, Bertolli is Italian, too."

He clutches his chest, stutters. "Get out. I can't believe you just compared Delphino's imported authentic olive oil to fucking Bertolli's! What kind of monster are you? It's the Irish. You have no appreciation for good food. What do you eat? Potatoes and cabbage?"

"Hey, don't insult my people because yours are glutinous heathens."

"Heathens? You're calling me a heathen now? Look at this table setting. It's fucking gorgeous. No heathen could do this. Da Vinci's *Mona Lisa* has nothing on the secrets hidden within the beauty of the placement of the forks and knives. Botticelli's use of color will never measure up to my palette. Michelangelo, despite having painted the Sistine Chapel which is singularly stunning, could never make a table setting this perfect."

Oh, we are screaming at the top of our lungs now, and it so much fun. And if the hard length poking out from Tony's apron is anything to go by, he's enjoying himself as well.

"You're so proud of the setting. Did your mommy give you the plates? Did she want her baby boy to have the best?"

"I bought everything myself. Like the fucking adult I am. What do you eat with down in your little hovel? Plastic non-biodegradable spoons? Great job contributing to the pollution of the planet."

Now that I have confirmation nothing on the table is a priceless family heirloom, I look over the setting while saying, "I know how I can make this a lot better."

"Oh please, enlighten me."

I take one of the smaller plates, one that would be used for an appetizer or to butter bread, and I throw it on the floor. The crash reverberates throughout the apartment: the broken plate heard 'round the world. He stares down at the shattered pieces then slowly turns back to me. There's fire in his eyes, and I know I'm going to get it.

I can't wait for him to give it to me.

"You didn't just do that."

I choose a large plate this time in response. The pieces scatter so far, they reach his feet, but that wouldn't take much now as he's advancing on me.

"Keep going, baby. Keep going."

I pick a nice-looking miniature bowl and chuck it down to join its broken counterparts.

He stares down at what's left of the bowl, then slowly looks at me, readying for battle.

"That was for the olive oil."

I think I've reached his limit.

I turn on my heel and run. He's got me around my waist and is picking me up while I'm cursing and kicking. I smack the side of his head and he grunts and throws me on his bed. I land on my hands and knees. I'm scrambling to escape but he grabs my ankle and jerks me back toward the edge of the bed. He's got fingers in my shorts and then all of a sudden, my backside is bare, underwear down around my knees, and a crack sounds from my ass cheek. It reverberates through my body, the sting spreading across my butt and into my thigh like a living creature. When the tingle reaches my pussy, I try my hardest not to enjoy it, not to start turning hot and melty down there where I want him most.

I look over my shoulder, trying to appear stunned. "Did you just spank me?"

"Fuck yeah, I did." His face is flushed. He undoes the apron and throws it off, leaving his distinct erection bare and sticking out from his body. The gleaming tip bounces, taunting me. "And I'm gonna keep doing it until you learn your lesson."

"What lesson is that?"

"I make the best table settings."

"You're insane." But I don't push him away as he presses a hand between my shoulders, lowering my upper body to the bed, keeping my ass high in the air. He's gotta see how turned on I am right now, how the liquid heat is starting to pool at my pussy lips, about to spill over.

"Wait," he pauses, comes down beside me on the bed. "Is this okay? The spanking?"

I want to growl at him for stopping and kiss him for being so caring.

"Yes, now get back to it." My body hurts from wanting him, impatient for everything he does to me.

"Right."

"Wait," I say, making *him* groan this time, tugging him back down to the bed. "Thank you for looking out for me."

"I got you." Tony kisses me fast, repositioning himself behind me. "Say *prosciutto* if it's too much."

I have to laugh at that, but the sound is high-pitched and frenetic. The crazy, sexy imbecile just gave me the most Italian safe word ever. I don't think I'll be able to say it with a straight face, but as his hand comes down to smack my other cheek, I lose all sense of hilarity. His hand is big and broad, and covers most of my large ass. And he doesn't stop talking, throughout the whole unhinged affair. He tells me I'm gorgeous. He apologizes for what he said earlier, then slaps my ass again and calls me crazy and sweet and greedy for his big cock.

It *is* a big cock, I can't argue with that. But every time his hand comes down on me, I curse him. Tell him to go fuck himself. His words get too hot, too much for me to keep arguing. I need to get to the main event now. My body is twisted and sweating, and I'm writhing in that perfect, beautiful agony a woman can only experience during sex.

"Shit," he curses after his hand smacks me particularly hard. My eyes are tearing, and each time his hand comes down on me I feel it all the way into my g-spot, up my spine and into my nipples. "If only you could see how hot you are right now. My cock is so hard. Every time I touch you, your ass jiggles and your body does this shuddering thing." His fingers touch my cunt, and he groans, pushing two inside me without so much as a second's hesitation. He slides right in.

"You're so wet, baby. You're creaming for it. You need my cock bad, don't you?"

"Just fuck me already," I scream into his sheets, offering my ass up to him.

"Tell me what I want to hear." His fingers curl and rub inside me, focusing on a spot he became intimately familiar with the night before. He's nowhere near my clit, but I'm squirming and babbling all the same.

"I'm never gonna say it."

"Then you're never gonna get this." He pushes the line of his cock against me. It's bare. He is completely naked behind me, and I can't see it. I mourn the thought and shove him away from me with a foot to his thigh.

"What the—Sophie."

I flip over and take him in. The apron is pooled around his feet. He looks like he's gonna yell at me, but I can see his brain stops when I stick my hand between my legs and start rubbing my clit as I stare him.

"Are you—" He clutches his hair in amazement, and his abs tense to perfect definition. "Are you fucking yourself and…are you getting yourself off from staring at me?"

I'm beyond words now. The smacking and the anger and the fighting, it's turned me into an animal. My ass hurts more now that I'm sitting on it. I'm a jittery addict in need of my next fix, and he's the dealer with the good stuff.

I think when I don't answer he loses himself a bit, like I have. He crawls onto the bed, takes my hand away then clambers on top of me. His cock is at my sex, nudging at me, and thank God I have enough sense to get out one word.

"Condom."

"Fuckingshitmotherfuckingcocksucker." He's shaking his head. "I can't believe I almost…" I see why he's angry, and it takes a chunk of the barriers around my heart out with wrecking ball. It's not that he's angry that he has to put one on—he's ashamed he nearly forgot to do it. He's always looking out for me and my comfort, never one to put himself first.

He grabs one from his bedside table, tears it open and rolls it on, muttering, "My prick is gonna break in half any second."

That just about pitches me over the edge of need and into full-blown lunacy.

Once he's got the condom on I reach for him, my hand behind his neck, and pull him toward me. He's in such an awkward position that he kind of stumbles over my legs. I twist and turn until I have him between my thighs again, then push off the bed until my mound is nudging the tip of his erection.

"Inside. Now."

"So rude, baby." His tone is playful, but his face is defenseless. He looks ruined.

My fervor is uncompromising. I've got my hand on his cock now, and I'm rubbing against him. He pushes forward, hands on my hips, guiding me slowly. I'm soaking the bed, and my pussy is swollen as hell, but he's still taking his damn time.

"Stop, Sophie," he says between panted obscenities. "I don't wanna hurt you. I'm huge right now, and I feel like I can fuck you into the floor."

In a move I'm not quite sure how I manage—I think he might be so far gone I can manipulate his body any way I want—I wrap my legs around his waist and spin him onto his back. I take his cock between my legs and push down onto it, embedding him deep inside my channel.

"Fuck, Sophie, fuck."

"What a mouth you've got," I tease.

Despite my statement, there isn't much talking afterward. I take what I need from him and give him everything he asks for in return. I have his groans, his cries, and his insistence, to guide me. The rise and fall of my hips against his is pitched and jostling. There's nothing romantic or sweet about this. Eventually I can't hold myself up anymore and come crashing down onto his chest. He uses the pause to flip us back over.

He lifts my legs up, resting my ankles on his shoulders, and starts pumping into me so fast I feel like there's an actual vibrator in my cunt instead of a cock. He's using an angle that doesn't touch where I need him to touch. I've got my hands on his head, keeping him close to me.

"Different. Need more."

His only response is to let my legs down. He's in the cradle of my body and he rolls himself against me, inside me, and Lord, is he hitting that good spot over and over now. He's holding my head, making me look at him. I only squeeze my eyes shut for a second before he kisses me and tells me to open.

He wants to see me at my most vulnerable moments. Doesn't he understand how much courage it takes to do that? Courage I don't have.

"Touch your clit," he says against my lips.

"Tony—I can't—"

"You can do it. I've got you."

He guides my hand down my body, and we touch the swollen bud together, rubbing and coaxing it into an orgasm that has me screaming his name.

When the pulsing subsides, he returns to our previous position, my feet up around his ears. His body is a machine, a jackhammer making love to me with molten satisfaction. He grips my thighs as he comes, clenching and shivering, his ragged sobs almost at a lyrical pitch.

When he's through and we're both spent, the full condom thrown over the side of the bed without a care, he comes down over me and nestles his head against my chest. We lay together for who knows how long, Tony's perfect dinner and smashed table setting completely forgotten.

He kisses my nipple, sucking on it like his favorite treat. It's tender and even his small kisses send chills across my skin.

"I can't so soon again, I need a break."

"I know, I'm turning you all soft and lazy before I tell you I did something you might not like."

That wakes me up. "What did you do?"

"I might have done a search for you on the internet."

"Why?" I groan.

"I wanted to learn more about you. And you know what I learned?" He doesn't give me a moment to respond, just slides up next to me and turns me to face him. "You're a fucking brilliant writer."

"I hate talking about my work."

"I figured, but I'm not gonna stop because I think you need to hear it. The points you made on deep equity—wow—I sent that article to my whole family."

"You what?"

"I didn't tell them I was sleeping with the woman who wrote it; I said look at this interesting article. They loved it. It's important stuff you're writing."

"Did you read my eminent piece on cat memes and the parallels they represent in our society?"

"Yeah, I did. It was funny."

I sigh, burying my head in a pillow. "I hate those articles."

"What? I can't hear you."

I turn onto my back and yell at the ceiling. "I hate those articles. I hate that I have to write them more and more now. My new editor doesn't give a shit about social justice. He's a privileged ass who has no interest in listening to what anyone else has to say. It's so frustrating working in a system like that. How can we progress as people when we refused to learn, to evolve? I hate to sound like a petulant child but it's really not fair."

"Have you tried finding a job somewhere else?"

God, there's nothing I want to do more, but as Gemma says, we have to grow up at some point.

"I can't risk that right now. I just moved into a new apartment; I have rent to pay. I barely have decent insurance. I might be unhappy at my job, but it's at least it's a stepping-stone bringing me closer to what I want to do. I've got to pay my dues."

"What you're doing is hard, baby. I admire you for it, and trust me, I more than understand."

"How do you understand?"

"My folks weren't well-off growing up." He turns us, pulling me up to rest my head on his shoulder. His hands trail through my hair. "My dad is an immigrant, and my mom didn't go to college. They married really young, and she became a stay-at-home mom right off the bat. Dad worked hard for us every day to make sure we had enough, not just to live, but to go to good schools, and live a life where we don't need to struggle or be unhappy. They both have jobs they love now, but I'm successful because he put me in a position to be successful. I'll always be grateful for that. I'll always be in their debt."

This snapshot into Tony's family has me curious. My journalistic qualities take over, and I start asking questions, delighted by the picture he paints.

"Your mom and dad still together?"

"Hell yeah! They are so in love it's embarrassing. They'd kiss in front of my brothers and me all the time, just to annoy us."

"How did your mom feel about not working?"

He looks at me askance.

"Not working? She raised three boys, although once Santi was old enough to watch us she got a job at an art gallery. She was the first person to take me to an art museum. But there's no harder job on the planet than being a full-time mom. You must know that."

"What does that mean?"

"Well—what I mean is—"

I see what's happening. There's no better way to get an inside scoop on my family life than social media.

"You stalked my Facebook, didn't you?"

"Why is your profile public? All that information ripe for gawking by assholes like me."

"It's a condition of working where I do. I need to have a public persona, let the world into my personal life, which you did without any compunctions."

I glare at him, but I can't be mad at something everyone I meet does nowadays. Looking a person up on the internet is normal, even though it will always feel like an invasion of privacy.

"It doesn't matter, but I should have asked first."

I kiss him, making sure he knows I'm not mad. "Thanks for saying that. It's okay, you can look."

"Is your Dad…"

"He's alive. Just out of the picture, or as much as I can make him stay out of the picture." I smile forcefully, unwilling to have this conversation right now.

I look through his bedroom door and into the living area, pieces of china scattered across the room like the aftermath of an earthquake.

"I'll buy you new plates." I can't believe I destroyed his personal property. Again.

"Don't even think about it," he says, eyebrows raised, promising he's not going to let my obvious subject change go for long. "I'm taking those broken pieces and putting them in a shadow box to frame on my wall."

"How do you even know what a shadowbox is?"

"I learned it on Pinterest."

And just like that we're laughing again. Later, when our sexual energy returns, he takes me on my stomach, spearing into me like it's the most natural thing, and he whispers enticingly dirty things in my ear until we come together.

Afterward we reheat the dinner in the microwave—much to Tony's chagrin—and eat at the table completely naked.

It's the best meal I've ever had.

8

TONY

LIKES FIGHTING WITH HIS SOPHIE.

One week into the fling that isn't a fling.

Sophie is a smartass, but a week into our fling—which I refuse to admit is a fling—I come to learn there are hidden depths, barriers even I have doubts I'll be able to crumble. She sticks to the rules, doesn't talk about family or anything too personal. But every now and then I get something, a glimmer of her life past what she presents to me.

Maybe it's because my family is always so open and brutally honest with each other, but I hate the boundaries she puts between us.

Tonight, we're hanging at her place, having a glass of wine and watching the news. No sex. Just normal couple stuff—despite her vehemently opposing the word. She treats it like an old man with no teeth hitting on her at a bar. If I didn't suspect she's got some major baggage where her relationships are concerned, I'd be a little offended.

"Be right back." She taps her stomach.

"You were just in the bathroom. Are you okay?"

"I ate too much. Don't judge me. Your food is delicious."

"No judgment." I tug her down for a kiss, gripping her ass. I seriously love her ass. "I like cooking it for you."

Her phone starts buzzing with incoming texts the second the bathroom door closes.

A lot of texts.

Worried it might be something important, I look over at the lit-up screen. They're from her sister.

FYI DAD CALLED ME TONIGHT.
HE'S ASKING FOR MONEY AGAIN BUT HE'S GOING TO PRETEND HE WANTS TO HANG OUT.
I'M NOT SAYING YOU SHOULD MEET UP WITH HIM, OR GIVE HIM MONEY, BUT AT LEAST THINK ABOUT TALKING TO HIM. IT'S BEEN YEARS. HE'S OUR FATHER.
IT WON'T KILL YOU TO TALK TO HIM.

Years? I've gathered things aren't great between her and her Dad. But she's mentioned he lives nearby. How has it been years?

He's asking for money again...maybe that's all he calls her for? I wouldn't blame her for resenting a man who was supposed to care for her but only saw her as a bank.

Sophie isn't well-off. She lives in one of the smallest apartments in the building and never has food in her fridge. I've taken to cooking her more dinner than she can eat, enough that she'll have leftovers to take to work.

It's a challenge getting her to have more than a cup of decaf coffee for breakfast.

Sometimes when I cook her dinner, she doesn't eat as much as she did at brunch that day. It's almost like she has something against my cooking. Maybe she doesn't like my food but doesn't want to hurt my feelings.

I've seen her devour food within seconds.

Maybe she doesn't like Italian food?

Oh, God. What kind of woman have I fallen for?

I return her phone back to its previous position when I hear the toilet flush. As she comes out I say, "Your phone's been blowing up."

"Thanks." She glances at it, her smile tightening as she reads the texts, then shoots off a quick message.

"Everything okay?"

She nods, taking a deep sip of wine. "Yeah, but I should head home for the night. I've got a little editing to do before bed."

"I could sleep at your place, if you want to do work together? I'm sure there's some crisis in Italy I could be dealing with."

She clears her throat, doesn't look at me. Why did I have to mention Italy? Isn't that the whole reason we're in this fling mess?

"No, I don't have energy for sex tonight."

"That's not what I meant by work. We could simply *be* together...doing things."

She shakes her head then gives me a scorching kiss before bidding me goodnight.

She's never let me stay over at her place. Not once.

The next night I convince her to let me come over...more like I meet her at the front door when she gets home from work and prod and push until she lets me in. But now she's in a temper. A sexy temper.

Sophie's yelling at me because I left the light on in her kitchen.

"Do you know how expensive electricity is in New York City?"

"Of course I know." I'm a Brooklyn boy, born and raised. "Do *you* know how expensive the electric can be here, you being from Staten Island and all? That's not a real part of New York City. At least not one that counts."

"You little shit," she yells and launches into a five-minute long tirade about how Staten Island is just as much a part of New York City as the other four boroughs. I knew this would spark a fight, but mostly I wanted to hear her Staten Island accent come out. It's so thick and sexy when she's pissed, especially when she's angry on behalf of her hometown. Which is hilarious to me, because when she talks about the island, it's in a very disparaging way. It's one of those distinctly New York traits of hers, a facet I connect with.

"Only Staten Island people are allowed to make fun of Staten Island. Anyone else does it and I'll bite their heads off. Yours included."

It's the same for me. I complain about Brooklyn all the time, but if I hear anyone talk shit about it, and they ain't from Brooklyn, I go off on 'em.

I sit down on her tiny couch and turn the game on. The Yankees are playing Cleveland. I'm a Mets fan, but I'll cheer for the Yankees if it pisses her off some more. She's fuming now.

She's yelling from the kitchen, turning the light on and off, asking if I care if she has an outrageous electric bill.

She's so red her freckles look like spots of paint speckling her face. All I do is grin back at her. She knows this is our game, and she plays it like a pro, but right now she's so far into it she wouldn't know fantasy from reality if it slapped her in the face like pigeon shit launched from a lamp post.

"What if I can't afford my electric bill anymore? What if I go broke from paying ConEd, and then I can't pay my rent and they evict me? Don't you care if I get kicked out?"

"Good riddance."

A sandal hits me in the back of the head.

I pounce on her.

By the time I reach her, I've got my pants undone and her shirt is halfway off her head. We make love on the floor like that first time, and yeah, sometimes I think of sex with her as fucking—actually most of the time—but right then, when I'm on top of her, cradling her face, going slow and long, torturing her as she's begging me to take her fast, I know we're making love.

Not that she'd ever admit it.

Afterward we lay together half-naked, petting one another. I trace as many freckles as I can reach, and her toes trip over a raised scar on my leg.

"Where did this come from?"

She always asks questions, never answers them.

"Family vacation when I was a kid. The biggest, craziest dog you've ever seen bit me. This thing must have been three hundred pounds at least."

She nuzzles deep into my shoulder, her smile resting on my skin.

"Don't laugh, it was scarring. Literally."

"How old were you?"

"Seven."

She raises her head then, eyebrows drawn down, her gaze on the scar. "Tony, that scar is massive."

"I told you. I had to get rabies shots. That's why I avoid Jersey at all costs now."

She sits up, reaching down to the scar and kissing it. "I'm sorry you had to go through that. That's more than scarring for a little kid. What happened to the dog?"

"It was a stray. Animal control probably came and picked it up. Ma and Pop never told me what happened to it. I think they were trying to protect me."

"I've noticed you avoid dogs sometimes." She massages the scar, as if it still aches all these years later.

I shrug, not wanting to admit my stupid fear. It's embarrassing, for Christ's sake. What grown man is afraid of dogs? She doesn't press me for it, but gives me a gift instead.

"One summer Gemma and I were visiting Mom in Cali, and we'd planned to see the redwoods at Muir Woods the next day. I felt something pinch my eyebrow but didn't think much of it. Later that night my eye was swollen shut. A bug bit me, and I had a massive allergic reaction to it."

She gets up stark naked and scrambles over to a bookcase. I stare at the freckles covering her long spine. She's small, but her back is muscular, rolling and flexing as she stretches to grab a photo album off the top shelf. Flipping through the dusty tome, she finds her quarry and tugs the 4x6 photo out. She catches me looking at her beautiful body. She blushes but her stride has a bit more sway as she returns to our spot on the floor. I love making her feel sexy. I've gotta do it more often.

Sophie hands the photo to me and it takes a lot not to laugh outright when I see it.

"It's okay, you can laugh. I was misshapen for a full two days. And Mom still made us go to the redwoods despite my throwing a fit."

A young girl, no older than sixteen, sits in the back of a pickup truck. She's wearing torn jean shorts, a Green Day T-shirt, and flip-flops. Her dark blonde curly hair, dyed pink on the ends, is swept up into a messy ponytail. Covered in freckles and zits, she glares at the camera as if the force of her gaze could make it melt. Her left is eye is swollen shut, and the brow is three times its normal size. A girl with wild red hair sits next to Sophie's younger self, smiling brightly and giving the camera the thumbs-up, clearly enjoying the younger girl's pain.

"You look like a miserable baby punk rocker."

"I was, and my sister took every moment to remind me how Quasimodo was a noble character, and I should be thankful to have his likeness. I was so mad at her for it." She elbows me playfully. "Who you calling baby punk? I was hardcore."

I kiss her, sipping at her lips, savoring the taste. "No doubts here."

"What did the Rodriguez clan do for vacations?"

I try to temper my excitement that we're having this conversation. These are intimate details we're sharing, each secret told creating a connection more solid than the last.

"Our equivalent of a family vacation was the Jersey shore. We couldn't afford to go far. Ma and Pop treated those days on the beach like the best adventures, and they were. I'd like you to meet them one day."

"I'll have tea with your mom, keep her company while you're off gallivanting in Rome."

Before I can remind her the job isn't a sure thing, she sees the light is still on in the kitchen, and jokingly chides me again. I let the topic lie, not wanting to spoil the contented magic between us tonight.

I smile and kiss her, and when I ask to sleep in her apartment for the night, I try to hide my disappointment when she says she'd rather stay in mine, citing my better air conditioning as the reason.

I don't push her, holding on to the little pieces she's shared tonight. Little by little, I'll make her melt. She'll come to me in her own time.

The problem is, I don't have much time left to spare.

Despite thwarting my continued attempts to sleep at her place, the next night my resolve to make Sophie mine only strengthens.

"We're going out for dinner tonight," she says, knocking on my door barely a second after I make it home from work.

"Where?"

"Somewhere nice, so look sharp." She's nearly bouncing off the walls, her smile is so big.

I'm not really in the mood for a fancy place. I've been working long hours, and my brother, Santiago, and I got into another fight. I'm stressed and in need of one-on-one Sophie time, but she refuses to be swayed.

"Baby, I'm tired. I want to stay in."

She frames my face and kisses me quickly. "If you don't get dressed and meet me on the curb in forty minutes, I will not have sex with you the remainder of the time you're in the country."

Not fair.

"Why are you being so mean to me?"

She slaps my ass. "Go get dressed."

I drag my heels but throw on some trousers, a blue button-down shirt and a jacket. I make it to the curb exactly forty minutes later, and I'm the only one there. It doesn't surprise me I'm the first to arrive.

Sophie's hair is as short as mine, why does she need an hour to fuss with it?

Okay, clearly I'm cranky, and whiny, and want to be naked in bed with Sophie.

I especially want to be naked in bed with Sophie when she finally makes it outside.

The creaky hinges on the main door catch my attention, and I look up. My mouth nearly drops to the floor and my pants become considerably tighter as Sophie steps out onto the stone stoop.

The dress she's wearing is long and flowing, the material blowing in the warm evening summer wind. The straps are thin, and from the angle they sit on her shoulders I can tell they make some sort of sexy pattern behind her back. The cut of the neck is modest, not showing any cleavage, but there's a belt cinching her waist and accentuating her luscious hips.

The shape of the dress is beautiful, but it's the colors that make her sun-burnished skin glow in the evening light. The deep dusky pink starts at the top then fades into a bright orange at the hem. It's a dress of sunsets, an evening spent on a beach walking along the sand and feeling the water trip against bare toes.

I grasp her hand as she comes down the stairs and press a kiss on her knuckles, try to be as gallant as I can. This woman deserves nothing less than a gentleman, and I'll do everything to meet those needs.

"You look very debonair," she says.

"You look like the sun, Sophie. You're so beautiful."

Her head dips, but she kisses me on the corner of my mouth, lingering there, her breath brushing my skin as she backs away.

"How are we getting to this mysterious location?"

She holds up her phone. A little dot on the screen tells me a hired car is almost here. I start to complain again, but as she turns toward the street, searching for the car, I'm confronted with straps of orange and pink fabric crisscrossing along her freckle-covered back, drawing attention to her delicate spine.

My pulse picks up.

"Are you sure we have to go out?"

I pull her against my body, gripping her waist tightly, making sure she feels how badly I want to stay home. Really, really badly.

"Yes." She's laughing at me. "Stop being such a whiny baby. You're going to enjoy this. I promise."

"I am so far from whiny, you wouldn't even believe it. In fact, I'm being the perfect gentleman."

"I have yet to see proof of that fact." She waves to our car as it pulls up.

"Baby, we're still going out, and your sexy dress is still on. That's me being a perfect gentleman."

When we settle into the car and close the door, I take her hand and bring it to rest against my groin. She shoots me a sharp look, but if anybody were to glance at us, they would think I was innocently holding her hand, our fingers entwined in my lap.

If I'm getting sexually tortured, then so is she.

Once in Manhattan we cross over to Madison Avenue and head uptown, eventually making a left onto 81st Street.

"Sophie, I know where this road goes." I've driven this route so many times, especially during undergrad, I know it like the back of my hand,.

For a long time, this place was my second home. Even as a kid I begged my parents to let me come here almost every day in the summer. My friends and brothers could have their video games —I wanted to spend my days at the Metropolitan Museum of Art.

It usually fell to Santiago to watch over me. He flirted with the ladies in the gift shop, the other teenagers forced to be there with their parents, while I drowned myself in culture and art, in perfectly formed lines and colors that confound the eye. I would sit and stare at a Titian drawing for hours and hours, forgetting to eat or drink, forgetting about whoever was accompanying me, forgetting about the world. When it was time to go, I'd run to the roof garden and hide among the current exhibit, staring across the magnificent view of Central Park.

I know I could easily get swept up in the magic of my home away from home, forgetting everything and everyone around me like I did as a kid, but it's a sobering truth realizing my childhood imaginings will never be as intense as what I feel for Sophie. I'd never forget she's beside me. She's a vibrant force, more powerful than any trance an ancient painting could put me under. I've barely talked about what it took for me to sever this part of my past, hardly a sentence or two, and yet she's seen what it meant to give it up.

She sees me.

No casual fling would do this monumental thing for me.

After we wait in a long line of cars, our driver lets us off in front of the imposing Greek columns. Men and women dressed to the nines filter up the stairs and into the museum.

"Shouldn't the museum be closed now?" I ask. She smiles coyly and tugs me inside, excited by whatever secret she has up her sleeve. I glance up at a banner in the grand entryway.

OPENING NIGHT:
ART AND LOVE IN ITALY; A SHARED COLLECTION.

A heavy stone drops into my stomach.

Of course I've heard of this exhibit. Some of these pieces have never been shown in America before; it's an historic international partnership between museums. I've seen ads for this collection on subway cars, the sides of buses, even the CEO of the company that bought our business, Mr. Petrov, is a sponsor for the museum. It's impossible to get tickets.

Sophie opens her small beaded bag and pulls out two tickets to the exclusive event.

I look down at her, dumbfounded. "How did you—"

"I have connections," she says fanning herself with the tickets.

"I have no idea how you did this," I lean down and whisper in her ear, "But I am so in awe of you. How will I ever pay you back?"

She wipes invisible lint off my jacket, takes my hand, then makes me fall for her all over again.

"This isn't about paying me back for anything, Tony. This is about letting you be who you are. I want you to wave your freak flag, and enjoy a night with me and all the art you so clearly love. Just because you chose a different path doesn't mean you need to forsake this one completely."

Her appraisal of my character sets me on my ass. The stone turns to molten metal inside me and grows larger.

She hands our tickets to the woman at a velvet-lined rope barrier then takes my hand and guides me into the bustling exhibition.

A man speaks at a podium. I don't hear a thing he's saying. I can't stop looking at Sophie. My Sophie.

I bring her hand to my lips and kiss her knuckles, making sure our eyes connect when she looks at me. Her smile lights up the room, and I'm the only one who can see it. Mine. All mine.

I can't let her go. It might actually decimate me if she won't be mine.

With the speeches concluded, the curtains part. Champagne is distributed in cut crystal glasses, and the exhibit opens.

I'm transported, as if the paintings can erase the past few years in the corporate sector and bring back a childhood guided by masters of the old world. Titian, Michelangelo, Da Vinci, Botticelli, Raphael, Donatello. These works instilled in me a love of art, one that has never abated and probably never will, no matter how hard I've tried to stuff it in a box and forget about it.

I remember who I used to be, and who I wanted to become.

"My whole family is artistically inclined," I say lightly. "I was never into applying it practically; I enjoyed the history and theory. I wanted to learn everything I could about these painters and their styles."

"What about your brothers?"

"Nicky's the actual painter—he's been making a name for himself recently. Santiago's love is music, like Pop."

"Do they work in business for day jobs, too?"

"No. That's just me." We stop at a darker painting, one depicting a hellscape meant to frighten, to warn against sin. "I'm the only one who gave it up. It surprised them, like nothing I've ever done before. They wanted me to see a psychiatrist. Ridiculous, huh?"

She doesn't look away from the painting when she says, "Actually, I think it's sad."

"Like pathetic?"

"No, sad you thought you needed to dissolve this part of yourself in order to become successful."

She sees inside me as if I were made of fucking glass. The stone grows bigger, amplified by each painting we pass.

We stop in front of a depiction of the Virgin Mary with baby Jesus, cradling her child, protecting him. I saw this one in Italy when I studied abroad in college. It didn't draw me like the others did, but now I want to stay here forever and apologize for not seeing its true beauty. It's been so long since I let myself return to my roots that it almost hurts. Like my eyes are crusted over after a long and restless sleep.

Sophie drags me to another piece I'm familiar with. I explain to her a little bit about Titian and his long life, his skill with color and brushwork.

"I'm sure when you travel to Italy you escape to the museums whenever you can."

"No, we're too busy. This last trip I barely left the office. They don't even know I have this interest."

"Oh." She looks dismayed, searching for words.

I understand why she'd think it's sad. The career I've chosen is the opposite of everything I wanted. And yet...it doesn't make me sad. Being in this museum makes me feel like an intruder in a house I used to live in.

"What do you talk about with your coworkers?"

"The usual. Sports. Meetings. Golf. I hate golf. My boss talks to me about golf all the time, and I can't stand it. It's the only thing he does on the weekend he deems worth talking about. Not the time he spends with his family or the high school soccer games he watches. Just golf. There's a picture of his kids on a shelf behind his desk. He never looks at it."

"My pop, no matter where he worked—the odd jobs, driving a taxi, whatever tiny space he occupied—it was covered in pictures of mom and my brothers. And me."

Sophie's fingers touch mine, they spread from a tentative skim to a full-on entwining of hands. I grasp with all my might, hoping she can feel everything I can't bring myself to say. Fear holds it all back. Frustration. After all the clawing and scraping I've had to do to get where I am at the firm, my fingers are so fucking bloody. When I first started I felt like an imposter, but now I don't think I belong here anymore either.

Christ, I'm surrounded by works I considered my lifeblood, and all I can think of is that tiny picture on my boss's shelf. And Sophie's hand holding mine, acting as my crutch as I battle with a part of myself I've been ignoring.

"When I'm my boss's age, I want to feel full and enriched by my passions. I want to be surrounded by people I love. I want to support them. I don't want to work hard for work's sake." I pull her hand to my stomach, holding it against the knot in my gut. "I don't think I could live with myself if my life were so empty."

"Look around you, Tony. Your life is anything but empty. You made a choice you didn't anticipate you'd have to make, and there's no shame in that."

I shove my hands in my pockets, walk toward a small sketch framed in glass. She follows, rubs my shoulders. I want to lean into the touch, but the unsettled feeling keeps pulling me away. If she touches me, I'll be forced to see what I'm afraid of admitting. I try to hold it back, but when she stretches on tiptoe to kiss my neck, the silence breaks.

"My brothers didn't give up what they loved. I did. I'm the sellout, no matter the reasons I tell myself. I can't keep using Ma and Pop as an excuse. They never asked for help. Nicky and Santi...they never understood my choice. We could have supported them together, but I had to take control. Had to take the credit."

Sophie makes me look at her, pulls my face down to hers.

"No, baby, you're not a sellout. You're the fucking opposite of a sellout. Every time you talk about your parents, the first word on your lips is sacrifice. *They* sacrificed for you, worked their asses off for you. You're the type of guy who needs to repay everything you feel you owe."

"They deserve the best. I wanted them to live a life without worry."

"Do you hate your job that much?"

"I don't hate it at all. It's a part of me now. I just—I'll always regret leaving this."

"That's the amazing thing about what you love so much, Tony. It will always be here for you. No matter how long you go away. The history of these paintings are like a good book. The story will be waiting." She strokes my cheek, pushes a fallen lock of hair off my face. "You're allowed to be more than one thing. I'm more than sure your parents, who sound pretty great, know that as well, and are grateful for what you've done for them. You're not a sellout. You're a good man."

I'm overcome by her faith in me.

"Let me take you to meet them Sophie. You will love them so much, and I know they'd love you." I hold her wrists, stroking the soft skin with my thumbs. "They already do, they read all of your articles and have no idea who you are. Who you really are to me."

"No, Tony."

"Why not? Just for dinner."

"That crosses a line. It's too serious."

I stroke her cheek. "*This* is serious. I'm serious about you."

"Let's not talk about this right now, let's not argue." She tries to pull away, but I won't let her go. "This is a good, happy night. Can't we just be here together, just the two of us?"

I can't, not after everything she's said to me. I know she wants more. She's just scared. Just needs to see how much I care for her.

"Sophie, you mean more—"

"Sophie?"

We look up to see a blonde woman wearing a black fitted dress approaching us.

"Adele," Sophie says, quickly pulling away from me to hug the woman as she joins us.

"I had no idea you were into art, Sophie."

"I'm the one who dragged her here," I say, making it obvious we came as a couple by draping my arm around her shoulders.

The woman eyes me up and down, taking my measure in a protective, familial way. It's only then I recognize her as the friend who posted a picture the night Sophie moved into her apartment. This is someone important to Sophie, and she clearly has no idea who I am. It fucking stings.

"Let me guess, you're the sexy neighbor who helped Sophie move into her apartment?"

"Wow, you told someone you know something about me. I'm shocked." I try to pass the comment off as a joke, but my tone is clearly biting and sarcastic. Why can't she admit we're in a relationship? She did this whole thing for me, who knows what she went through to get these tickets, but she still denies what I mean to her. It's infuriating, and frustrating, and all of a sudden the magic of the night drains and my aggravation takes over.

Adele eyes me for a second. "Sophie, you've been keeping things from Gemma and I, haven't you?"

"No," she says quickly, as if in trouble with a parent. "It's not like that. We're just here looking at the art. It's such pretty art, isn't it, Tony?"

I down my glass of champagne, the bubbles threatening to come back up and choke me.

"Hi, I'm Tony. Sophie didn't introduce us because I'm her dirty little secret, and she refuses to admit we're in a relationship."

Sophie's laugh is loud and hollow.

"Do you need more wine?" she asks me, her mouth thin but smiling, trying to keep up appearances. Nothing to see here. Just two people who obviously care deeply about each other but are not in a relationship, spending all the time we can together before I move. Which is not even a fucking done deal.

"I'm drinking champagne."

"Well you definitely need more of that. Adele, will you come with me, so we can get more champagne?"

I look away and grumble, "Yes, please go explain away our being together."

"What the hell is the matter with you?" Sophie whispers angrily at me.

I round on her.

"I agreed to the parameters you set, but I never agreed to keep this a secret. Are you ashamed to be seen with me?"

"Of course not, but we said no family—"

"I gotta think why you wanted that limit, Sophie. I'm dying for my family to meet you. Why can't you even introduce me to your friend?"

"Sophie, can you get me a refill?" Adele keeps her gaze on me as she speaks, cutting Sophie off before she can fight back.

Sophie puts her arm on her friend's shoulder. "This isn't necessary. We're just having a small argument." Sophie shoots daggers at me designed to disembowel.

Adele finally looks away from me, and I feel like I can breathe after being strangled.

"Sweetie, your hair is done. You're wearing makeup and a beautiful dress. You never dress up for anyone. I'm going to have a moment with this man whether you like it or not. That's what family does, Sophie. We watch out for one another. It might be good for you to remember that every now and then."

Sophie opens her mouth to argue, but Adele cuts her off.

"Don't say something you're going to regret. Gemma may accept your bullshit because you're her little sister, and she fears severing that connection, but I have a little sister of my own. One I don't get to talk to anymore or protect. But you will let me set this man straight." Adele turns her piercing glare on me, decision made.

Sophie and I swallow harshly at the same time.

Sophie glances back and forth between Adele and I, then makes what I think is the smart decision, and walks away, but not before narrowing her eyes at me.

Shit, I fucked up. Attacking her is not the way to persuade her to be with me. I fucked up bad.

I take a step to chase after her and apologize but Adele clears her throat, reminding me I'm about to get a talkin' to.

"Hi, Tony. I'm Adele. It's really nice to meet you. Do you know who I am?"

"I've seen you in pictures on Sophie's social media."

"I don't know who you are. Do you know why?"

"Does it matter?" I ask, the reminder that Sophie doesn't talk about me to anyone important in her life a constant burn.

"Listen up, big guy. Sophie never introduces men she's serious about to her family. Her family being her sister and me, because their mother wasn't sane enough to raise them, and their father is an incompetent loser, so it's very rare I get to meet the men in Sophie's life. Usually I'd be excited. But I'm not thrilled by how you're treating her."

"I appreciate your concern, Adele. Actually I admire it. But you don't know what is going on between Sophie and me, therefore you have no business butting your nose into our—into whatever it is we're doing."

"You don't know?"

"From no fault of mine."

She assesses me for a moment, takes my measure then makes a decision. She looks back over her shoulder, checking Sophie isn't approaching.

"When Gemma—no, sorry, let me restart. Gemma is my best friend, and Sophie and I became close as we grew older. When Sophie was ten, her mother had a breakdown. Their father was flawed but he wasn't a bad man; he did enough to make them think he cared about them. But not enough to convince his wife he loved her. He cheated a lot, and their mother Lillian caught him more than once. Eventually it just wore her down. She wasn't strong enough to be there for her daughters."

"That's a little harsh."

"If you had a child whose other parent was a waste of space, would you leave them with that parent? Let them raise your kid?"

"No, I would protect my child until my dying breath. It wouldn't matter what I was feeling—I would be there for them. But I can't presume to know what Sophie's mom was feeling. I won't judge her for it."

"I will judge her for it, because I was there, and I saw how it affected Sophie as she grew and the burden it placed on Gemma. Sophie's never had a lasting relationship. She's never even had a good role model for relationships. Gemma's first marriage...we don't talk about it, and her current fiancé is no prince."

"What about you? You weren't a role model for Sophie?"

"My family is even more fucked up then Sophie's, so no. Listen, Tony, the point of all this is Sophie isn't like other women seeking relationships. She avoids them because she's scared of the unknown possibilities."

"But I can see she's making an effort for you, which is more than she's done for any man in years. That alone would tell me you're important to her." She takes a step forward, lowers her voice, and presses her empty champagne glass against my stomach. "But if I even *think* you're treating her badly or talking to her the way you did tonight, I will break this champagne glass on the floor and use it to cut your dick off. She might not be my blood, but she's my family. Do you understand?"

I don't take my eyes off this crazy woman for even a second. If I do she might gut me before I can blink.

"You're from Staten Island, aren't you?"

"Damn straight."

She takes a step back as Sophie turns the corner to come back to us, no drink refills in hand.

"I understand." And then I add, "It's not usually like this between us. I fucked up. I'll make it right."

"You better." Adele faces Sophie, a cool smile painting her face, as though she didn't just threaten to maim me. "I'm here with a client, so I need to go. If you don't tell Gemma about him soon, I will do it myself. Clear?"

"Yeah, yeah, stop embarrassing me and get out of here." They hug tightly, the affection between them sisterly and deep.

Adele points two fingers at her eyes then aims them at me. I take the hint and raise my arms in surrender. The clack of Adele's heels fade as she returns to the main gallery, and then it's just me and Sophie and a few dozen old paintings judging me as I try to figure out what to say.

"I couldn't find the champagne." She looks everywhere but at me as she wrings her beaded purse, twisting it into a misshapen mess.

Taking the bag from her hands, I place it on a nearby table. I gently pull her arms around my neck then wrap my own around her small frame, and just hold her. It takes a long, unbearable minute, but eventually, she hugs me back. We stand like that for even longer, rocking back and forth, dancing to nothing but the sound of our heartbeats.

"I'm sorry," I say at last. "I don't have the right to be upset. We agreed this was a no-strings scenario. I crossed a line. It won't happen again."

She pulls back, bites her lip. "I can't do this with you if you're going to forget that line whenever these boundaries become inconvenient for you."

"I'm having trouble understanding how you can do this amazing thing for me and not want to be with me."

"You're moving, Tony. I'm not. There's nothing more to say. Do have anything more to say? Some new teleportation device that would make it easier for us to see each other?"

129

"Yes, it's almost done. I've just been too busy to work on it because of all the crazy sex we've been having."

She huffs, and I kiss her neck. Her body is pliant in my arms, but her next words are heated.

"I won't let you talk to me like that again."

"I know. I'm sorry. I had no right."

"I won't be so polite about it if it happens again, understand?"

"I like when you're impolite. Makes me hot."

She rolls her eyes as she steps back, but takes my hand anyway.

"C'mon, you idiot. Anyone who can withstand Adele's fury deserves something hardier than champagne. Let's go find the liquor."

"Then we can look at more art."

"Pretty art."

"Very pretty art."

I love the art, but not one piece is more beautiful than my Sophie.

But she's no more mine than any of these paintings, and she might never be.

9

SOPHIE

CARES FOR TONY MORE THAN HE KNOWS. AND IT'S
SCARY AS HELL.

Work is terrible today. It's step-in-dog-shit terrible.

It starts in my bed. Alone. No different from most of the days
I've been alive, except now I know what it is to have a Tony to
kiss and cuddle. To wake up enfolded in his arms, overheated
from the warmth radiating off his skin, despite the Air Condi-
tioner, yet reluctant to let go.

Because of Tony I know what it's like to be in the shower with
another person and not be self-conscious of my freckles, or my
chunky rolls, or where my thighs rub together. This man—this
amazing man—does nothing short of worshiping my body. His
hands roam every part of me with rough urgency, memorizing
each mark and divot. His tongue tastes me in delightfully weird
places like my inner elbow and outer hip. It's his way of saying
good morning, but I have none of that today.

Tony had a work retreat over the weekend, and it's the first time
I've awoken on a workday without him since our explosive
reunion.

"You gonna miss me, sexy?" He asked me as we kissed outside his pickup truck before he left.

"Nah." He wasn't too pleased with that answer, but after another wet, burning kiss I mumbled, "Maybe."

Christ, I do miss the bastard.

It's sex. It's really great sex and nothing else. My vagina has become a Tony penis addict and she's in withdrawal.

I repeat it like a mantra throughout my morning routine. *It's just sex.* My stomach pinches, a sure sign Gary the ulcer is acting up today. I shouldn't be eating all the heavy food I have been lately, but Tony loves cooking for me, and I can't turn it down. Every time he presents a new meal he looks so painfully hopeful, like he's sharing a part of himself with me. I can't tell him no, even if the acidic food makes Gary revolt in the worst ways.

I pop a few antacids and head into work, drinking herbal tea instead of anything with caffeine. And that's when the shitstorm hits. The subway stalls, causing delays system-wide. Once we're finally released from the sweltering prison, because of course the car I choose doesn't have A/C, I'm still not close enough to my office to walk. I hop on a bus, also without A/C.

The Gods of summer are laughing at me, taking bets to see how much shit they can dole out before I break.

The bus is packed full of noisy tourists, yet there are tons of people standing despite the empty seats next to a woman cooing to her restless baby. At first I think they're annoyed by the infant's cries, and then I overhear a catty woman mention the woman's hijab.

God, I hate people sometimes. But if these assholes want to give up a perfectly good seat, I have no problem taking full advantage. I sit right next to the woman and start up a conversation. Her name is Samaira, the baby is Sara, and she and her family recently moved to New York from England for her husband's promotion. She rides the bus instead of the subway because she and the baby got stuck on a train for an hour last week and came out dehydrated and ill.

A man across the aisle, overhearing us, pitches in with a subway horror story, and soon we've got a bus full of New Yorkers doing what we do best: complaining.

As my stop approaches, I give the standing idiots a bright smile and say, "Welcome to New York City."

My improved mood darkens the second I get to work when my incompetent boss beckons me into his office and starts yelling at me for nothing. I swear he's like a cartoon villain, curling his mustache and completely oblivious that Clark Kent and Superman are the same person.

A dickwad. He's a purposefully ignorant dickwad.

"You're two hours late, Sophie."

"The subway crapped out again—"

"You think you're the only one in this city getting stuck on the subway? Leave your house earlier. If you wanna be late for work, send me something worth publishing."

He slaps a printed copy of my latest article on the desk, the sound echoing around the room like a hammer on the nail of my pissed-off coffin. There are red lines and comments scattered throughout the document. Swaths of paragraphs are crossed out and the words "shit" and "snowflake mentality" mark the pages like a teacher grading a paper after taking five Jägerbombs.

"You printed this out?" I hold the document out like it's a cursed relic about to spread a plague. "You could have just sent an email with your notes."

"I could only express my contempt for this shit by writing on it."

He's serious when he says things like that. Full of drama, like he's a Harvard professor looking down his nose as some plebeian. He went to a fucking state school.

"Are you calling my article shit?"

I don't usually take his abrasive demeanor personally, but when he uses his antagonistic, high and mighty attitude to demean my work? That is a step too far. Especially a piece that has been so damn important me.

"Oh, I'm sorry, do you need me to spell it out for you? Don't leave your liberal sensibilities all over this website. It's not what our readers wants."

"It's exactly what they want." How out of touch can this idiot be?

"I don't want to read about politics."

"You've let me publish these types of pieces before, why the change now? Have I not reached my quota on cat memes this month?"

"You want to be a political advocate, go somewhere else and do it. We want entertainment here."

My heart sinks. Gary sends shooting pain through my gut.

"Are you firing me?"

"No," he says soberly, the threat hanging clearly over my head.

He might not be letting me go, but I'm dead certain I'll only get one warning.

"But the companies buying ads on our site don't want to see stories that aren't appealing to the millennial generation."

I stare at him, speechless for a moment, unable to comprehend his complete detachment from the modern world. I think of Samaira and her baby. The tourists on the bus who haven't a clue what it means to live here. I think of Tony, and how he accepts every demand, every urge to fight, like its natural. Like it's okay for me to speak my mind. It gives me strength. It shakes me from my stunned stupor.

And I speak my damn mind.

"And who are these old white men who think they understand the millennial generation? *My* generation. You think our sponsors know better than I do what my generation wants to read? The world is falling apart, and it's stories like this that will get people off their asses. Nothing's gonna change if we stay silent. I can't sit back in my comfortable life and remain blind to it all."

"You want to write about equity?" he yells, challenging me.

"Yes, dammit."

"Send me an article on why Idris Elba should be the next James Bond. Satisfied?"

His apathy is a slap to the face so hard I can feel the sting, followed by a creeping disgust.

"Get out. We're done. I want your next piece by tomorrow, or you *will* be fired."

That shuts me up, like he knew it would.

My stomach churns, the pain overwhelming. I slump down at my desk, not hearing my coworkers around me.

I can't stay here. I don't belong here. I'm worth more than this.

And yet I do what he says—not the exact thing he wants, but it's bland and has a lot of pictures of sexy men and adorable puppies. I feel ill and wrung out when I've finished, like I've lost an important battle.

I take the bus home, not speaking to any of the other passengers. We pass through Hell's Kitchen, pedestrians swamping the sidewalks. The kitschy diner Tony took me to for brunch is packed, but the thought of eating any of that fried chicken makes my stomach recoil.

Once we're over the bridge, my phone rings. I pick it up blindly, too tired to care who's calling.

"Hi, sweetheart."

"Dad." I rest my forehead on the window, feeling defeated before the conversation even begins. "This isn't a good time."

"It's never a good time for you. When am I going to see you? It's been so long."

I shrug, not caring he can't see it. "You have my new address."

"I don't want to intrude on your life."

"So, let's make a dinner date." I know what his answer will be, but I can't help but throw it out there, give him a chance to prove he cares. "You, me, Gemma, and Murray. Have you even met Gemma's fiancé yet?"

"No, you know how busy I am. Driving a cab is a full-time business."

"Dad, not even you can drive around 24/7. You're always complaining when we talk that you never see me. I am offering you the chance to see me."

"Actually, sweetheart, I'm out of town right now. I'm calling because I need—"

"How much?" I ask, stomping off the bus as it reaches my stop.

"Just two thousand."

136

I make pitstop at the bodega, buying a snack that will help me eat my feelings. Wine alone isn't going to erase this day.

"Two thousand dollars?" I ask, tearing the mini donut box open and stuffing one in my mouth. "What do you need that amount of money for?"

"My car needs some repairs."

"I don't have two thousand dollars, Dad." I swallow.

"If you didn't live in such a fancy place you could afford to help your Dad out every now and then."

Apparently, it's a full box of donuts night.

Tony's parking his truck as I round the corner onto my block. This morning I would have run to him, so excited by his return, but the impact of seeing his expectant smile while listening to someone who's disappointed me all my life makes me insensibly angry.

Tony waves through the front window. He looks happy to see me, and the thought gives me such a wave of anxiety I think I might puke up the donuts. I continue up the steps to the building, struggling to balance my bag, my phone, and the donuts while fishing for my keys.

It's Tony's fault my insides are so fucked up. If it weren't for Tony, with his stupid truck and his gorgeous body and his cooking and his eyes and his kindness, I would be able to handle this conversation with my Dad without wanting to crumble and cry. I would have the defenses to ignore how much it hurts that my father can barely spare an iota of concern for me. I would be fine if I'd never learned what it was to have a man hold me and ask how I'm feeling or how my day went.

I would be stronger if it weren't for Tony breaking down my barriers and convincing me it's okay to have expectations.

I can't let myself get lost in a man again. I won't. I won't.

"I have always given you every cent I have," I growl at my Dad, shoving another donut in my mouth because, seriously, fuck it.

"Why are you yelling at me, Gemma? You never yell."

"God, you don't even know who you're talking to. This is Sophie. *Sophie.* Your youngest daughter. Did you forget you have two?"

"Sophie yells at me even less. What gives? You shouldn't talk to your father this way."

Tony comes up behind me, rubbing my back briefly before taking my keys and helping me open the door. Our eyes meet, and the surety and confidence he has in me is glaring. He doesn't look at me like something to pity or feel sorry for. He nods at me, encouraging me to stand my ground. Tony believes in me, in the woman I want to be. He already sees me as that woman. It's scary as fuck and fortifying all at once.

I take a deep breath.

"Well, this is the new Sophie. I won't sit back and ignore how you only call me when you want something. I refuse to conveniently forget how you basically forced Gemma to become my mother after Mom had to leave."

"Your mother left me, Sophie. Why can't you ever be on my side of that argument? She left you, too."

"She left because you literally broke her heart and drove her nuts. She was so depressed she gave up on life. Christ, she wanted to kill herself."

My eyes meet Tony's as I say that last bit, laying bare the truth of my parents' destructive relationship. He looks…God, what is that expression? Pride and fear and concern and sorrow, all wrapped together in the perfect comforting package. Mental illness is a theme with my family, is that too much for him to deal with?

Well, it's too much for me to wait around and find out.

"Sophie," he says quietly, conciliatory, as if he can see me starting to freak out.

I grab my keys from Tony and run up the stairs to my apartment. I can't face him right now. I can't let him hear what I unload on my Dad.

"You were never there for us. Your abandonment was even worse than Mom's. At least she kept in touch, was transparent about what was happening to her. You spent just enough energy on us to keep us fed, clothed and alive. And yeah, I know other kids had it much worse, but I can't help but know deep down there was something missing in you. You never loved us."

I get to my floor but can't get into the apartment. I've forgotten which key goes in which lock. My hands shake as I struggle to find the right ones.

"We were a burden Mom saddled you with, and you were too self-centered to put any effort into being our father. If you had spared just a little tenderness, just a tiny hint that deep down you cared, it would have made a world of difference. But you couldn't be bothered. Not even to say you loved us."

"Sophie, I do"

I kick my front door. "Don't you fucking say it. Don't lie to me." I take a deep, rattling breath. "Text me where to send the money, and I'll give you what I can. But don't ask me for anything else. Ever. You either take my money and forget about me completely, once and for all, or you come out to dinner with Gemma and me and prove you're more than just an absent father."

He's silent for a moment. I can hear his breathing, long and slow, unconcerned that I've threatened to kick him out of my life permanently.

"I'll text you."

The line goes dead.

I bang my head on the door. Pain shoots from my forehead to my temples to my teeth. It does nothing to help. I'm so angry at everyone and everything. But mostly at myself.

Why, why did I offer him that chance? What was the point? I'm such a fucking idiot. Even in the heat of anger, I still hold out hope he'll come around. He never will, and despite my ultimatum, he'll still drunk-dial me on his birthday, asking why I haven't called to wish him well. Then he'll forget *my* birthday two days later.

Men in my world have always been unreliable. Tony will be no different. Better to cut the poisoned limb off before it infects the rest of the body. I ignore that the limb is actually my heart, and it has steadily been pumping poisoned blood throughout my veins since the moment I met him. I'm infected everywhere, with need for Tony.

Tony syphilis.

I grip my keys, pull my hand back to punch the door, letting my anger consume me, but I can't make the final thrust. Not for lack of trying, there's just a hand holding me back.

Tony doesn't say anything, just takes my keys.

"I need to be alone for a while," I say as he basically consumes me with his body heat, standing behind me and reaching around to unlock the door. "I'll call you."

All the bad thoughts I usually think before considering a relationship are crashing down on me. Memories of how Brian mistreated me, disrespected and became bored of me. The biting things he'd say to prove his superiority fresh in my mind, as if hearing them for the first time. I staved it all off for a while, but the dam is breaking, and I can't think of anything but the pain. What's the point of risking my heart when I know it will end like this again?

Tony's hands come down on my shoulders. They're so big. I have a seriously weird thing for how large he is. His gentle touch makes my poisoned heart pump harder, and I don't want that anymore, right? I want to be infection free.

"Let me in, Sophie. Let me hold you for a bit. We can sit on the couch, eat ice cream, and watch some period dramas. Or that movie you watch when you want to cry." He nuzzles my neck, wraps his arms around me. Just holds me. "Let me in."

Why does he have to be so wonderful? Why can't he keep being the asshole I met on the street? I would have fucked him then written him off. Instead he's caring and considerate and so sweet to me that falling into his embrace is almost like a drug.

I'm addicted to syphilis. To Tony.

The thought freaks me out so badly I shove him away.

"I said I want to be alone."

Tears prick the back of my eyes, and I can't let him see it. He hasn't seen me cry. It's only been four weeks since we met, three since we started spending a steady amount of time together. I'm so fucking scared I can't handle the wave of panic battering at my defenses.

My hands shake as I reach for the handle, but when I try to open my door it sticks, the humidity swelling the wood. I tug on it. Kick it. Slap my hand against it.

"Baby, don't push me away." He comes back, nuzzles against my cheek. "I got you. Let me in."

His words are an arrow, hitting the perfect spot in my battlements and making them crumble. I nearly fall to the floor, but he catches me around the waist and uses his considerable strength to shove the door open. We go into my apartment, and he lifts me into his arms. Like physically lifts me up, with an arm supporting my back and the other under my knees, as though I'm some damsel in distress. Shit, this feels good. I get now why all those damsels keep falling into distress.

It sure feels nice to have a hero sweep me off my feet.

But this isn't part of a fairytale. Tony hasn't saved me from a dragon or some dastardly villain—if anything, it feels like he's saving me from myself.

I'm sobbing now, and I have no fucking idea why. There is so much happening inside me, but he's there, cradling me, closing my door, sitting on the couch and holding me. Holding me so tight that at a certain point I can't breathe, and I love it. Then, as fast as it happens, he lets the tension in his arms go.

We don't speak. He surrounds me as I soak his shirt with my tears. He rubs my back, kisses the top of my head. I try to compare his gentle care with the apathetic attitude of my father and the callous indifference of my boss. I've always put men into one box: the unreliable. Yet here's Tony, holding me as I drool and drip nasty snot, and he stays with me anyway.

I can't reconcile his steady nature with everything I've known of men in my life.

Eventually I calm down, the sobs turning into hiccups, turning into deep breaths he helps me take. I match his breathing and take the glass of water he gets up to pour me. There are so many ways he could have made this about him, but instead he sits with me, my head against his shoulder. He plays with the curls in my short hair. I can tell they fascinate him. It's a little annoying, but I let him do what he wants because he's still holding me.

I adore Tony. I've never felt like this about anyone before. It's not love, it can't be, but it's a dangerous obsession, and I don't know how I'll ever willfully let him go.

In a month or so, he'll be gone, and I'll go back to being a woman too afraid to raise her voice or ask questions. I'll be the quiet writer, the hidden journalist, a role I was always comfortable playing, until I met a man who showed me how much fun it can be to raise my voice and scream my thoughts without a care who the hell hears.

"How was your day, honey?" he asks in mock peppiness.

I snort, burying my face in his shirt. "Awful, and not just this last part. The whole day was a pile of shit lit on fire and left in my underwear drawer."

My tears return, stinging my eyes at the reminder of every awful hour of this awful day.

"Will you tell me about it, please?" he asks after I've calmed down once more.

I'm hoarse and gross when I speak. "You heard the last straw, but earlier today, my editor rejected everything I've been working on the past few months. Rape culture in the schoolyard. That's what my story is. How the phrase 'boys will be boys' perpetuates rape culture and teaches children it's okay for men to treat women like something less than human, less than equal. It's really important to me to get this message out there. We're at a pivotal point in our society. We need to start teaching young women that 'No' is more than acceptable, and our men need to learn what 'Yes' actually looks like and how great and rewarding getting that yes really is."

I wait for him to respond, wanting to know what he thinks of it. I've been working on this article for months, handing in shorter fluff pieces to keep my editor at bay. This article is my gateway to something better, and sitting here in Tony's arms, I think I really need him to see that, to support me.

I'm such a shit. I expect so much and give so little.

"Did that—were you—" he stutters, and I realize his arms aren't just holding me tight out of affection. He's stiff and tense, he's freaked out. "Were you—"

Oh fuck, I see what's happening.

"No!" I look at him, understanding why he draws that conclusion. "Nothing like that has ever happened to me."

He thinks I was raped, that it's why I'm writing the article. God, he's torn up because he thinks I was hurt like that.

His body deflates as relief consumes him, and we hug for a long while. I get it. If I ever thought he'd been violated in such a way, I would have reacted just as badly—shocked and angry and wanting to kill anyone who would dare hurt this wonderful man.

I talk with my chin resting on his shoulder, his face in the crook of my neck.

"I interviewed rape victims, and women who feared their sons would grow to be men with the potential to rape." I grip the back of his T-shirt, still so angry at my editor. "Gay, straight, trans, asexual. Gender and sexuality doesn't matter. What matters is mutual respect.

"My boss doesn't respect me. He treats me like a five-year-old boy would treat a girl on the playground, and it makes me so mad. And this morning I saw a woman being ostracized because of a stupid stereotype, then my Dad...well, you heard that part."

Tony rubs my back, so open and willing to listen. He doesn't interrupt, doesn't try to impart manly wisdom or make excuses for my Dad. Just listens.

"I took it out on you." I need to look him in the eye when I say this next part, so I make him let go. I'm still sitting on his lap, but we're no longer glued together.

"I took it out on you," I say again, so regretful. "I'm sorry. I'm really sorry." I want to tell him about the sick panic that consumes me whenever I think about how much I've come to care for a man who'll leave me in a matter of weeks. But I'm still grappling with it in my head, so I keep it to myself. Confessions like that are pointless with a clock ticking over our head. We may have started this thing on the downhill slide of a roller-coaster, but it doesn't have to always be like that. I can be sensible now. Or at least I can try.

"Hey, we fight. It's fun. We don't apologize." He kisses me, with my nose dripping and tears running down my face. "Never apologize to me for crying, for sharing something with me." He tips my chin up, makes sure I see him. "Promise me."

"I promise."

"I'm really proud of you for standing up for your work. Will you let me read this new one?"

I nod, still shocked he's already gone to so much effort to research and read my work. Now he wants to read more? I bury my face in his chest, breathe him in, try to commit this feeling to memory.

Why does he have to go?

"Would you ever send it anywhere else?"

"No." I stay where I am, too transfixed by the lapels of his suit jacket to move. "I don't know if I can do that. It's too big a thing. I just...I don't want to think about this anymore tonight." I look up at him. "Distract me?"

"Baby, I am king of distractions."

He earns the title, though we don't have sex. He holds me, and we watch my favorite movie, *The Birdcage*, and we laugh together, especially when he starts saying the lines with the characters, and I realize he loves this movie just as much as I do. My laughs are still teary-eyed, and every time I sniffle, he kisses the sadness away, brings me ice cream, squeezes my breast playfully, teases me into happiness.

Something needs to change in my life. I'm on the precipice of an undeniable shift, crazy and drastic, and the thought of it fills me with equal parts anxiety and excitement. I can only hope that the excitement wins out.

I think of Tony moving to Italy...how it's most likely going to happen. But every time one of us brings it up we get awkward and the conversation halts.

He may put on a confidant front, but it's clear he's as confused as I am.

What a pair we make.

10

TONY

TELLS HIS FOLKS ABOUT SOPHIE.

"Ma, I don't think it's a good idea."

"Why won't you bring this girl to dinner? All you do is talk about her. What, you think we won't like her?"

"I know you'd love her."

"Why would I love a girl who fights with you? You say you fight all the time—that can't be healthy."

My ma, Rosanne Rodriguez, is a 5'5", fierce, Italian-American lady with graying black hair she has done at a salon every week, and a gap-toothed smile. Her parents came straight from Sicily, settling in America and working like maniacs until their kids could afford to have a good life. She works at art galleries and when I was a kid would volunteer at museums, just so she could sneak her kids in and give us a taste of culture and history. Without her I wouldn't have my love of art.

I know it's a cliché, but she's the model I hold women up to. Yeah, Sophie calls me a mama's boy for that, but I can hear respect and love when she tells me about her older sister and mother, so I know she gets it.

"My love, they fight from passion, from need for one another. It is his Colombian side." Pa claps my shoulder, his other thumb up in approval. "That is my boy."

My dad, Diego Rodriguez, escaped Colombia before the guerillas reigned terror and Pablo Escobar was the king of the country. Skin crinkles around his eyes as he smiles and laughs, flirts with my mom. We don't look alike; Ma's Italian side really won the genetic battle.

"Don't talk about passion to me, Pop." I make a face like the idea of him being passionate about my ma makes me gag.

"His Colombian side?" she says in outrage, stirring a pot of tomato sauce as it simmers on the stove. "Please, Italians are the passionate ones. Look at our people, look at the artists and scholars we have in our history." She points at her chest. "We're the passionate ones." She scoffs, waving her free hand at her husband. "Colombian side…gimme a break."

They bicker back and forth for a little longer, and I wonder if they fought like this when they were younger. It looks a lot like Sophie and me. Maybe I'm more like my parents than I ever thought.

Pop wins Ma over with a kiss. She smiles up at him, a secret between them I want to know so badly. I want what they have: a strange, undying love that thrives on an equal mix of mayhem and kindness. I think I'm almost there with Sophie. I can feel we're on the edge of something great, but she's holding back.

She's always holding herself back, protecting herself.

"What's wrong, son?"

Pop sits next to me at the round kitchen table, looking at me like I need to confess to trashing the car.

I sigh, knowing I came here not only for the food and to check on my folks, but also for advice. I tell my parents everything: how Sophie and I met, the week between, how she won't trust me enough to truly give herself to me. How Rome is a wall that will never bend or break, and not having her all to myself is killing me.

"I really like her, Pa."

"How you liked Natalie?" Ma asks from the stove without looking at me, her tone nearly screaming disapproval.

My almost-fiancé's name used to fill me with something akin to heartburn, but now there's nothing. Sophie takes up all the space in my heart, protecting it from old hurts like Natalie. She's the antacid to my Natalie heartburn.

Sophie would think that was funny. I want to text it to her, but don't know how to say it without mentioning my ex.

"No, not like that. Natalie was safe. I was gonna propose to her because it felt like that's what needed to happen at that point in our relationship. But I don't think Natalie and I would have been a good fit."

Ma drops the wooden spoon and lifts her hands up in the air, speaking to God. "Now he gets it. Years of me telling him she was not good for him, and now he sees."

Pa and I smile at her very familiar routine.

"But your Sophie?" Pa asks, leaving Ma to her conversation with God.

"She's...fire and ice and wind and rain. It actually hurts when I'm not around her."

And with those few words, my parents look at me like I'm a different person. My ma always said to find a person who would be the sum of the earth to us, the four elements. You can't live without them. Well, it's only been a few weeks, but the thought of being without Sophie makes my heart ache.

"So, she is keepin' distance between you because of Italy?"

"Yeah…I want—I can't say it."

"You want her to go with you. To live with you in Rome."

I nod at Pop, exhausted by the intensity of the passion and need I feel for Sophie.

"Have you told her you feel this way?" Mom asks from the stove.

"No. I can't. She'll run away if I do."

Ma looks at me sternly. "Antonio Miguel Luis Rodriguez, we did not raise you to keep secrets from the woman you love."

I never said anything about love, but I guess I don't need to with them.

"I don't want to overwhelm her with talk of dropping everything she's ever known and moving to another continent with me. She's skittish, to say the least, and she hasn't had a good track record with men." I scoff at that understatement. "I'm pretty sure she's never known a single trustworthy man in her life. Her dad's a total deadbeat."

Ma turns the stove off, and Pop jumps up to move the giant saucepan to an inert burner. She kisses her husband on the cheek then takes a seat next to me and holds my hands.

"Sweetheart, you are very handsome."

"Ma, stop."

"No, listen to me, I'm not trying to blow up your ego. It's big enough as it is. You're handsome and successful, you know how to cook, and we raised you to be a kind gentleman. To any woman you would be an irresistible dream they'd chase to the ends of the earth to keep. To a woman who hasn't known many men she can trust, who didn't have good male role models…she probably doesn't believe you'll keep your promises. She's probably scared shitless."

"Ma, language." I tease, because I don't want to face what she's saying.

"I just want to prepare you, sweetheart. If you ask her to go with you to Italy, and I know you're thinking of doing it, be ready to fight for her."

"Fighting for her was never gonna be the problem, it's how much she'll fight for me. And I can't do long distance. Not after Natalie."

"You'll never know what the future holds until you ask her to go with you."

"It's too soon."

Pop stands, takes mom's hands. They turn to me a unit, a partnership. "Love can bloom in a day or over fifty years. You need to grab happiness while you can."

"Thanks, guys. I'll think about what you've said."

"When are you moving?" Ma says, tapping my nose like she did when I was a boy. "We need to have a going-away party for you."

"No, no party. I swear, Ma. Just a family get-together. And that's only *if* I move. It's not a sure thing yet."

"You kidding?" Pa asks, clutching my neck in that weird hug-thing-that-isn't-a-hug he does. "We're throwing you a parade.

But really, when's the date, because they would be *pendejos* to not give you that office. We need to plan our first visit."

I look over at the calendar, my heart seizing. "If I get the job, they'll send me at the end of next month."

"Barely a month left," Mom says woefully. "What will I do when you're not in this country anymore?"

"You have two other sons to occupy your time."

"Don't you mean one?" Dad looks away for a second, thinking of the tension in our family because of Santiago and his stubbornness.

Mom tries to change the subject. "So, tell us, obviously we are inviting your Sophie for dinner this weekend. Do you want the family to come?"

"She won't come."

"Because of your stupid fling rules? Please, just don't tell her."

"Ma!"

Pop laughs, shaking his head. "You're so devious, *mi amore*."

Spanish and Italian is interchangeable in this family.

"It's better to ask forgiveness than permission, and she'll never trust you if you don't show her your life, your vulnerabilities."

Sophie is going to be so pissed with me if I bring her to meet my family, but Ma's right, I need to risk it. She's too important to me to keep hidden away like a dirty secret.

"Why not? She might as well meet the whole brood."

"Do you think Santi will come?" Pa asks, his shoulders hunched in a way I've never seen before.

"I don't know, Dad, I'll talk to him." Even if I can't stand the sight of the jackass after what he's put Ma and Pop through the last few months.

I've got a quick trip out of state tomorrow, but it won't take the whole day. My flight gets in at four in the morning, then I'll go see Santi when he gets off shift at the theatre. I'd much rather go straight home and curl up around Sophie's warm and sexy body, but Santi needs to meet Sophie, whether the bastard wants to or not.

And I need to figure out how to get Sophie over to my folks' place without letting on I'm breaking one of our fling rules. I'll do every underhanded, dirty thing I can that will lead her to say yes to moving with me. The steps I need to reach my goal are clear.

She needs to know my family, and more importantly, she needs to know I've gone and fallen in love with her.

11

SOPHIE

IS PISSED, AND TONY'S IN A SHIT-TON OF TROUBLE.

"Stop wiggling."

"I'm not wiggling."

"Your leg is shaking like a maraca."

"I'm nervous; what do you expect? Can't you go five minutes without critiquing me?"

It takes two days, lots of amazing sex, and some pathetically adorable begging, but Tony finally convinces me to meet his brothers, citing a small gathering of friends. Grudgingly I admit it can't hurt to get to know some of the people in Tony's life. With any luck, I'll hate every one of them and judge Tony for his choice of friends, which will make it much easier to keep him at a distance.

He also bribed me with a whole tiramisu cake. Baked from scratch.

He plays dirty.

"I'm not critiquing. When you do that your breasts jiggle, and I can't stop staring at them in that killer dress you got on, and I don't want to say hi to my brother with an erection."

I look at Tony, really take him in. His signature devil-may-care smirk is present, but it's paired with a ruddy tinge to his cheeks. He's joking, but he isn't. In fact, he looks almost as nervous as I feel. What has he got to be nervous about?

"My twitching leg gives you a hard-on?" I say it low in case his friends are on the other side of the door eavesdropping. He's got two brothers, who knows what kind of shenanigans they get up to.

He leans down, kissing just beneath my ear, and whispers, "Baby, everything about you gives me a hard-on."

The door swings open.

"Bro!" A tall man instantly pulls Tony into a hug. It's clear they're related, but when they separate it's easy to spot the disparities.

Pitch-black hair lacking the gold-painted natural highlights in Tony's. Eyes a little lighter, more green than hazel, skin slightly darker. A full, thick beard and a man bun top off the hip look. Nothing like Tony. Then he smiles down at me, and I see bright white teeth, and even with all that beard and the way his eyes crinkle, my heart warms with affection. He's handsome, in a unique, creative way. Different from Tony but the same. More charming. Definitely family.

All of sudden I'm more excited than nervous to meet Tony's brothers. Would they share the same naughty sense of humor and quick wit? Maybe I can convince them to tell me every embarrassing detail of Tony's adolescence.

"Sophie, this is my little brother, Nicholas. Nicky, this is my Sophie."

Nicky comes at me for a big bear hug so quickly I don't have time to melt when Tony calls me *his* Sophie. His. I like being his.

I'm lifted off the floor, Nicky's arms pinning mine. He twists back and forth, dancing with my legs dangling a foot off the ground. Good Lord, these Rodriguez men are tall.

At Tony's beckoning Nick sets me down, but not before kissing me on both cheeks. Twice.

"All right, all right, you mook." Tony puts a hand on Nicky's chest, pushes him away. "Stop trying to piss me off."

"Oh, I'm sorry. Did I step over a line where *your* Sophie is concerned? Does *your* Sophie not like to be hugged? *Your* Sophie might want to prepare herself, she's in for a full night of huggers and loudmouths."

Every time Tony says *your Sophie* my stomach flips pleasantly, despite Nick's teasing over the very possessive claiming. Tony's actually blushing, and I can't let *my* Tony get teased on my behalf.

"*His* Sophie can answer all your questions if you addressed them to her like a civilized human being."

Tony barks with laughter, pointing at Nicky's stupefied face. The shock doesn't last long, though. Nicky beams down at me.

"Oh, I like you," Nicky says, all teasing gone.

"Boys," a female voice within the apartment calls. "Bring the girl inside, for goodness sake. Are you going to make her eat standing in the hallway?"

"Sorry, Ma," Nicky calls back, waving Tony and I inside. "I was just razzing Tony and *his* Sophie."

"Ma?" I look up at Tony, panicked. "Did he say Ma? As in *mother*?"

"Yeah." Tony scratches his head, looks up at the ceiling. "I may have forgotten to mention this is less of a hangout with friends and more of a dinner."

"A dinner."

"With my family."

"Your entire family?"

"Well, not aunts and uncles and cousins, third cousins, second cousins once removed, dead grandparents...but yeah...sort of. My parents and brothers."

I look away, trying not to stomp on his foot.

I'm going to kill him. I'm going to strangle his thick neck.

"I told you no families," I say under my breath.

"I'm sorry, but I know you'll love them. Relax, this will be a great night."

"Whether I like them or not isn't the point, I can't believe you tricked me—"

We're interrupted by a woman stepping into the doorway.

"Oh, let me see you." A petite woman with short, dark hair striped with gray and a figure so tiny she couldn't possibly have taught Tony how to cook and eat Italian food, comes at me with outstretched hands. "Let me look at you." She grips both my wrists and holds them out to my sides, examining me. I should be petrified. This is precisely the type of thing I prefer to avoid. Parental affection and approval comes with too much pressure. If they don't like me, it will only screw with the time Tony and have left. But instead of feeling judged or disliked, she looks back and forth between Tony and me, a gleeful smile on her face, so infectious I can't help but grin back.

"Oh, Tony. You were right—she is gorgeous."

I look over at him with my eyebrows up in the stratosphere. He told his parents I'm gorgeous? Me, with freckles covering every inch of my body like a pox survivor?

"Is he not telling you how beautiful you are?" She drops my hands to wave a scolding finger at her son. "I taught you better than that, Antonio Miguel Luis Rodriguez."

Oh shit, that is a great name. That is one sexy name. I am going to scream those four names the next time we fuck—if we ever have sex again because I'm so pissed at him it's entirely possible we never will—just to make him laugh. Oh, even better, I'll scold him like that when we're fighting and *then* moan the epic name.

"Ma, I swear, I tell her she's beautiful every day. I mean, how could I not? Even when I can see she's now plotting something after discovering my hundred names, she's obviously gorgeous." He smiles down at me cautiously, probably worried I'll freak out and start a fight right in front of his mother.

He deserves a fight after pulling this stunt.

"Hi honey, I'm Roseanne. Call me Rosie." Rosie kisses me on the cheek and hugs me close. I feel weird and vulnerable with her arms around me, a longing for my mom rising to the surface like a tank slowly filling, about to overflow. I glance at my feet and clear my throat when she pulls away, only looking back up after I'm sure I have control over my emotions.

"Thank you for inviting me to your home," I say. "Something smells amazing."

Rosie pulls me inside, and I glance over my shoulder at Tony. He's leaning against the doorframe, smiling contentedly.

"*Thank you,*" he mouths silently.

I don't respond, still angry. But I won't hurt Rosie or insult her hospitality by acting petulant.

"Well, I'm glad you say that, because we have a bit of an odd meal for you tonight." She guides me further into their apartment.

The place looks new. I think Tony told me it had been recently renovated, with new kitchen appliances—ones Tony handpicked if I know him at all—and new paint. The focus of the apartment is a floor-to-ceiling brick wall covered in old records, with an ancient but well-cared-for record player as the centerpiece.

As we walk into the living room, and Rosie offers me a seat on a large and comfy couch, I spot another heavily decorated wall filled with pictures. Little boys running turn into young men graduating from high school and then college. In what could be a custom, reclaimed wood frame, Nicky grins cheekily at an art show. In a series of unframed canvas prints, each brother shows their personalities. Nick covered in paint on one end, and who I'm assuming is the older brother, Santiago, on the other, holding a guitar and looking dramatically past the camera. But my eyes are drawn to the center, to Tony, looking absolutely miserable dressed in a suit and glaring at the camera, but in a hilarious way. It has to be an inside joke of some kind.

This wall…I want to examine every single inch of Tony's life, of his family's culture. Every captured moment looks so blissfully perfect, it weirdly makes me jealous for not being a part of it. But I'm also satisfied Tony was privileged enough to grow up in a happy home.

I force myself away from the gallery wall, one I'll examine in further detail later on, and turn back to Rosie.

"How so?" I ask about the dinner, intrigued by her worry over my approval of the meal. This woman could feed me bread and gruel and I'd still be overjoyed.

"I started making a classic Rodriguez family Sunday dinner, very Italian."

Very Italian means very high acidity levels, which will not be great for my stomach. I prepare myself for a hard night filled with acid reflux and indigestion. But it will be worth it if the food tastes as good as it smells.

Nicky rattles off the menu as he sits in a wing-backed chair next to the couch, a beer in hand. "Penne, antipasti, fish, garlic bread and—"

"Fried calamari. The best." Tony says calamari like *galamar* and where before I might have found that annoying, on him it's sexy. He offers me a glass of white wine, kisses me on the cheek, then sits down next to me. He tries to take my hand, but I clasp the wine glass with both, not wanting to encourage him. I'm in his family home, I'll play nice, but I won't forget what he did to get me here.

I catch Roseanne watching the interaction with a critical eye.

"That sounds delicious, not odd. My stomach is trying to eat itself I'm so hungry."

She pats my shoulder, the awkward moment between Tony and me passing. "Well…that's not all you're getting." She turns to Tony with a roll of her eyes. "Your father got a little whiny and decided Sophie should have traditional Colombian instead. So now, we are eating a mix of Italian and Colombian and it's going to be the strangest dinner I've ever fed to a guest."

"What?" Tony groans, then looks over his shoulder and back toward the kitchen. "Dad, what the hell? This was supposed to be Italian night. We would have done Colombian next time."

"So sure there would have been a next time?" I say below my breath so only Tony can hear.

"Yeah, I am," he whispers back. "Give them a chance."

"It's not your family who betrayed my trust and dragged me here under false pretenses."

I turn back in the direction of the kitchen with a smile as someone emerges.

A man walks out holding a large porcelain soup tureen. He's taller than Rosie, slim profile, a head full of salt and pepper hair, and a small patch of beard on his chin. Thin glasses soften his features, making the goofy smile on his face intelligent, sly. He wears the heck out of a maroon button-down shirt and gray trousers, so sharp looking. He clearly takes pride in how he dresses, and has a sense of humor to if the apron stating Colombian food is better than Italian food is anything to go by. I can't help but grin in glee when I see it.

"Yeah, this is my pop." Tony gets up and takes the heavy container from his father, placing it on the dining room table. "Pop, this is my girl, Sophie. Sophie, this is Diego."

No matter how angry I am with Tony, each time he claims me warmth spreads throughout my body. Which in turn infuriates me even more. Betrayed not only by him, but my own damn emotions.

I stand, and Tony's father practically dances his way over. He's an older man, but still smooth and graceful as he kisses my cheek and wraps me in a hug.

"Welcome, my dear. Welcome to our home." He holds me at arm's length. "Tonight, you will taste both sides of Tony's heritage." He glances over his family and says with emphasis, "Each just as important as the other."

They all groan and wave him off. I take one of Diego's hands in mine, knowing how pushy and prideful Italian New Yorkers can be.

"I am very excited to try authentic Colombian food, Mr. Rodriguez. I've never had it before."

Hopefully it won't make Gary the ulcer any bigger. Lord, I am not looking forward to the aftermath of this meal. Just thinking of staying up all night in pain is making me anxious. Why couldn't I fall for someone who eats bland food? A Midwesterner, maybe.

"Call me Diego. And my dear, you won't be trying anything tonight. You'll be—"

"Experiencing."

We all look over at the newcomer closing the front door and walking into the apartment. He's clearly older than Tony, wearing jeans and a T-shirt. His hair is pitch black like Mr. Rodriguez's, but his eyes are so pale, the blue almost silver in color, with a darker skin tone similar to Nicky's.

I wait for someone to introduce me, but all I get is a very awkward silence. Everybody seems to be waiting for the man to say something. I look over at Tony, but he and the rest of his family only have eyes for who must be the older brother. Before I can break the silence, he stiffly says, "Pa, are you torturing Tony's girl with your magical tales of how enchanting Colombia is?"

"It is a magical place, Santi." Mr. Rodriguez puts an arm around me and shakes a finger at his eldest son. "My home country is filled with wonder and beauty. You do not appreciate it enough."

"Right. Been hearing that a lot lately." He looks at me, earnest despite the awkwardness. "Hi, I'm Santiago."

We shake hands, and I notice the markedly different, and almost cold way, he greets me, at least compared to the rest of his family. Everyone else has hugged and gushed over me, and where a handshake might be a normal manner of greeting in another family, in the Rodriguez home it's almost glacial. This Rodriguez son looks tired, worn down. Like he might wish to be anywhere else. It concerns me to see someone with hints of Tony's features looking so haggard.

I squeeze his hand as we shake, cupping it with my other. This man should be smiling, just like his brothers and parents. I want to make him smile, but I don't know how. I'm terrible at this meet the family shit, which is precisely why I never wanted to be put in this situation in the first place.

"I'm Sophie. It's wonderful to meet you."

He pauses for a second as we shake, then squeezes my hand back, a small smile tipping the corners of his mouth. We separate, and he holds a hand out in the direction of the table.

"Are we ready to eat?" Santi asks.

Nicky walks over and pulls his big brother into a hug. They slap each other's backs in that very manly way, and I swear I can see something regretful and painful in Santi's eyes when they separate. Nicky mumbles to his brother, they both nod, smiling at one another.

Tony, on the other hand, takes me to the table, holding my chair out for me as I sit. I watch all the other members of the Rodriguez family greet Santi in the same way. All of them except Tony, who has kept his distance.

Something is happening here, or has happened—a disharmony Tony didn't feel the need to warn me about but is weighing heavily on this family.

I look at Tony as he sits next to me, questioning. He only shakes his head. A denial. Okay, if he doesn't want to tell me, that's fine. I'm not a part of this family, and families have their secrets. It isn't appropriate for me to pry, and I have no right feeling left out or alienated from this dining party by my ignorance of a tension-riddled family conflict.

It's fine. I'm fine. I was dragged here against my will and am now sitting between Tony and a brother he's clearly having some sort of issue with, like a buffer. But hey, I live for familial animosity. This should be awesome.

Said no one ever.

Rosie and Santiago sit as Diego and Nicky bring platters upon platters of food out onto the table. There are things I recognize, like the pasta and calamari, then there is the stew dish Diego put into the tureen and some little flat pancake things.

When all the food is set, Diego stands at the head of the table, subtly commanding our attention.

"Tonight, we are so, so happy to welcome our Sophie to our dinner table."

Our Sophie. So quick to claim me, just like Tony. It seems like love is a fast and hard fall for the Rodriguez clan.

"I think you mean Tony's Sophie, Pop," Nick jokes, ribbing his brother. "He's a little possessive."

Tony smacks Nick upside his head, inciting a small riot of slaps and shoves until Rosie says, "Boys, be quiet and listen to your father."

They all turn back to Diego, and I'm suddenly happy I only grew up with one sister.

"Sophie may be Tony's, Nicholas, but Tony is ours. So, by extension she is ours tonight."

They all look at me like I might argue this point, but all I can say is a meek thank you for being offered a hand to join this family for the evening, even if it is only on the periphery. Even though they'll probably never see me again.

Diego nods, satisfied by my response, and continues. "We are also so happy to have our eldest son here with us tonight, who has been away for far too long. Santiago, no matter what you have a home here. We are your family, forever and always."

Diego clutches his chest, overwhelmed by the depths of his emotion. "I am overjoyed to see you know this."

Santiago isn't looking at his father, but down at his hands in his lap. For a second I think he isn't going to respond, but he looks up at Diego, a fierce respect and love for his father emanating from his every pore. "I know you're my family, no one else."

Its obvious he means it, though his tone is laced with hesitation.

"As long as you know that, we can overcome anything."

Nicky and Rosie are smiling, relieved by Santiago's words. Everyone is touched, satisfied. Except Tony, whose eyes are hard and unforgiving as he glares at Santiago.

Rosie catches his eye and frowns at her middle child, silently chastising him.

I turn away from the subtle exchange, so absolutely furious with Tony by this point fora million reasons I don't even know where to begin. I make a list in my head I can use against him when we're fighting—not sexy fighting, ugly fighting— later:

1. You lied to get me here.
2. You are mad at your brother and using me as a buffer.
3. You didn't tell me about whatever is happening with your family to at least give me some advance warning of what a night with them might be like.
4. You've given me a glimpse of what a healthy, functioning family is supposed to be, and I'm more envious than ever.
5. You've made me like your family, and they'll be gone, out of my life the moment you are.
6. I hate you for putting me in this position.
7. I hate that I don't think I could ever hate you.

Tony pats my thigh under the table, and I push his hand away in a knee-jerk reaction, keeping my focus on Diego.

"Now, to the food," Diego starts, sitting down then spreading a napkin over his lap with a flourish. "Dear, Sophie, we have traditional *ajiaco* made with guasca—"

"Essential for the *ajiaco*."

"Thank you, Nicky—"

"Impossible to find here in a non-dehydrated form."

"Shuddup, Nick," Santi says congenially. "Let Dad finish."

Tony shakes his head, like he's unbelieving of his brother's congenial behavior. Diego continues, either unaware of the tension at the table or willfully ignorant.

"A beautiful stew made with chicken, corn, sour cream, avocado, capers, yucca, potato, and yes, guasca."

Santiago points at the little pancakes. "These are *arepas*, they're like cornmeal bread. Put a lot of butter on it, or cheese. It's really good."

It's Nick's turn, picking up a fried little pocket of something and shoving it in his mouth. "Empanada. Yum."

Rosie lightly slaps his hand. "Don't eat before our guests, Nicky."

"Sorry, Ma."

He's not sorry at all, and everyone knows it, too charmed by his winks and smiles to care.

"*Arroz con coco.*" Tony picks up the serving tray and dishes it into a tiny bowl next to my larger plate. His expression is pinched, awkward, and of course now I feel bad for pulling away from him in front of his family. But it's not the friction between us creating tension.

"What does that mean?" My Spanish is awful, but I know what arroz means. I'm annoyed with him, but I want him to relax, fearing some sort of outburst is on the horizon. I put my anger aside for a moment, and focus on Tony. The pain he's in is so obvious it aches just to look at him. Something happened between him and Santiago, and they're both hurting. I won't let my resentment get in the way tonight. This dinner isn't about me, it's about the Rodriguez family, and I'm here as a witness, or a neutral party. I'll do what I can to put aside the roiling confusion simmering in my heart and smooth the way.

I place my hand on his thigh and squeeze, smiling. It isn't a full smile, I can feel how hard I'm trying, but the sinking of his shoulders tells me it's working. After he passes the dish to Nicky, he grabs my hand, gripping it hard.

"It's rice cooked in coconut milk, with salt and pepper."

I kiss his cheek, and I can almost hear the tension deflating like air from a balloon.

The dinner progresses, the tension constantly there but

remaining at a low level. Rosie and Nicky gladly tell me embarrassing stories about Tony, how he was a moody teenager, mooning for hours over a painting at the Metropolitan Museum of Art. They claim he was in love with a woman in a fresco.

"I can't believe you're ragging on me when Nicky is the one who's the actual painter. He's the moody, artistic one."

"My moods are poetic," Nicky says, holding his glass of wine elegantly. "Yours are petulant."

Santiago doesn't say much, at least not to Tony. But as he's sitting on the other side of me, and the conversation shifts to the recent Mets game between the other four Rodriguez family members, I turn to Santiago.

He, however, gets to me first.

"Not a fan of Italian food?" he asks quietly.

"Oh, no, I love Italian food. Tony cooks for me all the time."

"Yeah, he's a great a cook. Better than Nick and I, that's for sure." He nods at my uneaten plate of pasta. "Do you not like the sauce?"

"It's very good, I'm taking small bites. Savoring."

"She's a slow eater, Santi. Leave her be." Tony interjects, his voice acerbic.

"She's eaten plenty of the ajiaco and the arepas."

"She also ate some antipasti and calamari. Why does it matter what she ate?"

Okay I get there's emotional strain between them, but this is getting ridiculous.

Santi ignores Tony in favor of talking to me. "Italian food is heavy. I like Colombian food because there's plenty of flavor, and it's never spicy."

Yes, that's why I've had two bowls of the ajiaco. The broth is like a balm to my stomach and the arepas are perfectly soft with hints of savory sweetness. It might be the most delicious thing I've ever eaten. Rosie seems to think so as well because she hasn't touched anything but the Colombian dishes, just as Diego has only devoured the pasta and calamari. They argue that their dishes are the best, but they support each other in such a subtle yet lasting way. This is where Tony gets his passion.

Not wanting Tony to think I haven't like all the Italian food he's cooked me, I dip my fork in the pasta and twirl it until it's circling the fork like a spool, manageable enough to eat. I take a bite, relishing the hints of garlic, onion, and basil as they wash over my taste buds.

It's delicious, of course, but not without consequence.

"Happy?" Santiago says over my head to Tony. "Maybe she didn't want that, but you guilted her into it."

I seriously can't believe this is the argument happening right now.

"Sophie loves Italian food, don't you Sophie?"

"Yes, I—"

"See?" Tony practically snarls at Santiago. "Now why don't you stay out of things that aren't your business? You're so good at walking away."

"Enough." Rosie silences them with barely a raised voice. "Boys, go get some fresh air on the roof. *Now*." She turns to me with a smile. "Would you help me clean up a bit, Sophie?"

Rosie stands and heads into the kitchen without waiting for me to respond. I grab a few plates and follow, looking back over my shoulder at Tony and Santiago as they stare each other down like wolves challenging for dominance.

"Go on boys," Diego says. "Nicky, make sure they don't kill each other on the way to the roof."

"Watch as they kill each other. Got it, Pop." Nicky sounds far too happy with his appointed task.

"Come here, Sophie." Rosie garners my attention. Her petite face is pinched, her shoulders bunched up against her ears, as if she's trying to escape some uncomfortable, disgusting thing.

"My boys are passionate, especially Tony. He thinks defending his father and me is his sole purpose in life. As if he has nothing else to live for, as if he has no other passions or pursuits that matter."

The plate she's cleaning clangs as she drops it into the drying rack. I place my hand on her shoulder and gently push her aside to take over the task.

"Are you talking about the art history degree?"

She takes her glass of wine and sips delicately, nodding furiously as she swallows. It's easy to see why Tony holds her in such high regard yet thinks he needs to protect her. Delicate strength. Hard beauty. Tony's family is filled with dichotomies.

"Tony lied to us for years about that, all throughout his Master's. We thought he was learning Renaissance paintings, the difference in paint strokes between Michelangelo and Da Vinci, topics he's been obsessed with since childhood. Instead he's taking classes on stocks, and financial reports, and business strategies. It wasn't until he told us he got a job at that firm of his that we even realized he'd misled us all that time. For *years*. He didn't come to us, telling us he was worried for our future; he took matters into his own hands and made the decision by himself. I tried to explain he needed to live the life he wanted, he kept saying this is what he wants. Always sacrificing for his family. That's my Tony." She sighs deeply. "He'd lie till the end of the earth if he thought it would protect or serve someone he loves."

"He does that a lot, doesn't he?" I ask, a clearer picture of who Tony is forming in my mind.

"So often I want to tear my hair out where he's concerned. Being the middle child is not an easy thing, and he's always felt he needed to make his mark on the world. But the need to provide for us won out. He's very successful, not that he'd show it. Frugalness, thy name is Antonio." She smiles at the saying, resting her wine against her cheek. "The one big splurge was this building."

"What do you mean?"

"He bought us the damn building, so we'd never be tossed out in the rain, hired a trustworthy management company to run it. Claimed it was a good investment. And it has been, but he's never done anything as extravagant for himself. He never thinks about himself. I was thrilled when I heard he'd be moving to Italy. He'll finally learn the meaning of self-care, to indulge in his own dreams."

Tony never thinks about himself, always sacrifices. Would he sacrifice moving to Rome for me? Is that what she's trying to get at? That he'd give up this adventure to stay in New York?

I look Rosie in the eye, making sure she knows I'd never take this away from him.

"Tony is going to Rome. Nothing will change that."

Rosie smiles, briefly plays with the curls in my hair, just like her son.

"I think you're wrong. And I wouldn't blame Tony if that's what he decided. He's a good man, Sophie, and good men are hard to find. Remember that."

I can't handle the intensity of this conversation, so I force it back into frivolity.

"Are you saying I should forgive him for dragging me here even though I didn't know I was going to be meeting you and Diego?"

"Yes, because it was me who convinced him to trick you." Rosie looks like the cat in the cream as I stare at her in shock. Like mother, like son. "You're a sweet girl. I like you. You're angry with Tony, yet you're there for him. He'll probably need you a little bit more before the evening is through."

"Maybe you can tell me what's going on between Santiago and Tony?"

"That's up to Tony to tell you—it's a family matter."

The truth stings, but I take it in stride.

"And I'm not family, I get it."

Rosie quirks her lips thoughtfully.

"I really think you could be, if you took a chance on my boy."

And leave my life behind, move to Rome. Neither of us speaks the truth, but it hangs over our head like the sword of Damocles.

Seeing I can't speak on this subject, Rosie saves me with a request.

"Can you please go up to the roof and make sure my sons haven't murdered each other? Nicky doesn't take refereeing seriously. I'll finish the dishes."

"Sure."

"And Sophie?" I stop at the exit to the kitchen, look back at Rosie. "You're welcome here anytime, whether to eat Colombian food or Italian, whether Tony is in this country or not. Our door will always be open to you."

Pinching my mouth to keep the well of emotions from rising, I leave the kitchen.

Diego gives me directions and a pair of old keys. I climb a recessed set of stairs out in the hallway and use the key to unlock a metal door. The exit leads out onto a magical rooftop escape, transporting me to another world.

"Wow!" It's all I can say.

Little awnings decorate the roof creating secluded seated areas. Each awning is adorned with twinkling lights, giving the space an ethereal quality. Rugs and pillows under each canopy contribute to shape a cozy atmosphere. Small tables are decorated with distinct personalities, one with a deck of cards, another with pads and pencils for sketching. An old boom box sits on one end of the roof, connected to an mp3 player.

It's a rooftop urban secret garden. It's a beautiful escape, nostalgic and secluded. Or at least it would be, if weren't for the massive argument erupting between Tony and Santiago.

"You abandoned them," Tony is yelling, nearly chest-to-chest with his older brother. "Who cares if Pop isn't our biological father? He's still our dad. He still raised us."

Damn, that's…this baggage is heavier than Rosie's tomato sauce.

"You don't understand," Santiago returns, his voice calm in comparison to Tony's vibrant passion. "You never take time to listen to what I'm thinking."

"It is our job to support them now that they're older—"

"*You* made it your job, Tony, your responsibility. Don't resent me because I didn't give up on my dreams for our parents."

I get between Tony before he can lunge at Santiago. He stops short.

"Get out of my way, Sophie."

"Go stand over there." I point to where Nicky is scribbling something in a small notebook. When Tony doesn't move, I evoke Rosie and harden my tone. "Now."

Tony takes a deep breath and expels it quickly before moving over to his little brother. Nicky makes a whip sound, and I want to smack him for it.

I cannot let that slide.

"Great job keeping them from killing each other, man bun."

Nicky shrugs, not looking up from the paper. "This fight's not something I haven't heard on repeat the past few months. You see the same episode again and again, it gets boring."

I think that bland statement affects Tony more than anything I could say to him. He scrunches his hair in his hands and tugs just a bit, turning on his heel and marching to the other end of the roof, not nearing any of his brothers.

I whistle, garnering Nicky's attention. He rolls his eyes at me when I nod toward Tony and give him a look that in no uncertain terms says, *get your ass over there and talk to you brother or so help me God I will smite you.*

As Nicky reaches Tony I hear him say, "Your girl is mean, Tony."

"Shuddup, Nicky. She's perfect."

Men. Why are men so stupid, and when will I ever be rid of them? My life would be way easier if I were a lesbian.

Yeah, keep on dreaming.

I move to the edge of the roof and look out over the skyline. New York is beautiful at night, especially in the summer. Everything is so raw and bare, nothing hiding the dirty underbelly of this beastly city.

"It's the best place on earth, huh?"

Santiago stands next to me, his hands gripping the railing. His face is pinched, and he's biting his bottom lip, his chest is still heaving, the anger not yet abating.

Still pissed, but at least he's talking to me.

"Yeah, but I haven't seen much else. I like California whenever I visit my mom…but I don't think I'd want to live there."

"Would you ever live anywhere else?"

"Yes, I think I'd like to try other places."

"Maybe some other countries?"

I give Santi a good deal of side-eye. "You're fishing."

He chuckles, relaxing a little. "Can you blame me? I want my little brother to be happy."

"Could have fooled me."

"He's the one being an antagonistic little shit."

"Tony doesn't get mad without reason." I nudge him a bit. "Want to talk about it?"

"Tony is an idiot." The sentiment is released on a huff of breath.

"I think that myself quite a bit. This evening alone, the thought's run through my head at least a thousand times. What does that have to do with your argument?"

He looks away, shifts his stance.

I place a comforting hand on Santi's shoulder. "You don't have to tell me if you don't want to. I'm not going to run away because there is a Rodriguez family secret I'm not aware of. I'm not part of this family."

"I should slap my brother. He's clearly not treating you right."

"It's unreasonable to think that way. We've only known each other for a few weeks, and in another few weeks he'll be gone, and I'll be here. I'm a temporary fixture in your life, one who won't be around to judge or have opinions. Use that to your advantage. You can talk to me."

"Did Tony ever tell you our mom and dad met and after a day he asked her to marry him?"

Fuck, no, he did not tell me that. Of course he didn't tell me that. Because he's smart, and if I know anything about him that hints at something more than a fling, I freak out and get pissed. He knows me well...but I'm getting tired of this game of treading lightly and not crossing lines. I want him to know all of me, just like I want to know all of him.

"It was a different time," I say, deflecting. "Courtship was different. The world was different."

"I really don't think it's any different."

"You're stalling." And I'm changing the subject. "What is this horrible secret?"

"I like you, Sophie. You'll make a good sister." Before I can protest that title, he takes a deep breath and dives in. "Earlier this year, my doctors found testicular cancer. Nothing they couldn't cut off real quick, if you get my meaning." He wiggles his eyebrows at me, but I don't find it funny. I wrap an arm around his shoulders, and he leans into me, the playful edge to his story disappearing and the real crux of the matter coming out.

"The cancer got us brothers to talking, about other possibilities. Who could donate bone marrow and all that, if needed. Blood types, other health things we wanted to clear up with our parents. When we asked them about it, they got cagey. It was weird."

He takes a deep breath before saying it. "Long story short, Diego isn't our biological father. He's sterile, always has been. His brother, who passed a while back, donated sperm for all our conceptions."

"Oh, shit." I squeeze him close, hearing the pain in his voice. I look behind us to see Tony and Nick watching us. They know what's happening, and I'm grateful to them for staying away, letting me have this moment with their brother.

But I can feel Tony's eyes on the back of my neck throughout the rest of the conversation.

"Nicky and Tony, they accepted it like it was nothing. They knew right away that the biological shit didn't matter. It was love that mattered. But I felt betrayed. Even now, I can't explain it. I'm the oldest. Pop should have trusted me enough to tell me. I got real angry. Tonight's the first night I've talked to our parents in two months."

"And Tony didn't like that you weren't speaking to your parents."

"That's why he's an idiot. To Tony our folks can do no wrong. He's got this idea in his head that it's his job to take care of them, that he needs to give up everything he ever wanted to ensure their safety and security. He expects Nick and me to act the same way."

"But you don't believe that?"

"No, because I'm not an idiot."

This is going nowhere. I square off with him, intent on getting the truth.

"So, you wouldn't do all you could to help your parents?"

"I would die for them. Even feeling how I do about Diego right now, I would give up everything I have ever loved and wanted for them. But I know I don't have to. I can love them and take care of them and still live my own life, achieving goals I set for myself, being selfish. There's nothing wrong with being a little selfish.

"Tony never seems to understand that. He's mad at me for not setting my hurt aside for the good of the family, and he's been mad ever since. He always needs to please everybody, and that's just not who I am. But this was nothing compared to how he acted with Natalie."

I look at him quizzically.

"Natalie. The ex he proposed to?"

White noise fills my ears, and the image of me cracking Tony over the head with a sledgehammer twirls around my head like a cartoon.

"Oh shit, you don't know who she is, do you? Well Tony pissed me off tonight, so I'm going to do something to piss him off." Santiago takes pleasure in laying it all out for me. "Natalie was Tony's sweetheart all through undergrad. We were sure they were gonna marry. Tony bought a ring. She got a job somewhere in Chicago, and she moved away. A month later he goes out to visit, to propose, and she breaks it off."

"Do you know why?"

"No. All I know is she wasn't worth an inch of him. She was materialistic, ambitious and vain. The whole family rejoiced when they separated, but Tony took it hard. Didn't date for a long time after that. Still doesn't really date, now that I think of it. Until you, that is."

Ex-girlfriends. Proposals. Failed long-distance relationships. I should have met Tony's family sooner. I would have understood his motives way better.

"Thanks for telling me."

"You gonna give me some sage advice about this fight with my brother?"

I think about it for a second. "Stop being a jackass."

"I will if he does."

"Don't forget, it may confound you that he's sacrificed so much, possibly needlessly, but he'd do it for you in a hot second if you ever needed him to."

"I know. I love the dumb idiot." He points at me solemnly. "Make sure he knows I love him."

"Tell him yourself."

"How about I pick you up and carry you over to your boyfriend, so you can tell him?"

Santiago advances on me.

"Don't you dare."

"You're daring me? Now I gotta do it."

I scream, running to Tony as Santi chases me. I love every second of it. Nicky picks me up before I can get to Tony and spins me around with my legs flailing out behind me. Tony is there when I tell Nick to stop because I'm gonna puke. He lifts me into his arms, and I look into his beautiful golden hazel eyes.

I hug Tony, especially after everything I've learned about his family. It must be difficult having a rift between him and Santiago. It probably feels like a limb is cut off. I don't think I'd function if I ever fought with Gemma like this.

I squeeze Tony close, brushing his silky hair. The moment is tender, and the other guys don't bother or tease us; they leave us be. So, I can't blame Tony when he looks at me all shocked after I tenderly whisper, "You're so in the fucking shit house."

12

TONY

MESSED UP. BUT HE CAN FIX IT, RIGHT?

I'd never admit this out loud, but I might actually be a little scared to get in the car with Sophie. She hugs each member of my family, ignores my annoyed eye roll as her arms wrap around Santiago, and promises to invite my mom for sangria after Rosie demands she stay in touch. They've all fallen in love with her. And when she turns her back on them, coming down the brownstone steps and toward my truck, the glare she gives me makes my balls shrivel.

I open the passenger door. She accepts my help getting onto the seat. That's a good sign, right? And the way she's squeezing my hand like she's trying to make my nails shoot out of my fingers is her way of saying thanks. It's an Irish thing, her aggressive appreciation.

I wave bye to my folks—it may be the last time, if Sophie kills me—then hop into the driver's seat. We're on the road for a few minutes and she's quiet, but the tension is killing me. She usually lays right into me whenever she's got something on her mind, but right now she's stewing. It's her silent anger, the real anger. When Sophie stews, nothing good comes of it. She's thinking of plans and ways to say how I've done everything wrong, each way probably harsher than the last. Natalie was great at this piercing kind of silence— it's how we'd argue. No knockout, drag-out fights. No screaming and yelling our feelings at the top of our lungs. Silence. It was agony, and I can't bear to have Sophie be this way with me too.

As I'm making the turn to get on the BQE, I can't take it anymore. It's only been ten minutes, and she's already got me crumbling.

"I'm sorry. I know you're pissed. I broke our rules. Fuck, but I knew they'd all love you so much. Please, Sophie, I don't want to leave this on a sour note because of some stupid shit I did."

"Leave what?" she asks quietly, still not looking at me.

"Leave me. I know I crossed the line—"

"I'm not leaving you," she sighs, but her hand comes over mine in a conciliatory gesture I'd never suspect from a woman in a rage. "I'm working stuff out in my head; let me be for a few minutes."

It takes all I have to stay quiet for a whole thirty seconds. She says she isn't ending the fling, but what happens when she's done working things out?

"See, I'm trying. I really am. But every second that goes by, I feel like you're trying to make up some reason to keep being mad at me. And usually, that would be awesome because for us it leads to sex, but that's not what this feels like."

"No," she says quietly staring out her window. "This wouldn't lead to sex."

She looks at me and I'm gutted because whatever is upsetting her is really turning her inside out.

"Do not mistake me, Tony. What you did, tricking me to get me over there, was fucked up, even if it was your mom's idea. I specifically told you I did not want to meet your family, because of course I'd love them. Anyone who raised you would be awesome. What I'm trying to wrap my head around is how you don't seem to care what it does to me to become so entrenched in your life for such a short period of time, especially knowing what you do about me."

She glances at me sharply. "I know Adele told you about my parents. But even she doesn't understand how bad it got at times with my mom. Mom would sit and stare at the wall for hours and hours, catatonic, when my dad would disappear for a few days." Sophie's hand clenches on the door, her knuckles turning white, the freckles appearing darker. "She was ill, clinically depressed, and I know it isn't her fault but…from anyone's point of view, the things that happened in that house would have been deemed neglect."

"Sophie—"

"You don't know how lucky you are, Tony. Your family is great, and despite your gripe with Santiago, he's pretty great, too. He's honest and open and he cares so much about you. He misses you. There will come a time when your parents will be gone, and you'll need your brothers. Don't let this come between you. He has a right to be angry with your parents after the truth bomb they dropped on you guys, and though in the end, blood doesn't matter, your father is your father, you each have a different relationship with your parents, and Santiago is the oldest. Your dad trusted him to take care of you two a lot, didn't he?"

"When Pop would be working late, and Ma was out of town, yeah. Santiago would be in charge."

"There's probably things your dad relied on Santiago for that you don't know about. That's always how it is with the oldest sibling: they take on a burden, so the younger ones don't have to."

I sigh, rubbing my head as we sit at a stoplight. "Then after all that, he finds out there's something he didn't know. Something big."

She nods encouragingly. "And it feels like betrayal."

"But to not talk to them for two months…"

"It's not your job to take care of your parents."

I want her to forgive me, but I won't bend my beliefs to appease her.

"It's every kid's job to take care of their parents. Why do people keep saying that?"

She squeezes my hand. "It's not your job alone."

Every word she says chops my legs off, inch by fucking inch.

"I know that. *I know*. But you didn't see Pop working himself to the bone. You didn't see Ma staying up till dawn, helping us with our school projects, canceling plans with friends when we were sick. They gave up so much for us; it's time for me to give back."

"Tony, that's what parents do, or what they're *supposed* to do. They signed that contract getting into the gig. And you have given up so much. You gave up your dream for them…though I kind of have a feeling there was another reason for that." She sets a foot on the dash, her sparkly sandal glittering in the street-lights, and says, "One that starts with the letter N."

She's looking at me now, and the delicate compassion from before has turned into something more familiar. Anger. And where normally I'd welcome a fight, tonight I only want things to be right between us. No matter the consequences.

"I was almost engaged." I don't mean to say it out loud, but the words just vomit up. She looks a little surprised by my answer, but doesn't laying into me for not telling her. She listens.

"We met at orientation, were together through college. After graduation, I told her I wanted to spend the rest of my life with her, and she moved away for a job the next week. She said she was committed to me, that despite the long distance, she'd still be mine. But it crumbled so fast, and she didn't try to do anything to stop it. I went out there to surprise her, to propose. She told me no, flat out."

I swallow hard, trying to get the words out. They stick in my throat like peanut butter on dry bread.

Sophie's quiet for a bit, but keeps holding my hand. Really tight now, too.

"I wasn't enough for her. An art historian didn't make what she needed to be supported." I smile sardonically, hating these words still have an effect on me. "She only wanted someone with a real job. So, I went home, sold the ring, and used it to pay for some of my grad school tuition."

"You're worth more than a hundred thousand women like her."

I squeeze her hand back, her words choking me up for a whole different reason. I'll never be worth Sophie, not in a million years. She's scared of what we can be together, and yet she hasn't used what I did or how I acted tonight as an excuse to end things. She's still here, comforting me when it should be the other way around.

"A hundred thousand, that's a pretty steep number."

"I'm willing to bet good money on it. I'm all in."

We pull up in front of the building, my spot open and waiting as it should be, and I really look at her.

"All in?"

She glances down at our hands, fused together so tightly they could become one. When she looks back up, there's determination in her luminous green eyes. "No more rules, Tony. Let's be together while we can."

I frame her face and kiss her, pour everything I am into the kiss, everything I am willing to be for her. My Sophie is so fucking brave. Hurt in a thousand ways, and yet she's here with me, trusts me. There's no greater gift in the world.

Sophie comes willingly, unbuckling her seatbelt and crawling over the bench of the truck to get closer.

"Do we get to have argument sex now?" I ask after we come up for air.

"We didn't really have an argument."

"Well, you got mad at me, that's gotta count for something. We could have sex without an argument."

"Let me go break a few of your plates and then we'll talk."

"Baby, you can break all my plates, and I'll still want your beautiful body."

"One of these days I'm going to mar one of your fancy kitchen appliances, and you're gonna regret saying that."

I lean in and rest my mouth against hers, breathing in her sweet scent, feeling like we've turned a page, are moving forward.

"Never gonna happen."

We walk up to the building hand-in-hand, and as I start to unlock the front door I turn to her in all seriousness and say, "But if you touch my Vitamix, this is over."

She rolls her eyes then kisses me with laughter on her lips.

13

SOPHIE

AND GEMMA FLANAGAN CONQUER THE WORLD
WHILE DRINKING SANGRIA.

"You did what?" Gemma nearly spits her drink out when I tell her how Tony and I met.

I always say my older sister is the wild one in the family, throwing herself head first into life, whereas I can't help but take things slow, my pace likened to a glacier's. Everything is backwards now. She's engaged to a predictable egotist and I made a split-second decision to screw a man I'd just met.

"I can't believe you fucked a guy five minutes after meeting him, then didn't tell me about it. That's not you at all." She takes a large swig from her oversized wine glass. "I'm not judging you for it. I'm just...surprised. And you're still seeing him?"

"Yes, I know it's crazy," I exclaim, slapping my hands on the tiled café table.

It's our favorite spot for afternoon sangria and no summer is complete without the sweet, fruit-infused wine. The outdoor patio is shaded by trellises covered with ivy and other thick-leaved plants. Flowers and succulents decorate the brick wall leading back into the open door main room, the A/C blasting so high we can feel it outside.

"At a certain point, it felt like I became a different woman. He started yelling at me, and I yelled back, and I was a goner."

Wow," Gemma deadpans. "True love."

I throw a crumpled napkin at her, but I'm laughing. My big sister always makes me smile.

"I think the humidity's getting to you, hon."

I wouldn't be surprised if that were true. This summer is turning out to be the most stifling in all my years living in the city. The stench of the garbage rotting on the sidewalks is enough to make a person pass out. Commuters take the subway at their own risk—the damn thing has breaks down every other train, causing major delays and headaches. There was even a fire in a tunnel on the D line. So yeah, I might believe the heat and chaos of the summer is getting to me, but where Tony's concerned, I'm in full possession of my faculties.

"No, I'm serious. I don't know what it is about him. One second we're fighting like cats and dogs over absolutely nothing, and the next thing I know, he has me against the wall. We can't fuck without fighting. It's like foreplay."

Gemma's eyes narrow. "He's never hurt you, has he?"

"Thanks for looking out, but no. It's not like that…it's fun. It's exciting. Gives me good goose bumps."

Gemma scrunches up her face. "That sounds exhausting."

"It is. I've never been so tired in my life. I can barely keep my eyes open at work."

"I doubt that's because of the fighting."

I grin, so at home in the world Tony and I have created. "Sometimes we wake up in the middle of the night just to fight. He's a very argumentative person, and I can't help that I'm right all the time."

Like when Tony hollers at my open window from the sidewalk, yelling at me to move my ass or we'll miss the movie we planned to see. I'm right when I threw a spoon at him, barely missing his face. We didn't make the movie.

"So...what's bothering you?" Gemma sets her oversized glass on the table, leveling me with a knowing frown.

"What do you mean?"

"You're clearly crazy about him, and no matter what you say, there has to be more than sex that keeps you together. So why does everything you're telling me sound like it has a big *but* on the end of it?"

I can never hide anything from my big sister; it is equally annoying and comforting. Adele was right to force my hand, so I'd tell Gemma, and it feels like a reprieve, getting it all off my chest.

"He's...there's another side to him, a very sweet and attentive side that kinda surprises me every time it comes out. He sent an edible bouquet to work the other day." The card simply read *I got you.* "It had chocolate-covered bananas and strawberries. Then, the other night I complained I never have any ice cream in my freezer when I want it, and the day after I found four pints of Ben & Jerry's. All my favorite flavors."

And one of his, so he could sit with me and eat. I told him he could always eat my ice cream, and then we laughed as we composed more double entendres to match the unintended ice cream comment.

"And those are bad things? You have doubts." She points her

spoon at me. "I can see them in the back of that meandering brain of yours."

"It's not that I have doubts...it just can't last." I tell her about Rome, about the clock hanging over our head, ticking away. "It can't be anything more than a fling. A couple months of sex and cuddling and some good times. That's it. Then he leaves, and I'm still here."

"How does that make you feel?" Gemma's hands wrap around the stem of the oversized wine glass, her thumb playing with the decorated edges of the cup. I watch the movement, try to get the words out.

"I feel," I clutch my tank top over my chest, rubbing it, unable to finish my sentence. "I don't know what I feel. Lost. Scared. Eager to see him every moment of the day. But mostly in agony that it's going to end before we can even start. The pressure keeps building."

"Don't ignore the pressure, Sophie. It will build if you do, taint what you've got going."

It would be smart to take her word for it, no doubt Gemma's speaking from experience. Her first husband kept a secret for so long it buried them in the end, forever changing who Gemma is.

"You sure it's not just lust?"

I think of the ice cream, the first dreamy brunch we had together, how he fed me fruit from his plate. I think of all the sex —most of it angry and crazy, the rest of it sweet and tender and so, so, long and slow. I think of how we hold each other at night and stare at one another like love-struck idiots. I think of how we joke comfortably about the levels of stink in the bathroom after our morning coffees kick in. I think of how he's read almost every single one of my articles, cat memes and all.

It's more than lust. Maybe it started that way, but now it's much more. Which makes how he's embedded me into his life so much harder to stomach. It won't last, and it will destroy me when it's over.

"I met his family last night."

"Yowza."

"Yowza is right."

"You never meet families. How did that even happen?"

I explain Tony's trickery, how pissed I was.

Gemma's smile is catlike. "You don't look angry now."

"No, I liked them a lot." So much that when Tony moves away, it won't only be him I'm aching for, but also his rambunctious family. He keeps giving me beautiful, precious gifts, but they've all got time limits.

This fling is so burdened by strings I'm becoming a puppet.

"When am I meeting him?"

"Huh?" I look at her dumbfounded.

"I want to meet him. We'll go on a double date. It will be fun."

"Didn't you hear the part where I said any sort of relationship with him is doomed? Why would you want to torture me?"

"Don't care. Set it up. This Friday. Murray will want to pick the place." She sends a text to Murray then looks at me with a reflection of the carefree Gemma she used to be, the devil in her eye. "Does he even know you've never been in a real relationship?"

"I have!" My outrage is a bit dramatic. "I don't know why you say that. I dated Brian for two years."

"You were in college. That shit does not count. And he was a dick."

I nodded, agreeing. "He was very much a dick."

Gemma raises her glass. "To not dating dicks anymore." We toast then swallow healthy doses of our sangria. No better medicine.

"Speaking of not dating dicks, how's Murray?"

"He's good." Gemma's smile is strained, setting alarm bells off in my head.

"Just good? What are you two working on?"

"Defamation case. Pretty standard. We'll win it, no problem." She focuses on the stem of her wine glass again, the artificial tone of her voice betraying her true emotions.

Gemma has a real gift for showing the world only what she wants it to see, but every now and then, when the pressure surges and the past comes back to bite her in the ass, her true self shines through. If I'm honest, what I see when that happens really worries me.

But focusing on Gemma's past isn't the key to luring her out.

"What aren't you saying?" When she continues to prevaricate, I pull out the big guns. "If you don't fess up, I'll tell Mom the real reason you came home late when we visited her back in 2014."

She narrows her eyes, grits her teeth. "You wouldn't."

I lean forward and whisper, "Try me."

She rolls her eyes, the obnoxious younger sister routine a familiar one. But I wouldn't use it if it didn't work every time.

"He's been working late a lot since the engagement, that's all."

I need to be delicate here. If I'm fucked up by my trust issues, then Gemma should be in the psych ward. It's the only reason I can guess as to why she presents a false image to the world: self-preservation.

"Do you suspect him of doing something other than working?" I ask lightly.

"No. If Murray has a shining quality, it's his surplus of honesty. Cheating isn't his style. He's been stressed and snapping at me."

"Need me to shake him down? Use my journalist intuition to get to the real story?"

"The real story is he's under a lot of pressure, and the added wedding planning has only exacerbated the problem."

"Well, you share the wedding planning stress together, no?"

"Yeah. That's what I meant. We. Us. We're both stressed." She waves her hand, erasing her words. "Enough about Murray."

It's obvious she doesn't want to talk about this, but I scrunch my face in suspicion anyway. Gemma laughs.

"Don't give me the patented Sophie side-eye. We're fine." She grasps my hand and squeezes briefly before returning to her glass. "What's going on with work? Is your boss still being a jackass?"

"Yes, he's refusing to take anything I'm working on seriously. It was never this bad before they hired him."

"Have you ever thought of quitting?"

"Are you crazy? I can't quit; I just got an apartment in one of the most expensive cities in the country."

"At least you're not living in San Francisco."

"True, that would be idiotic. I'd need to have a million roommates."

"You'd barely make enough to afford rice."

"Except I'd have to have all the latest technology to even function in that city."

"Or you'd be kicked out on principle."

I raise my glass. "To not living in San Francisco."

Gemma matches me. "Why Mom chose that foggy city to live after her recovery, of all places, I'll never understand."

"I'll drink to that."

Our glasses clink, and the sun glistens off the white sangria, lighting it from within like a flame. The crisp liquid singes my senses, gives me a jolt. I'll pay for this glass later when I add it to all the heavy food Tony's been cooking, but it tastes too good to only stick to one.

"How's Gary?" Gemma asks, seeing me pat my stomach.

"Testy as always, but manageable."

"You better treat him right, or he'll bite you in the ass." She rolls her eyes. "I can't believe you've got me calling it Gary."

"It suits him."

Gemma doesn't question my peculiarities anymore. She knows its futile, and I'll never change.

After brunch we go our separate ways. Instead of heading straight home, I decide to get an extra-large iced chai tea and hang out in Times Square for a little tourist watching.

Most native New Yorkers avoid Times Square like the plague, unless they work here or are forced to play host to out-of-town relatives. But I'm not a normal New Yorker, and I effing love it.

I love the pandemonium of lights and sounds, and the fake cartoon character costumes, especially the creepy Elmo. A street performer dressed as the Statue of Liberty makes a tourist jump when she photobombs their picture. It's a classic moment, replicated a million times every day, but it never fails to make me laugh.

I sit on the steps at the TKTS booth and sip the icy chai, basking in the hubbub of the hectic crowd. This city is part of my lifeblood. The people born here—or who move here and decide to stay—understand. Leaving would be like cutting out a part of my heart.

Then my treacherous brain starts to imagine what it would be like if I was still here, but Tony was no longer my neighbor, my lover…my boyfriend? How would it feel to be in a New York City without Tony? How would it feel to come home and not have a meal cooked by a man hoping to impress and take care of me? No cuddling on the couch when I'm sad and watching the same move twice in a row. No cheering together when a subway rider makes it by a hair's breadth onto the train? No seeing the deep and almost painful way he smiles at me.

Empty.

There would be millions of people crammed onto this tiny island, and it would feel completely empty.

Hoping to catch Tony before he heads out for his dinner plans, I go home, needing to see him. I stop in the front lobby to check my mail and my phone rings.

"This is Sophie."

"Sophie Flanagan?" A woman replies, her voice light and airy.

"Speaking."

"Great, I was worried I had the wrong number. My name is Gina Lee from *New Yorker World*. We're a new online publication started by *The New Yorker*."

"Oh, I've heard about that. Are you guys releasing articles yet?"

"Not yet, right now we're building stories, creating our brand. It will be another month or so before we're ready to go live. We're seeking a way to reach the new, digital generation. The ones who come after the millennials."

I idly flip through my mail, tearing up credit card offers and putting aside bills. "I would totally be into reading that."

"That's good to hear, but I'm not calling to ask you to read it. I'm calling to ask you to write for it."

I nearly drop the phone. "What? You want me to write for *The New Yorker.*"

"A new online subset of *The New Yorker*, something that will keep us ahead of the game. Your piece on intersectionality was spot-on. Your words are powerful, and we need that strength on our team."

"How did you get that article?" I lean against the metal mail-boxes, not trusting my knees to keep me standing. "It wasn't even published. I mean, it was, but it was chopped to pieces and—"

"Subversively hidden within your fluff work? Yeah, that's what we're looking for—the writers being forced to hide who they truly are just to stay afloat in this new digital, instant-gratification world. We want to get back to traditional journalism, without the constant 24/7 news feed, or the cat memes."

This woman is feeding my creative soul, but I can't sound too eager. I think of Tony and his business acumen. What would he do? He'd play hard to get, make them want him even more.

"A cat meme every now and then never hurt anyone."

"True," she laughs. "But if it's all we see it will become tedious. Lose its appeal."

"So, what would I be writing for you? What would I add to your publication?"

"You're a native New Yorker. We want that perspective, especially someone from the forgotten borough." I walk up the stairs to my apartment, listing to her intriguing idea. "Staten Island is the most conservative yet neglected borough in the city. I'd love to hear what it was like growing up a liberal in a red patch hidden among all of New York City's blue. An investigative journalist digging up the dirt on her hometown and other spots around the city."

I stop at my door, leaning against the wood without bothering to look for my keys. These are all topics I'd love to write about. Her description of Staten Island as my forgotten hometown is perfect—it's so often overlooked or dismissed. I'd love to bring its positive qualities to light while remaining truthful to the dark and sharp edges.

But there's something else I want first.

"I can do that...but, well," I clench my fist, crumpling my mail, and take a chance. "There's actually another piece I have that I'd like to get out into the world. My editor shot it down recently."

"Send it to me," she says without hesitation. "I'd be happy to read it, and we'll see if it's a fit."

"Wow. That's just—wow. I'm speechless." Be cool, Sophie. "Thank you for this opportunity."

"You've got a great voice, Sophie. It should be heard."

"Thanks, Ms. Lee."

"Call me Gina, and you're welcome. We'll talk again after I read your article."

She hangs up, and I shut my eyes, unable to believe that actually happened. The giddiness takes over, and I do a little jig in the middle of the hallway, chanting in my mind. *I'm gonna quit my jo-ob. I'm gonna quit my jo-ob. Someone likes my writing. They think I have a great vo-oice.*

I turn around in a circle, fist pumping to a heavy bass beat no one can hear but me. When I open my eyes, Tony is leaning against the railing, his arms crossed and a brilliant smile on his face.

I don't stop dancing.

"Give me a minute. I'm not done."

"Don't mind me. I'm enjoying this."

"Not as much as I am." I spin around a couple more times, shimmy a bit and then finally lean back against my door, mirroring Tony's position. "Okay, I think I'm done now." I jump one more time. "Nope, now I'm done."

"Gotta admit, baby, you're crazy cute when you're all happy and giddy. Care to tell me what brought this on?" And I can see from his open smile he really means it; it touches him that I'm happy. It affects him when I'm sad. My general well-being is a constant thought in his mind, and after meeting his parents and talking with Santiago—after the night we shared—I would be an idiot to think Tony wants to remain emotionally detached.

What he told me about Natalie pops into my mind. She deserted him during a long-distance relationship, put that distance between them on purpose so she could leave him, seek out better things.

Even if I wanted to keep Tony, he'd never settle for long distance. It would be all or nothing...which means what? I'd need to move to Rome to be with him? Leave my family? I can't do that. I won't. Particularly not now that I've got this poten-tially amazing job opportunity.

No matter how much it hurts, I can't give Tony what he wants. And sharing this small, important pieces of my life with him will only entangle him further into my heart.

"Oh, it's nothing. Gemma is letting me choose my maid of honor dress. I thought she'd force something ugly on me." It's the truth, just not the one he wants.

"Okay," he nods, crossing his arms and looking away for a second. He sees through the lie but doesn't complain. It's hurting him, how I won't give min completely, and I hate it. I hate putting that tight expression on his face. "Well, I've got plans tonight."

"I know."

"I'll see you tomorrow." He takes one step down the stairs before I stop him, running to throw my arms around him from behind.

"Wait." I kiss his cheek, his neck, hating to part ways like this. "I told Gemma about us. She wants to have dinner—a double date. You, me, Gemma and Murray."

"When?"

"Friday. Is that okay?"

He turns into my arms for a full hug, rests his chin on my shoulder as he whispers in my ear. "I'd love to meet your sister. I'd love to meet your whole family. I'd love to be a part of your life, if you'll let me."

I take a step back, my throat tightening, the clock hanging over us ticking louder with every second. "What happens when you're gone?"

He has no answer for me.

I kiss him on the cheek, then head into my apartment.

With the door closed, with the world and Tony safely shut away on the other side, I allow myself a moment to imagine what it would be like to have Tony fully immersed in my life, tangled up in each other, making decisions based on what the other would want.

It would feel like this, like it does now, like he's already burrowed into every corner of my life.

And that is scary as fuck.

14

TONY

The week flies by, my time with Sophie going so quick I can almost see the end, creeping up on us like the mother of all deadline. Soon, it's Friday, and we're heading out for a double date with Sophie's sister, Gemma, and her fiancé, Murray.

The restaurant Gemma's fiancé makes a reservation at has me questioning his taste right off the bat. It's the type of place I'm forced to go for business dinners, when we've got an investor we're trying to impress, and we need to shell out some money to convince them to sign with us. When Petrov Incorporated bought out my firm, we considered taking him here. Somewhere expensive, meant to show we're not afraid to play with big money.

I tolerate the pretentious atmosphere for work, where it serves a purpose. But on a double date? I mean, what's wrong with getting a slice of pizza at Gino's and then seeing a Mets game? That's a normal double date.

But no, I've got to put a fucking suit on, my second for the day, as I just shed the one I wore for work. But what's really shitty, is even though Sophie is sexy as sin in spiky heels and a little black dress with strappy bits that go across her back, it's obvious she's miserably uncomfortable.

I listened to her chat with Murray about picking a place last night, and how exasperated she sounded every time he interrupted her. I was ready to call it off, reschedule with Gemma alone, but then he made Sophie laugh toward the end of the call, her smile genuine, and I figure the guy is just a little pushy. He represents Wall Street stockbrokers, and you gotta be a stubborn jackass if you're gonna get anywhere there. Maybe I should cut him some slack. He might be a decent guy who just has a taste for pompous, look-how-much-money-I-have restaurants.

I offer Sophie my arm, like I'm escorting her into a ballroom. The gesture seems to delight her. Her smile is so brilliant I just have to cradle her cheek with my free hand and kiss her. I sip at her luscious bottom lip, and the taste of her is better than any aged wine I'll have at this fancy restaurant tonight. I trail my lips to a particularly large cluster of freckles right near her jaw and bite just a bit. She snorts.

I love her snorts. Like, I have a strange obsession with them.

"We should go in. They're probably waiting. Murray is obnoxiously punctual." She kisses me this time, a hand gripping my lapel. "You smell so good. What cologne are you wearing?"

"I don't need to wear cologne now that you've drenched my bedroom in it. The fumes have permanently seeped into my pores."

"Hashtag no regrets."

I'm the one snorting now.

We go to check in, and the hostess clearly thinks she's hot to trot because she gives me a look I'm a little too familiar with, her eyes lingering on certain body parts. I don't give a crap about her attention, just hold Sophie closer to me, resting my hand on her waist and playing with the soft fabric hugging her body. The hostess is wearing a black dress similar to Sophie's, but it doesn't look nearly as good on her as it does on my girl. I glance down at Sophie again, so unbelievably happy to be with her right at this moment, and feeling lucky.

Things have been touch-and-go since the dinner. Sometimes I can feel how ready Sophie is to give herself to me completely, to dispense with the fling bullshit, and then other times she's distant and careful, like she's reminding herself every second we're together that I'm moving away. It kills me each time I see her body get tense, or the obvious ways she keeps me from staying over at her place, as if it's some state line I can't ever cross.

Maybe it will always be like this. Maybe she'll never accept me. She didn't tell me about the job offer. I heard all of it, and then she lied to my face about a maid of honor dress. What do I have to do to get her to trust me?

What do I gotta say to get her to move to Italy with me?

We follow the hostess to a table where a beautiful redhead, who looks nothing like Sophie, and a guy on a cell phone are seated. The woman smacks her companion on the arm, and he raises his shoulders in a sorry-not-sorry kind of way. She rolls her eyes then stands to greet us.

Gemma and Sophie hug, and I get my first real look at my girl's big sister. There aren't any outwardly physical hints that these two are related, but the way they hold themselves, the little smiles, and how Gemma smacked the guy—who I'm assuming is Murray—are definite traits the Flanagan sisters share. Where Sophie has a unique beauty, Gemma is classic. She's got curly, red hair pinned back in a bun, but from the substantial mass of the knot, I'm guessing it's pretty long. Her skin is clear and smooth like porcelain, and her eyes are a light green. She's taller than Sophie but not by much. I wonder where Sophie gets her coloring from, they really don't look anything alike. When Sophie introduces me, and I give Gemma a kiss on the cheek, I tell them so.

"You sure you two are sisters?" I point back and forth. "You don't look anything alike."

Gemma grins. "Oh, by the end of the night you'll see it."

I hold out Sophie's chair for her to sit, then rush around to do the same for Gemma since Murray is still on the phone. Gemma looks annoyed but not surprised by his rudeness. Sophie frowns at the man, and when she snaps in his face, something so weirdly out of character for her it almost makes my jaw drop, Murray finally relents and hangs up.

"Sorry, Phie."

Phie? What kind of nickname is that? Sophie is not a Phie.

"Client is freaking out over some tanking stocks. He wants me to sue his broker. He doesn't get that the market's like waves, it goes up and goes down."

"That's very poetic, Murray, but your client can freak out some other time. We're at dinner. This is my...friend, Tony Rodriguez."

Friend? Really? She can't say it, like the word boyfriend will strike her dead.

I roll my eyes at her before shaking hands with Murray across the table as the waiter arrives, bringing a basket of bread.

Sophie grabs a piece, splits it in half and gives the other to Gemma.

"Nothing for me?" I ask.

Gemma shakes her head. "Sister privilege. I come first. Better get used to that, Antonio Miguel Luis Rodriguez."

I groan, turning to the traitor sitting next to me. "You told her my million names?" I clutch my chest dramatically. "How could you?"

When the waiter returns, Murray orders a couple bottles of wine for the table.

I would have liked to see a drink menu first, but it seems they know him here, so I don't step on his toes. Before the waiter leaves I do make sure to ask for a menu. After dinner with my family—mostly thanks to Santiago's nosiness—I've come to realize Sophie has a weird stomach. Even though she dove right in and ate everything my parents put in front of her, I couldn't help but notice the extra-long time she spent in the bathroom later in the evening, and the ten tums she popped, claiming she was fine while grimacing and rubbing her chest. I don't want her to eat anything too heavy today, for fear she'll be in pain again. Maybe I've been cooking too much tomato sauce. I should switch to alfredo or vodka.

But my tomato sauce is so good.

"Don't worry about the menu," Murray says with a confident grin. "I'll order the food tonight."

Sophie rests a hand against my thigh. I grip it without thinking and try to keep my voice as cool and genuine as possible.

"While I'm sure you know better than all of us what they have here, I'm interested in taking a look at the menu. I've never been here before, and I consider myself an amateur chef."

Murray leans forward, his gray eyes lighting up. "No kidding. What's your cuisine of choice?"

"I've taken classes on traditional French technique"

"Butter, butter, and more butter."

"Too right, man." Okay. If he knows about cooking, maybe he's not as terrible as he appears. He's probably one of those guys who needs to act like a big shot, but once he's more comfortable the abrasiveness of his behavior abates. New York does have millions of people with big personalities in it.

I glance at Sophie, she's smiling encouragingly at me, her freckles bunching. My gut clenches. Maybe I'm the one with the stomach problem.

The waiter returns with the wine, displaying and pouring it for Murray to sample.

"My maternal grandma is from Italy and my father emigrated from Colombia forty years ago. Mom and Dad are avid cooks."

"Home cooks are the best, in my opinion," Murray lifts his glass to the light, examining the color of the deep red wine. "Their food has a rough shine, but there's nothing more authentic."

I hate the word authentic when it comes to food. Who decides what is authentic? Everyone has their own definition. I don't argue about it, wanting to be friendly.

"Agreed. You've gotta try my Grandma's gnocchi. The best you'll ever have."

"Oh, gnocchi is my favorite," Gemma says, rubbing Murray's shoulder.

"I thought it was penne?" Murray turns to her with a frown.

"No," she laughs, brushing his jaw affectionately. "My favorite Italian food? Always been gnocchi. And—"

"Fried polenta," Gemma and Sophie saying in unison, lifting their water glasses in a toast.

For a moment I hear the same person, their laughter too similar to distinguish one from the other.

"Creepy, isn't it?" Murray asks, giving the waiter the go ahead to pour the wine for the table.

"I dunno, I'm a little mesmerized by the two of you. Gemma, tell me every embarrassing story about Sophie. I want all the gory, ill-behaved details."

The waiter hands me a menu, and Murray tries to stop him.

"Tony, I appreciate your love of food, but trust my judgment on this. I'll bet you one hundred bucks I know what you'll order."

I take the menu, opening it over my table settings. "My taste might surprise you."

Murray shrugs, looking a little too pleased with himself. "Suit yourself. You'll find more than rustic Italian fare here."

Gemma places a hand over Murray's. "Babe, I told you we need menus for Sophie's ulcer. She has a limited diet. You know that." Her tone is gentle, but the exasperation is clear.

Wait…an ulcer? A fucking ulcer?

I stare at Sophie with wide eyes and she looks everywhere but at me. She's caught.

"You have an ulcer?"

"She's named it," Gemma claims in amused astonishment, shaking her head at her little sister.

My brain can't even begin to comprehend this. "You have an ulcer and you named it?"

"Maybe," Sophie evades. When I don't respond she finally relents. "It's a baby ulcer. It whines a little when it's upset."

"You ate every heavy and acidic thing I've been putting in front of you, and you've got an ulcer? That you *named*? I can't believe you didn't tell me this." I scratch my head, not knowing what to make of her. "Putting aside the fact you named it—and to be honest, I may want you even more for that—why didn't you say anything?"

"I love your food. Nobody ever cooks for me. I didn't want to put you off."

I cup her cheek, rubbing her smooth skin, soothing any pain I may have inadvertently caused her in the past. God, why can't she just talk to me?

"Have I ever given you the impression I would be mad if you told me what I fed you caused you pain?"

"No…not exactly."

"Uh-oh, trouble in paradise." Murray jokes.

I do everything I can to keep from dragging Sophie outside and kissing her until she tells me all her secrets. These barriers are gonna kill me in the end.

"No trouble." Sophie sounds exasperated. "It's not a big deal."

"It's a big deal," Gemma says in a very older sister tone of voice. She turns to me, giving me the rundown. At least someone is willing to tell me Sophie's secrets. "She ignores it. I keep telling her one of these days she's gonna go Downton Abbey on us and spit blood all over the dinner table."

"Is it pathetic that I actually know what she's talking about?" Murray asks me, Gemma gives him a kiss on the cheek in response.

"No, you watching period dramas with me is one of the many reasons I love you."

"Love you too, kid," he says with an exaggerated wink.

Something bugs me about the condescending way Murray says "kid." I turn back to Sophie, needing to clear the air about her freaking *ulcer*. She's barely over thirty, and she has an ulcer. That's insane.

"Your horrible eating habits are stopping today. I am doing every bit of research I can on ulcers, and we are changing our diet to suit whatever it is you need."

"What do you mean changing *our* diet? It's only me that has the ulcer."

"Yeah, but it wouldn't be fair to eat what you can't right in front of you. I'm not that big an asshole."

Sophie stares at me a second before glancing over at Gemma, secret sister communication volleying between them. She soon smiles at me in this adorably embarrassed but pleasing way. "No, not *that* big."

"Wow, that was too cute a moment." Gemma says. "I like you, Tony. Make my sister eat right; that's what a good man does."

We finally order our food. Sophie and I get a salmon and chicken dish we'll share. Gemma chooses a duck entree she exclaims is divine, and I want to punch Murray a little when he orders steak. As the food comes out, Sophie looks at the slab of meat like she's dying. She loves red meat. She eats burgers like they're popcorn.

I rub her back as I feed her a piece of the chicken.

"This is good," I say, not wanting her to think she's missing out.

"You're sweet." She kisses me, hints of butter, rosemary, and thyme on her lips. My new favorite flavor combinations.

We chat lightly as we eat, nothing too serious. Murray tells us about his firm, and I discuss what it is my company does. I don't mention Italy, and it seems like Gemma notices because she and Sophie exchange not so surreptitious glances throughout the entire conversation.

"So, Tony." Murray starts, holding his glass of red wine like he's a sommelier. "What are your intentions toward my soon-to-be sister-in-law?"

"My intentions…are to treat her like the goddess she is." And convince her to move to Italy with me, then marry her, support her as her career blows up, and grow old together in whatever way suits us.

"Right answer." He salutes me then takes a healthy sip, his hand cradling the bowl of the glass.

"How about you?" I ask. "What are your intentions toward this lovely lady?"

Gemma waves me off, feigning embarrassment.

"Oh, you know, barefoot and pregnant within the year."

It's a joke; I know he didn't mean any harm by it, but Gemma looks as if he's stabbed her in the heart. Sophie puts her silverware on the table, nice and slow, but I recognize it for the way she sometimes gets before freaking out.

Quiet and dangerous.

"Seriously, Murray?" Sophie asks softly. "I know you've got a loud mouth and sometimes that filter of yours doesn't work like it's supposed to, but you can't be this callous."

"What did I say?"

"Barefoot and *pregnant?*"

"Christ, why are you so sensitive about this?" Murray grumbles. "Gemma doesn't care, so why do you?"

"Sorry, Tony." Gemma addresses me quietly as Murray and Sophie continue to argue in hissed whispers.

"I don't know what you're apologizing for." I try to keep my tone light, not liking the wounded look on her face.

"Guys, stop fighting. That's enough." They ignore her, and she turns back to me with a shrug. "Murray sometimes forgets I can't have kids. I have the BRCA1 gene mutation, and made the decision to get a hysterectomy last year."

"What's BRAC1?"

"Oh, you sweet innocent man. BRCA1 and BRCA2 are genes that help suppress cancer tumors, but when they're mutated, the suppression doesn't work properly so I have a higher chance of getting breast or ovarian cancer."

"Shit, that's a thing?"

"It's big thing. I'll most likely be getting a double mastectomy in the next couple years as well. I froze my eggs. I won't be able to physically have a baby. It's something I accepted and moved on from a while ago. I'm fine with it. Sophie's overprotective and Murray is...Murray."

I take her hand and squeeze, because now I see the resemblance between Gemma and her sister. The strength and courage shared between the two of them could conquer the world. "That's really brave of you, Gemma."

"A million women experience worse than me every day." She glances at Sophie, who is now gesticulating like a mad woman at Murray, their voices still miraculously low.

CERI GRENELLE

Gemma's smile is far too Mona Lisa-esque when she says, "Don't worry, Sophie doesn't have the gene."

A breath I didn't realize I was holding expels from my body like an air cannon. "Thank you," is all I can think to say. "Thank you."

Not that how I feel about Sophie would change if she couldn't have kids, but the thought of her potentially getting cancer invokes the pain and shock I felt with my brother's diagnosis. But in this more possessive, intimate way, the pressure close to debilitating.

"You're a good guy, Tony," Gemma says tenderly, her slender hand patting my arm. "I hope Sophie lets herself go with you."

Taking a leap and relying on my instincts, I let Gemma see everything Sophie has come to mean to me in a scary short amount of time.

"How do I get her to trust me?"

"Be there for her. Support her," Gemma glances away briefly, taking a hard, deep breath. "Trust she knows her mind, and let her make her own choices."

For a split second, Gemma's put-together exterior melts away and darkness fills her light green eyes, turning them dull. The self-possessed magnetic woman of a few moments ago is gone, and the person left is unrecognizable.

Before I can ask if anything is wrong, or give her some sort of comfort, the wistful tone turns hard, and her gaze comes back to mine. It's instantly clear why Sophie says she's kick-ass at her job. This is the Gemma who deals with stockbrokers and lawyers and the toughest, most unrelenting assholes in the city.

"But in the end, Tony, you're leaving. And this is Sophie's home.

214

What do you think will happen? I see how she looks at you, how enamored of her you are."

"You think she shouldn't be with me?"

"No, that's not what I mean. I think you're good for her. You make her happy, even if it's just for a short while. But I can't see a happy ending here."

Before I can tell Gemma my plan of asking Sophie to move with me, asking her to make the sacrifice and give up her home and life here—which I know isn't fucking fair to her, but I wouldn't do if it if I didn't think Sophie would thrive in Rome—the loud clink of diningware brings my attention back to the argument.

Sophie's cutting up a piece of chicken, her shoulders hunched and her mouth pinched in frustration, staring at the savory meat like it's her sworn enemy.

Murray, on the other hand, is relaxed, leaning back in his chair without a care in the world, treating Sophie like a child.

"C'mon, Phie. It was a joke. Let's drop it."

"Please don't call me that, Murray," Sophie says through gritted teeth, all semblance of pretending to like Murray gone.

"But it's such a cute nickname, just like you, Phie." His tone is teasing. Mocking. It grates on my nerves.

"Hey, man," I interject, rubbing Sophie's back. "She doesn't like it. Better listen before she really gets mad." Or before I punch Murray in the face.

"Got some experience with her moods, huh? She as tempestuous in the sack as she is during the day?"

This time it's Sophie gripping my hand, keeping me from doing something that will get the cops called.

"Don't be crude, Murray," Gemma butts in, but he doesn't

listen, only paying attention to her when he needs something, or when it makes him look good. I don't think I've ever met a more narcissistic bastard. How can Gemma be marrying this guy?

"Your lack of a filter is gonna get you in big trouble some day, Murray." Sophie isn't even attempting to hide the vitriol in her voice.

"Look where we are, Sophie. You tell me I have no filter? You can't even wait to scold me until we're out of the restaurant? God, I mean, I get it. You're an artistic type, and you wear your weirdness out in the open, but can't you cover it all up for once? Nobody wants to see all that."

And I fucking know he's not talking about her outspoken nature, he's waving a hand at her freckles. He does it on purpose, trying to hurt her. The asshole wants to hurt my Sophie? I'll fucking kill him.

I stand, the chair scraping behind me. I don't know what I'm gonna do, but I need to do something. Before I can say a word or take a step, Gemma turns to Murray with fury in her eyes.

"This shit needs to stop," she demands of her fiancé. "What has gotten into you lately? You've been on the phone nonstop, you've been biting my head off, staying at work hours past closing, and now you insult my sister? My baby sister? The most important person in the world to me. Who the fuck do you think you are?"

"Hey, I'm your fiancé, remember?" Murray leans forward, his hand on the back of Gemma's chair in an intimidating manner I'm not a fan of. I circle the table, make sure I'm close in case this argument goes a bad way. "The one your baby sister treats like shit on the bottom of her shoe."

"She only treats you that way because that's how you've been acting."

"You think I've been acting like shit?"

"Like rat shit, more specifically."

Sophie grabs my hand and tries to tug me back down into my chair. I must look awkward as hell standing there staring at their argument, but I refuse to move.

I'm more than impressed by Gemma. Murray may be her fiancé, but Sophie is her sister, and that is an indelible connection the two of them will clearly fight for. My esteem for Gemma keeps on rising, just as my opinion of Murray plummets.

I'm glad I don't sit when Murray removes his napkin from his lap and slams it on the table, the first loud noise or indication that there is an argument happening at our table. The other diners in the room look over, startled, but Murray goes about his business.

"If I am such a pile of rat shit, as you so delicately put it, then I'll leave you three, so you don't have to deal with the smell."

He storms off, already dialing someone on his cell phone.

I glance at Gemma, seeing how she's taking this mess, and am shocked by her composure. No tears. Not even a scrunched brow. She exemplifies propriety, and it pisses me the hell off. Is Murray like this so frequently that she's numb to it? Gemma is Sophie's family, her closest family, and I won't let anything hurt her. Not even her own fiancé.

"I'll be back."

"Tony, don't do anything stupid," Sophie warns.

I kiss her forehead. "I'm a model of decorum."

Without looking back, I walk after Murray. I find him outside the restaurant, chatting animatedly. I hear the word stocks, and my brain goes numb with fury. He's not even bitching about the fight to a friend. He's on the phone with a client, like hurting his fiancé wasn't a blip on his radar.

I grab the phone away and end the call.

"What the fuck—"

"Hi, again." I keep my voice hard but level, unwilling to give this douche an inch of reaction. "We're gonna have a little talk about what happened back there."

"It's none of your business. It's between me and Gemma. Figures Sophie would find the most obnoxious wannabe cook in all of Manhattan to date." He groans, raking his hands through his perfectly coiffed hair. "Why are women so frustrating? Can't they just shut up and be there when you want them?"

I want to punch him. I need to punch him. My fist is practically twitching for it. He's kvetching to me like I would fucking agree with him. I take a less violent but no less distasteful tactic and spit at his feet.

"What the fuck, man? Are you a goddamn savage? These are Jimmy Choos."

"After the way you behaved tonight, the only savage I see is you. If I ever hear you talk to Gemma or my Sophie that way again, you're gonna be worrying about a lot worse than ruined shoes."

I leave. If I stay and listen to him rant, I will definitely crush the little bug. When I return to the table, Sophie is waiting for me.

"Is he still standing?" she asks, welcoming me into her arms.

I grip her hips and rest my forehead on hers, breathing her in, taking solace from the way she holds me.

"Yes, unfortunately."

"I guess I should thank you for not killing him. I almost did."

"You okay?" I ask, letting her tug me into my seat. "Where's Gemma?"

"Said she needed to go to the bathroom, and no, I'm not okay."

I tap her bottom lip where she's gnawing it raw like a bone.

"Tell me what's wrong."

"Something isn't right. Gemma said Murray's been acting weird for a month or so now, ever since they got engaged."

"He wasn't always a complete douche monkey?"

"No—I mean, he was always full of himself—but he used to be more…lighthearted."

She cranes her neck, looking for Gemma, then slumps back down. I kiss her cheek and whisper, "I got you. You know that, right? And by extension I got your sister."

She leans into me. I nuzzle the top of her fluffy hair. It smells like sweet roses and coconut.

"I know. I know I can rely on you."

"Do you?" I ask, unable to ignore the doubt.

"Of course I do."

"It doesn't always feel that way."

Her hands squeeze the lapels of my jacket.

"Sometimes I forget you're moving, when you're like this. So determined to keep me after such little time together."

"Time doesn't matter. I know you, baby. I know us, and I know you're supposed to be mine."

"It won't work—"

"We'll make it work."

"Tony, I—"

"Imagine it. Us together. No time limits."

I can practically see the image form in her mind, especially since it's all I've been thinking of. The two of us without barriers. Cooking together. Reading. Going for walks. Going to the beach. Complaining about traffic. Arguing over everything and nothing. Making love on the floor so frequently our bodies form an imprint in the wood. She sees it, and how fucking amazing it is, and she wants to say yes. The word hovers between us, thick as summer lightening.

Tell me you love me. Say you want me forever.

The possibility of a life together expands, takes shape, then pops like a needle striking a balloon.

"I can't talk about this right now." She sits straight in her seat, disengaging, and I nearly curse across the restaurant I'm so frustrated we never seem to get the words out. "I need to go find Gemma. I'm worried about her."

She looks to me for help, like she thinks I can do something to make the night better. I put aside my need to know what Sophie might have said and swear to myself Gemma is going to be smiling and happy again before dawn, if it's the last thing I do.

"Go to her. I'm gonna make some calls to salvage this night."

"What do you mean?"

"Do you trust me?"

She stares up at me, worry for her sister apparent in her eyes, but more than that, surprise.

"Yeah. I do."

I feel that shift again, the one telling me we're about to move forward, take the next step, if it weren't for the miles between us.

"Go on, then."

Sophie leaves, and I dial the first person that comes to mind, putting aside the rift between us, because Sophie needs me, and I really need my big brother.

"Hey, man," I say when Santi answers. "You working tonight? I've got a favor to ask."

15

SOPHIE

IS FALLING IN LOVE.

The waiting room outside the ladies restroom at Murray's stuck-up restaurant is gilded, layered with satin, and pretentious as fuck. People glance at Gemma and I as they pass by, craning their necks to get a hint of whatever drama transpired, but they can suck it. All I care about is if Gemma is okay.

Everything is fine, she keeps telling me, reassuring me when I should be doing that for her.

"I'll be fine; Murray will be fine. The wedding planning, on top of this big case he's got, and tons of clients to juggle, and not a lot of staff to delegate to, it's stressful. I'm sorry he was such an ass to you. He shouldn't have——"

"I get it honey, work sucks." I rub her arm, brush nonexistent strands out of her face. I would dab at her tears using one of the fancy, not-quite-paper-not-quite-fabric napkins the bathroom attendant hands us, but Gemma isn't crying. She looks like she should be crying, but I haven't seen her cry in years. "And yeah, it can be stressful, and we all get pissed, but you don't take out your shit on your fiancé when you come home. You find solace in one another."

"What romance novel did you read that in?" She scoffs, cold cynicism in every word.

"Every single one. That's what's so awesome about romance novels—you always get the happy ending with two stupid people loving and supporting each other. It's genius. You should try them sometime."

"Romance isn't practical. My life with Murray is practical, and its real, and in real life people fight." She stands, looks in the mirror and brushes nonexistent lint from her dress, keeping up the facade of perfection. "Love isn't some linear progression, Sophie. It's backward and forward and up and down, side-to-side. You can't put Murray and me in some stereotypical, romantic box."

"Hey, who's supposed to be lecturing who here?" Though at this point it sounds like she's giving herself a pep talk.

"Murray isn't perfect, but I'm not either." She turns to face me, resolute. "You should see us at work together; we are a kick-ass team. Everything is great there."

"And at home?" I ask gently.

"At home there is family stuff to deal with and neighbors and friends."

I try not to think that I'm part of the family stuff adding to her problems, but Gemma's always felt responsible for me. I wish there was some way I can make it up to her.

"This is New York, who talks to their neighbors?"

She grins and pushes me gently. "Stop making me laugh; we're trying to have a serious conversation."

"That's exactly why I want you to laugh. You're serious all the time. I miss crazy Gemma. I miss us stealing Mrs. Goldstein's convertible and watching you drive it to the Jersey shore with your hair flying behind you. By the time we got there, you had an afro the size of the state."

We both chuckle at the wonderful memory. It had been such a gloriously perfect day in the middle of a shitstorm. That was the summer Mom and Dad split up. And we hadn't actually stolen the car; Gemma had "rented" it by offering to clean the old woman's house the rest of the summer. I hadn't known that till later, when Mrs. Goldstein left a golden embossed feather duster to Gemma in her will. She'd done it for me, so we could have a sister day away from the turmoil in our family.

Gemma pats her tightly twisted curls at the base of her neck. "My hair is still crazy. But I don't live in a world where doing things like that is possible anymore."

"That's what the weekends are for."

"I need to be practical, Sophie. I need safety and security. That girl is gone. She died when—" Gemma shakes her head and turns back to the mirror, her fists clenching at her sides. "This is who I need to be."

I hug her from behind, my chin on her shoulder.

"I lived a practical, safe life for a long time, Gemma. It was free of pain, but it was boring." I sigh, letting the things I feel for Tony seep into my being and sock me in the face for the millionth time that day. "It wasn't living. I was alone."

"I'll have Murray."

"Will you? Or is it going to be late nights and sarcastic barbs forever?"

She moves away from me, her mouth tight. "I'm gonna pee then we can go. Think you guys can drop me off at my place?"

I don't press her for an answer, seeing the fine line she's walking. But I can't let Gemma marry Murray if this stoic, cold woman is who she'll be with him. Despite her conviction, this is not who Gemma needs to be. She's so much more.

"Nope, you're crashing with me tonight and we are watching *The Birdcage* five times in a row."

"You're obsessed with that movie." She locks the door on one of the private stalls.

"For good reason," I call back.

I run into the dining room to check in with Tony, and to my surprise, he's standing outside the bathroom entrance with three paper to-go bags.

"Hey, is she okay?" he asks.

I smile up at him, so thankful he's not an asshole, no matter how much I call him that in jest. In fact, he's much more than not an asshole—he's a genuinely good and decent human being. "She says she'll be fine, but I'm gonna have her crash at my place tonight for some girl time."

"Perfect. Except, you'll have to save the girl time for later."

"Why?"

"We're going out. You, your sister, me, my brothers."

"Brothers? Including Santiago?"

"I may have listened to this blonde bombshell telling me my fight with my older brother was stupid."

He keeps doing these amazing things for me. Over and over. Small and big.

"Tony, I am so happy you're talking to Santiago, but I really don't think she's in the mood for a night on the town. And, I'm sorry, but my heels are killing me."

I stick out a foot, pointing to the blisters forming on my ankles.

"I know, I saw those blisters starting earlier. We're throwing those shoes out. The feet are the workhorses of the body; you gotta treat them right or they're gonna stop supporting you."

The feet are the what?

"But you love how these shoes make my legs look."

"Yeah, I also love having a *girlfriend* who isn't in pain all the time. Baby, you can wear wooden clogs with that dress, and you'd still be hot as shit."

"I love when you call me hot as shit." I kiss his cheek, pointedly ignoring his emphasis of the world girlfriend. Everything about where Tony and I are in relationship status is so far out of bounds it's flown into the stratosphere. I feel like I'm floating in space when I'm with him, unbound and limitless, the cosmos at my fingertips.

"We're not doing something that requires a lot of walking?"

"Walking is involved, but we'll stop off at our building to change into jeans, sweats, whatever. Sneakers. Something comfortable."

"Comfortable sounds amazing," I groan in relief, wanting to get the hell out of this dress. "What do you have planned?"

"It's a surprise, but it's something Gemma sorely needs."

I'm overcome. I don't even know what he's planning, but he's clearly put a lot of thought into it in the small amount of time we've been huddled in the ladies room.

"Thank you."

"For what?"

"For being a wonderful man. For dealing with Murray's douchiness without punching him—wait…did you punch him when you followed him outside?"

"No, and it was a great sacrifice on my part."

"Good. We're gonna talk about you standing to defend my honor."

"I wasn't defending your honor. I was defending your beautiful freckles. I know this isn't the right place to confess something like this, but I gotta tell ya." He leans over and whispers in my ear, my heart pounding, frantically wondering what he's about to say. "I have a serious love affair happening with your freckles. My love for them can't be contained. They're more beautiful than the brush strokes on a Botticelli."

"The Botticelli you mooned over for a summer?"

"The woman in that painting has got nothing on the majesty of your freckles."

I laugh, half-relieved and weirdly half-disappointed he didn't fall to his knees and confess his love for me.

Decide what you want, Sophie. You can't keep moving back and forth.

It's time to decide.

Look at what he's done for me. I don't want to be alone forever —that realization shocking enough—and I don't want to settle for a man like Murray. Good to me when it's convenient for him, a narcissistic terror when it isn't. I want someone who will support me, who will buy me slippers so I don't have to walk on cold floors in the mornings, someone who makes innuendos in a weatherman's voice, who fills my fridge with ice cream and holds me when I cry. A man who rallies his family, so my sister will have a good night.

I want Tony. God, I want him so terribly. I want him to stay in New York and be with me.

I hug him as tight as I can, holding onto him while he's still here, breathing in the spiced cologne he can't wash off.

"Never forget, no matter what happens." His forehead rests against mine. "I got you."

He does. Has all of me. He always will.

After Gemma emerges from the bathroom, Tony drives us to the apartment so we can change. It feels so good to be dressed comfortably and ready for whatever shenanigans he has planned.

"Why didn't you leave your hair down?" I ask Gemma as we exit the building in shorts and sneakers, the nighttime humidity oppressive.

"I wanted it off my face. Who knows what we're getting into tonight?"

I can't remember the last time I saw Gemma's hair down and free, another part of my sister I miss.

A car pulls up to the curb just as we meet Tony on the sidewalk. I can't tell who's driving, but Nicky hops out of the back with a baseball bat. He's grinning so wide and stupid through all his beardedness I can't help but laugh.

"What is going on?" Gemma asks, pointing at the idiot with the baseball bat. "I'm mad at Murray, but I'm not gonna pull a *Lemonade* and smash the windows of his car in."

"As satisfying as that sounds," Santiago says as he steps out of the driver's seat, "We're just gonna go hit a few balls." He raises a hand to clarify. "Not man balls."

"Batting cages?" I ask Tony, and he grins down at me with a nod. This is perfect. Something fun and silly with his brothers, while providing Gemma an outlet to release pent-up anger. I'm so excited and grateful I can barely speak.

"Yup, there's a place in Ridgewood we like to visit, and we know the owner."

"Ah, a little New York favor." I make my accent really thick. "I hope he doesn't ask you to whack anyone in return."

Tony says, "Pay no attention to the cement bricks in the truck bed. But I was really hoping your sister's got a little bit more grace to handle the bat than your uncoordinated self. Don't want to be embarrassed in front of my mafia buddies."

There goes my being grateful. Without even missing a beat, Nicky tosses me the bat, which I catch, to Tony's surprise, and proceed to chase my smartass boyfriend around with it for a bit.

"C'mon, let's go!" Gemma cries from the front seat. "I want to go hit some balls." She smiles coyly back at the Rodriguez brothers. "Man balls not excluded."

They start to plead and beg her to be kind to their family jewels, making her laugh every time they say something outrageous. I haven't seen Gemma this happy in a while, and it only reaffirms my belief that Murray isn't right for her, no matter how much practicality she claims to want in life.

Santiago gets behind the wheel, and Nicky, Tony, and I clamber into the back.

"Hey," Nicky complains. "How come the redhead gets to ride in the front?"

"Eldest children always ride in the front," Tony responds. "It's to remind them they'll reach their dotage faster than us."

"Damn, Tony," Gemma sighs. "And I was just starting to like you."

"Gemma, you already love me, I can tell. Let me introduce you to my crazy brothers. The old fogey behind the wheel is Santiago."

Santi salutes her silently. "We'll show them old fogey at the cages."

"And this young whippersnapper is Nicholas."

"Call my Nick. Or Nicky. Or your slave. Hi, pretty lady."

"She's engaged, Nick."

"Damn." Nick scratches his beard. "Sophie, you got any more gorgeous family members?"

"My mom is single."

"Perfect."

Tony reaches over me to smack Nicky upside his head.

"What was that for?"

"Have some respect for their mother. How would you feel if someone said that about our mother?"

"Have you seen how massive the three of us are? Nobody would say shit about our ma."

Gemma takes stock of all of them before whistling. "There is way too much Italian male happening in this car."

"Technically there's only like one and a half Italians and one and a half Colombians."

"Colombian and Italian?" Gemma's wink in my direction is

equally lascivious and ridiculous. "No wonder you banged him the first night you met."

The reaction from the Rodriguez boys is nothing short of hilarious. Santiago nearly runs a red light. His jaw is on the floor, and he's sputtering nonsense. Nicky squawks out a *"Whaaat?"*, followed by highly suspicious coughing that is probably laughing.

It's all very amusing, and usually I'd join in the hilarity, but I can't focus on any of it. Their shock is more than surprising—it means Tony didn't instantly call his brothers after our passionate rendezvous to brag. Any other guy would have touted about it like a trophy. Not Tony. He kept it a secret, a special memory held just between us. The thought of him keeping that first time together close to his heart means more to me than I can ever say.

My heart aches. I rub my knuckles over my chest. I need to make a choice. Soon.

The pressure is building. I feel it in my teeth. In my bones. I don't know if it's possible, but my toenails are feeling it, too. Overwhelming pressure. Not from Tony, from me and my stupid heart.

Our eyes meet. His cheeks are slightly red, embarrassed by the attention. But he's not ashamed. He's proud of how we met, how we returned to each other after a week of radio silence. When he looks at me like this, I feel treasured.

I feel loved.

My stomach somersaults like a pair of Russian gymnasts. I have to look away, try to pay attention to the conversation. The intensity of his gaze alone strips me raw. He puts everything into one look, and I do all I can to accept it, keep him from feeling rejected. I try, but I don't think I'm doing enough. He needs more, deserves better than my inability to be fully present in a relationship.

Being the wonderful, caring man that he is, despite the chaos in the car, he takes my hand and kisses it gently. He sees my worry. He sees me, freckles, hang-ups, and all. He sees me and wants me…because all of those weird, wacky facets make me who I am. And that's who he doesn't look away from.

"What?" Nicky yells again, breaking me from my revelry. "You guys did it on the first date? That is—no, I can't believe it. Tony is not that much a badass."

"It wasn't even a date," Gemma continues. I glance over at Tony again. He's got this stupid grin on his face, and I don't know whether it's because Nick called him a badass or because he might finally get the chance to boast about how we met. I don't blame him for wanting to, after all this time. It was pretty hot.

"They had an argument about a parking spot, and then ten minutes later were fucking."

"Whaaat," Santiago joins in his brother's exclamations, swerving the truck around a double-parked cab. "I can't believe this is the first time I'm hearing this."

"This shit is crazy." Nicky slaps his knee.

"Our brother the playa."

"I was like the opposite of the playa," Tony corrects. "It's Sophie who's the playa. I mean, we had sex once, and that was it for me. No other woman will do. I'm addicted."

I bump his shoulder to get his attention.

"Thank you for not shooting your mouth off about how we met, but you can go ahead and brag if you want. Even I can admit you were a little bit the playa."

The memory of Tony crushing me against the wall then taking me on my bare floor with boxes strewn about the empty apartment is the single hottest image in my sexy fantasy bank. I refuse to call it a spank bank.

"Wait, really?" He lowers his voice and whispers, "Because I have been dying to give them the details. It was like the sexiest thing that's ever happened to me, but I didn't want to tell them because I know it embarrasses you a little."

"How I behaved embarrasses me, not that we had sex right away. That is my fondest memory in my new apartment."

He leans his forehead against mine, scary and powerful sentiments passing wordlessly between. "I got you" has quickly become the most romantic phrase ever to be spoken in the English language. I don't need to hear him say it, it's so ingrained into the fabric of who we are together, but I still enjoy it when he does.

"Sorry, guys," Tony says as they egg him on for more details. "A gentleman never tells."

The pressure builds. I'm fit to bursting.

We arrive at the batting cages in Queens and instantly find a parking spot near the facility. An older man stands outside, waiting for us. I tease Tony when the guy takes turns kissing the Rodriguez boys on both cheeks like an old-world mafia boss. When he does it to Gemma and me, Tony makes a face behind the guy's back, mimicking Don Corleone, and gestures like an old-world Italian. After a reminder of some rules for the boys, who apparently spent a few high school nights here getting drunk with buddies, we're in the building, and to my surprise, have the entire place to ourselves.

The Rodriguez brothers are like kids in a candy store, and obviously they've done this before, as they know where all the equipment is and how to work it. Santiago and Nicky give Gemma and I a quick tutorial. To my great annoyance, Tony is right about Gemma being able to handle the bat better than me. But to be fair, she played high school softball and was pretty good at it. I can't even play baseball video games successfully. He shows no leniency in his teasing when I attempt to make this point.

About a half-hour after hitting some balls, we've all got a good rhythm going, alternating with one another so we can watch the machine. Santiago and Tony are quiet with each other, the tension still present. But it's clear Santiago is happy to have been invited, and is putting aside his own resentment to bring them closer. It will take a while to get them there, but I have faith they'll return to normal before long.

Family is precious and should be treasured. I'm proud of Tony for putting aside his hurt…and he did it to help my sister.

I try to focus on the conversation instead of watching Tony, fantasizing about a future we can't have. Or maybe we can. It will be a lot of work, but maybe after all he's done for me, it's time I trust in us. We can make it work.

"How do you guys have this hookup?" Gemma asks, taking a stance to hit the ball.

"We all worked here as kids," Santiago answers. "Coached the little leagues that use the facility. Dad never paid attention to the baseball team in Colombia, but when he came here, and futbol—soccer—wasn't such a big thing, he fell in love with the sport and met Danny, the owner. Danny is Nicky's godfather, that's how much our pop loves baseball."

"All our godfathers are nonrelatives," Nicky jokes. "I don't think Pa understands the concept of godfathers."

"Godfathers can be friends of the family; they're not always relatives," I say after missing a ball.

"What do you know about it, you Irish heathen?" Tony heckles me.

"You really want me to hit you with a bat tonight, huh?"

"You know I love it when you chase me, baby."

A little ping echoes across the cages, and the guys razz Gemma for not turning her phone off before entering the batting zone. She steps out of the line of fire to check her cell. A strained but true smile stretches her cheeks.

She looks over at me, gives me a thumbs-up then points to her phone. "Murray says he's sorry if he hurt your feelings."

I hand my bat to Tony and walk over to Gemma, preparing myself to just give it to her straight. I promised to never get between her and Murray, but I can't let my sister marry a man who doesn't make her happy.

"Gemma—"

"He also says he'll pay Tony back for the meal. He meant to treat everyone anyway, since he picked the place."

Christ, I hadn't even thought of that. That meal must have cost a fortune, and Tony paid for it all like it was nothing.

"Listen to me for a second, please."

"No, Sophie." Gemma holds up her hand. "I know what you're going to say, that Murray and I fight too much. We're not right for each other."

"I haven't seen you this relaxed," I wave at the batting cages, "Since you met Murray. That means something."

She tugs me further away from the guys and starts telling me off in that quiet, older sister way. Like she knows best.

"You know what else means something? That Murray doesn't

care I won't be able to have kids. It means something that he knows about my ex-husband, and he would never lie to me like Frank did. Not many men are able to take on the emotional baggage of a widow. But Murray did, and he made me stronger."

"Murray loving you despite all that is not how it's supposed to be. You shouldn't feel grateful to him for that, a good person would support you no matter what happens to your body or the things you've been through in life."

"I can't believe you're attempting to give me advice, you don't know anything about relationships—"

I ignore the jab, needing to get my point across. "He should love you because you're brave enough to do what you have to do to survive. You're so courageous, Gemma. You shouldn't settle for a man who can't see that. You're making a mistake." I hold up my hands in surrender. "I promise that's all I'm gonna say. Let's go hit a few more balls, and then I'll drop you off at Murray's place."

"You can't drop a bomb like that on me then cut the conversation off." The guys call us back over, and Gemma sees this isn't the place for an argument. "We're not done talking about this. Rather I'm not done talking to you about it, because I'm through being talked at by you."

I nod, wrapping an arm around her shoulders.

"Like you know best," she mutters.

"Sure thing."

"I'm the oldest."

"I know. And you're so much smarter because of it."

She groans but leans into me. I'm gonna get it later, no doubt about it. Gemma will rip me a new one when the glow of an evening laced without worry over an asshole fiancé fades. But for now, we're relaxed and we're happy.

We walk back to the cages, and Tony tilts his head, silently asking if things are all right. I shrug, because I don't know. My sister is making a mistake, marrying Murray, but I'm glad I've said my piece. From now on I'll try to support her in whatever she chooses to do.

"Hey, Gemma," Tony calls out. "Come over here and show my brothers what hittin' like a girl really means."

Gemma smiles at me and says, "I like your guy, Soph. Don't fuck it up." She runs over to Tony and proceeds to hit at least three home runs in a row, or at least that's what the guys say they would be if we were in a field.

The image is surreal, my sister with Tony and his brothers, playfully mocking each other while simultaneously cheering one another on. As though we're a family. The Flanagan girls and the Rodriguez boys fit together like corners of a puzzle gone missing centuries ago. And here we are, finally connected again.

Tony's mouth drops open as my sister hits a ball at a particularly high speed. He looks over at me in shock, pointing at Gemma like she's something out of this world.

Does he know that's how I feel about him? Should I tell him I see him as this otherworldly creature come down from another planet to abduct me? He steals me away from earth, and at first, I want to resist, but once I let myself open up, there's so much he has to show me. Distant stars and undiscovered planets. That's what every day with Tony is like.

And it's all so wonderful. I want to tell him, but even though the words are in my head, I can't get them out of my mouth. There's a surge of emotional crap rising inside me whenever I try to express how perfectly imperfect he is. All I can come up with is, he's got me, and somehow that's enough.

After another hour, the guys volunteer to take Gemma home in a cab, since she lives on the Upper East Side and Tony and I are in Brooklyn Heights. I check if she's okay with traveling with the rowdy Rodriguez brothers, and all she says is, "Please, I can handle these mooks."

"Who you callin' a mook, princess?" Nicky asks, which earns him a smack on the back of his head from Tony. If they keep doing that to each other, they'll fall into a permanent concussive state.

Tony and I watch them get into the cab then head back to our place. It's late, neither of us in the mood to talk, and when I reach over to take his hand, intertwining his fingers with mine, I see him smile out of the corner of my eye.

We park the car and make it up the stairs to my floor. The elevator is out of service, as usual.

"You going to grab your PJs before coming up?" he asks in front of my door, watching me unlock it.

"No."

The pressure in my heart resumes its relentless force, filling my chest and spreading to my throat in painful need.

I take his hand and pull him into my place, shut the door without a word, and lock it behind us.

He glances at the locks, an incredible expression on his face. He can't comprehend what he's seeing, and then when it hits, when he realizes what I'm asking for, his shoulders sag, and a great breath of pent-up emotional frustration releases on one big wave.

Acceptance. That's what he looks like. The next step.

We usually end up at his place. It's bigger, always tidy, and has a better kitchen. I live like a slob and only have almond butter and leftover Chinese food in my fridge, but those aren't the real reasons I tend to pick his apartment, and he knows it.

We've spent time at my place, hung around and watched movies, fucked on my floor and my couch, but staying in my apartment, in my bed, is an intimate thing I was never ready for. Seeing him sprawled half-under my covers as morning light shines down from my bedroom window. Watching him eat breakfast in his boxer briefs at my kitchen counter. Getting out of bed in the middle of the night to pee, only to come back to him, curling into my welcoming arms and falling back asleep. Allowing him into my personal space at night, at my most vulnerable, trusting him to be here and be with me without ruining the special place I've claimed as my own.

This one spot, in all the millions of apartments in New York City, is mine. It has my mark on it. But without realizing it, Tony has left his mark on my life, just as I've left a mark on his.

And oh, it is sweet.

A barrier crumbles, one I'm always keenly aware of but actively ignore. I have obvious hang-ups that keep me from moving forward in relationships, but I'm trying to let it go. Struggling.

"This won't last," I say, the words bursting out of me like fire-crackers. "I want it to, but it won't."

"Baby, we're the only ones standing in the way of us making it. I'm all in, Sophie. I am here for us all the way, and I will do whatever it takes to make that happen."

A bubble forms in my throat, preventing me from responding. He raises his hands.

"You don't need to say anything if you don't want to. I only felt this was the right moment for me to tell you that. I'm fine waiting for your moment." He steps forward, cups my cheek, streaks fire over my lips where his thumb skims. "I'll wait for you forever."

He doesn't push me up against the wall or bend me over the couch. Instead we walk into the bedroom, his hand in mine, and then slowly undress each other. I revel in his insistent but soft caresses against my bare arms, my neck, my lips. He's marking me, memorizing every inch of me, and I'm doing the same.

I touch the stubble on his chin, enjoying the abrasion against my fingers. I trip over the sharp angles of his jaw, the thickness of his neck, the beautifully lush color of his tanned skin. His hands go to the edge of my shirt, but before he can tug it up, I rise on tiptoe to kiss his neck. I can't help it—the color calls to me, like a tree full of honey calling to a cartoon bear. And my kiss is almost cartoonish, or at least it would be if I weren't so hungry for him.

I bite and suckle the space under his jaw—a spot just to the right of his Adam's apple—then the dip in his collarbone that I tug his shirt down to get to. I focus on small, exciting pieces of him, delicacies to be savored, yet through it all I'm so hyper-aware of the rest of his body. There's tension in his muscles and a distinctive and delicious hardness skimming over my pussy. He isn't rubbing against me, not yet. I can tell he wants to, the rigidity of his jaw and the short breaths he takes projecting his eagerness to keep going, to see this through.

Our joining is usually fast and furious, but tonight I need something more. He's in my personal space, and I want him there till morning. I want him with me for much longer than just the morning.

I need to wake up from the safe numbness I've lived in this past decade. I need love, and I need Tony to give it to me. Only Tony.

We can make this work. He said he'd wait for me.

Tony presses down on my shoulders, putting me flat on my feet, then strips me of my shirt and bra, his fingers trailing after the falling garments. I think his speed might pick up because his breathing is deep, and I can tell he's anxious for me. But he stops. A full stop and stare as I stand there before him in nothing but my jeans and sneakers.

It's appallingly provocative to be looked at in such a bare, hungry way.

He cups both my breasts first, playing with the weight of them in his hands. His mouth is slightly open, and the bellows in his chest pick up speed. I can't stop smiling through the delicate and almost innocent pleasure he's getting from this. He's a kid in high school getting to second base for the first time, testing the feel of my breasts, not knowing what to do.

Except he absolutely knows what the fuck he's doing when he licks both hands then starts to manipulate my nipples into stiffness. I gasp and tip my head back, staring at my ceiling and holding onto his forearms. Then his mouth is against my nipples, and it's wet and dirty. Teeth skim the plump sides of my breast, biting me just hard enough to leave a mark. My hands are in his hair now, keeping him pressed against me. I feel awkward and uncomfortable, like my skin is on fire. The wetness between my legs is overflowing, so slick, and my pussy is swollen beyond belief. It almost hurts to stand still. I can't take much more of this, and we've barely undressed. He still has his shirt on, for Christ's sake.

Tony pulls my hands off his hair to get away. I make a pathetic, needful sound when his lips leave my skin. Any other man would have smirked, celebrated how destitute I am without him. Not Tony—he says things that makes my blood boil and my confidence surge.

"I know. I know, baby. I need to feel you everywhere, too." He helps me out of my jeans and sneakers, kissing my shins as he's kneeling in front of me. My shins become the most erotically sensitive spot on my body. "I just—" His eyes flick up, and he sees how wet I am. How can he miss it? I'm dripping down my thighs.

He groans and leans his face right fucking against my wet pussy. His lips are touching my lace underwear, not moving, not doing anything, until I feel his tongue press against the fabric. It's the barest of strokes, but the knowledge that its Tony's tongue doing this to me, and that he can taste my sex and liquid, is enough to make me come. I almost do; I start to pant like I'm gonna. Then I hear him, and my focus shifts.

The sound he makes is feral, almost wild in its abandonment. I never thought a man would ever be willing to make that sound with another person present. It's private and guttural, scary in a naturally violent way, a facet of his inner self only I get to see. It's the same thing that happens with my little whimpers. I know Tony won't make fun of me, won't think me weak for showing a little vulnerability, because he feels the same way.

We're both falling into a deep well, a miasma of greed and agony and sublimity. It's graceful and horrifying, silent and cacophonous. We're consumed by each other until there is no ending or beginning, just the mess of our hearts and bodies, and the hope we won't fuck this up.

He pulls the lacy fabric down and helps me step out of them. My knees are shaking, and I'm on the edge of coming, but I'm so focused on him and his every move that I can't think about myself. He leans in for another taste of me, but I step back.

I swear to God he growls.

"Let me do the same for you. Tony, I feel—" I don't know how to express it; I just hope he sees my distress and understands.

He stands and a thrill shoots through me because it's my turn to get his damn clothes off. I kiss his chest as I push his shirt away. He's looked and acted the proper gentleman all night, but I need him to be low and filthy with me. I squeeze his ass when his jeans and underwear fall to the floor, then lightly push my finger into the cleft between his cheeks, rubbing the tight bundle of nerves that make up his rim.

He jerks in surprise but leans back into it with eyes closed tight, which has to be the sexiest thing in the world. I kneel then, his bobbing cock stiff and jutting toward me like a treat I get to suck on. I don't take my finger away from his hole, just keep rubbing and massaging.

There is a copious amount of precum dripping from his tip, making the head glisten like a piece of candy, tantalizing me with every bead. Without a word I pop the tip of his cock into my mouth. I don't go far, just to the ridge, then swirl my tongue around the slit, licking up all the delicious wetness he's given me. The taste of him is hotter than it ever has been before, his smooth flesh scalding my lips.

He grunts, the sounds turning harsh and deep as I push him further into my mouth. I've barely had time to suck on him slowly, moving back toward the slit again, when he pulls away, leaving me bereft. The loss of him feels like he's pulled out of my pussy, not my mouth.

"You're amazing at that. One lick and I'm almost coming." He takes my hand and pulls me up, like some fancy lord pulling a lady out of a deep curtsy. But fantasies of lords and ladies dissolve as he pushes two fingers into my cunt. "Shit, you're wet."

The talker is back. He has all this energy, but since we're not fighting then fucking each other against a wall, he needs to expend it some way. "And you're squirming on all of it. You feel so juicy down here, baby, and I want to lick all of you up."

"No, it's my turn." I really don't fucking care that I sound like a petulant child. He took my toy away, and I want it back.

He smiles at me with eyebrows raised, and I snort at myself, the moment turning sweet and embarrassing. Of course we can get what we want at the same time; my head was just so full of him I forgot there was anything but taking turns.

He walks me backward until my calves hit the bed. I bend my knees to sit but he brings me back up again, turning me around until his cock is pressing into my ass. Not grinding, not humping, just lightly pressing and nestling so gently it almost tickles. Except the tickle is molten heat scorching my skin, turning me into some sort of impassioned beast.

He moves around me and sits, crawls up the bed—my bed, which makes me shudder in an uncontrollable way seeing him on my patterned comforter—then turns around until his head is by me, at the edge of the bed.

"Crawl over me. Let me lick you while you suck my cock."

"You're mine," I say, and the words are so proprietary and out of character for me I almost shock myself out of the lustful puddle I've melted into. I'm self-conscious until I hear his reaction.

"Yes, shit, yes, you don't know what it does to me to hear you talk like that. My dick is so fucking hard...I can come just from watching your lips touch it. I don't even need to feel it. Just to watch you get so turned on makes me go like a teenager."

I'm crawling over him as he's talking. I make sure to stay low, so my nipples brush his chest hair, abrading and scratching the stiff points to painful sensation. He skims his hands over my hips, my stomach, my calves. Again, such an innocuous spot now feels like he's kissing my lips or squeezing my ass.

Finally, I'm at his cock. It's almost purple in color now, and I can believe he might come the second I touch him. He pulls my hips back until they're right over his mouth, and then starts to lick me. I'm scared now, not for what's happening or to suck his cock—something I really, really, really want—but I need to feel him inside me tonight, and I think I might cry if he comes in my mouth then passes out...which has happened before, so I don't really think it's in the realm of impossibilities.

I set aside all pride, and while he's busy licking at my pussy like a bowl of cream, so sloppy and dirty I feel my orgasm start to rise and twist in my gut, I turn back to him and blurt out, "I really want to suck your cock but if I lick you will you come in my mouth? I love when you do that; I love the taste of you, but I need you inside me more than anything tonight."

He pauses, but doesn't say anything. Well, that's it. I just ruined the night. Our rhythm was perfect, we were completely in sync, and I had to go and—

He sits up, tipping me forward into my pillows.

"Sorry, I just—I don't know if I, if anyone, has ever been so honest with me in bed. You like it when I come in your mouth?" He adjusts me so that my face is no longer mashed into my pillow. I don't know what position he's aiming for, so I try to go on my hands and knees, thinking he wants me from behind, and in a way, he does, but this is something different. I don't think I've ever done this before.

He goes into my bedside drawer for a condom, and once he's got it on he asks, "Is this okay?" Always checking in with me. Making sure I'm comfortable and content.

I'm sitting over his bent knees, his chest to my back. I feel his powerful thighs beneath mine, the hairs on his legs chafing my skin. He props me up and places his cock at my entrance. "Can I have you now? Let me have you." His voice is in my ear, and I'm thrust into a new stratosphere of yearning. No woman could have ever felt this way before.

"Yes, Tony. Always." It's not a moan or a whimper, but an agreement. A promise.

He pushes inside me, slowly. I feel that stiff length stretching me, driving me past my limits. His hand comes around and rests over my mound, just lays there as his hips begin to roll. It's slow and sensual, a dance we both know so well by now, yet I love learning the steps again, thrust by thrust. He doesn't slam into me, doesn't fuck the life out of me like I've felt him do so many times before. I love when he does that—it's fun and crazy and fueled by a frantic passion—but this is essential. It's life and pain and joy. It's connection. It's love. It's everything I swore I didn't need in my life, but I'll die without.

I twist to him for a kiss, and his rhythm falters as our mouths meet. I bite at him, lick inside past his lips, fuck his mouth as he's driving into me. I squeeze my inner muscles, wanting to hold him there, push him to madness, as he's doing to me. The hand covering my clit slides over our joining.

"Touch this," he says against my lips.

I can't keep my eyes off him. Sweat dews on his temples. He keeps licking his lips, kissing mine, gritting his teeth.

"What?" I ask, breathless, uncertain what he wants.

"Where we're together."

He takes my hand and places it right into the depths of us. I touch his cock as it spears in and out of me. I close my eyes and just live in the moment. It's wet and messy and dirty and so perfect and right.

"You're inside me. Push deeper inside me, Tony."

"Your pussy squeezes me so tight, baby; I can't last much longer."

But he does. We keep going until we're both panting and groaning, to the point of pain. He's rubbing my clit with both our hands, and the angle is hitting a spot inside me I so rarely found with anyone else. He's grunting on every thrust, and I'm moaning so loud we're probably keeping my neighbors awake. They're rolling their eyes in their apartments, talking about how those people are going at it again.

I moan louder at the thought.

"Gonna come, baby," he groans against my ear, grasping my breast with his free hand and kneading it. "I need you to go with me."

"It's too much. I'm too worked over. I can't."

"Look at me."

I open my eyes, and he tickles my clit with a few delicate and quick strokes. I feel my orgasm crest, waiting at the rim of a bowl inside me, just needing that extra amount of liquid to spill over.

"You can. I got you." He presses down on my clit and strokes inside me in a weird and different angle. It stops my pleasure in a moment of uncertainty, and then as I embrace it, it sends me flying. My body crumbles. There is no Sophie left—I'm a vessel made for sex, and I'm surpassing any expectation of what I was created for. But I'm not alone; I'm not empty like I've felt in the past, after this large and intimate moment takes me under. Tony is with me, and he's riding this excruciating wave alongside me, stoking my eagerness, feeding it back to me.

"Tony," I yell before he takes me in a kiss as his cock jerks inside me. We're both keening into each other, the sounds muffled but no less sharp and desperate.

After an eternity, it ebbs. My sex stops pulsing, and he begins to slip from me. He grunts, and I reach down, holding the base of the condom as I slide off him. He pulls it off, tossing it in the garbage by my bed. I sit back against my pillows, breathing deep and staring at him.

He's sweating, like crazy sweating. I see spots on my comforter from where his legs were. His cock is soft, but still a little intimidating to see, even though I've had him in me many times this past month. His chest is rising and falling as fast as mine, and he's doing the same thing I am. Just staring, taking me in.

We're a beautiful, sweet, disastrous mess, with a great big ocean between us we might be able to cross. Just maybe, if we work at it. If we put aside the fear.

I hold out my hand to him, and he takes it without a second's thought. He curls up next to me, and we spend the next moments touching and kissing. I wipe the sweat off his brow, and Tony plays with my frizzed-out curls. His kisses take on odd patterns, then I figure out he's mapping my freckles, playing a sexy kind of connect-the-dots.

I put my hand on his chest, directly over his heart. I can feel the beat of it beneath my hand, and it makes me smile. I look up at him, not attempting to hide anything I'm feeling in this moment. I embrace how terrifyingly and wonderfully raw I am.

He's a beautiful man, but the person he is within, the kind and funny and somewhat cocky guy, is everything I never knew I wanted. He takes me for who I am, a neurotic, freckle-faced, argumentative weirdo, and he likes every bit of it. Maybe even loves. Hell, there could be love in the look he's giving me right now. It's soft and stunning, so forgiving and caring.

I kiss him then, because what else is there to do, aside from telling him I love him?

God, I do.

I love him so, so much the words are bursting from my heart, but my stupid brain keeps holding me back. At this point, the mental chains my mind has cinched around those words are starting to hurt. If I can't break those chains soon, I'll start to bleed.

I sigh and bury my face in his chest. His arms come around me, and we start to drift, the air conditioning cooling the sweat off our bodies. I can stay like this forever.

Tony's cell starts to ring.

And rings, and rings. It doesn't stop ringing. When it finally cuts off, it starts again fifteen seconds later.

"Tony, just get up and get it."

"No, we're having a moment."

I'm relieved I'm not the only one in the moment's thrall, but I'd rather he just deal with the call so we can go back to having the moment. "Please answer it."

He fetches his jeans with a curse, tugging the smartphone out of his back pocket, then answers. He doesn't walk out of the room to talk, leaving me to wonder what the call's about. I like it. Maybe if we were at dinner with friends I would have been annoyed, but here in the intimacy of the night, I like that he's standing naked in the middle of my bedroom and talking in that rapid mix of Italian and English.

He covers the phone receiver and turns to me. "Baby, there's some sort of emergency. I need to go and deal with this."

"No, stay. You can work here." I crawl across the bed, well

aware my bare ass and pussy are shaking in his face. I grab my laptop and set it up on the bed. He downloaded his network access on my Mac the week before when his computer went on the fritz. I've got it all booted up and ready for him, so I scoot back with my legs spread wide and pat the bed. "Here."

He looks like he's in pain. "I don't know what you're trying to say." The phone is resting on his shoulder now, forgotten. I can hear a very annoyed Italian voice screaming at him from the other line. "All I'm seeing are your legs wide open and your wet pussy staring at me."

"Sit here. I want——" What I want is intimate and embarrassing to admit, but after what we just shared I can't shy away from it. "Sit between my legs, rest against me." I pat the bed again, staring at the covers instead of him. "Stay with me."

I look up, and he's right there, crawling over to me. The phone is forgotten on the bed covers. He holds my face and kisses me, a strong echo of the pain and joy we felt a little while ago.

"I'd really, really, really like to do that. Are you sure?"

Seeing him off balance and unsure of himself is a little endearing. "Yeah, I asked you, didn't I?"

With a blinding grin he grabs his phone and settles into the cradle of my thighs, but I'm the one who breathes a sigh of relief and contentment as he leans back against me. I ignore what he's saying; I can't understand half of it anyway. Instead I focus on the vibrations of his voice pulsing from his back to my chest. It's so easy. We're both buck-ass naked so the hairs on his legs and back are abrading my skin a little—hell, I've basically got rug burn on the back of my thighs from that position—and my still distinctly wet core is smooshed up against the base of his spine.

Neither of us seems to care. His legs are crossed, and he's got the computer in his lap, the phone in the crook of his neck, and whenever he isn't typing, his hands are sliding up and down my legs.

When his voice raises a little, frustration showing, I massage his shoulders then pet his hair. The tension drains from his muscles, obviously and instantly, like I've got some sort of magic in my fingers.

It's only me. I did that. I made him calm and relaxed. My presence, my company, can soothe this wonderful man, who indulges my need for play by verbally sparring with me, who supports me, who calls in reinforcements to help my sister heal from a fight with her own useless fiancé.

He stops talking, cover the speaker on his phone, and turns to me.

"What's your ulcer's name?"

Oh, God, this is mortifying. I'm gonna kick Gemma's ass for telling him this.

"Don't you have business to worry about?"

"Yeah, I'm fixing yet another shipping company contract that's taking advantage of our lack of knowledge of the Italian markets, but all I can think of right now is you have an ulcer, and you named it. I have to know."

This will either make or break his feelings for me. "Gary."

"Why Gary?"

"I knew a Gary in elementary school. He was whiny and annoying. Like the ulcer."

He doesn't answer, only shakes his head and smiles at me. He doesn't seem appalled by my weirdness, doesn't judge me. He actually looks…delighted?

Acceptance. That's what it is.

I can almost feel the walls around my heart melt, and it's the thought of how he treats my sister that does it. He treated her like family, like his family treated me. He looked past his argument with Santiago to help support Gemma. He really would sacrifice everything for the ones he loves. He shouldn't have to. He should be happy. I want to make Tony happy.

I love him, I think again, giddy. I rub my face along his back. Mouth the words against his skin.

I'm in love with Tony, and though I can't say it yet, I hold him close against my chest, trying to speak through physicality. Sometimes that's all I'm able to do in any situation, the words getting jammed up inside me. But I think he understands. He says something quickly on the phone, then puts it down and turns to me.

"I'll be a few more minutes, then we can sleep. You sure I can stay here? I wanna wake up in the morning next to you."

I kiss the corner of his mouth. His cheek. His temple.

"Stay forever."

And God, I mean it with all of my heart.

I'm screwed.

16

TONY

IS RUNNING OUT OF TIME.

I kick my apartment door closed and rest my laptop bag on the floor. I know Sophie's home; she's been sending me adorable texts all day about some big news she has for me. There are a thousand things running through my mind, but of course, today of all days, I think that maybe she's ready to talk about us, talk about a future together…in Italy.

I pull a folder out of my bag then bring it to the kitchen island, flipping through the pages one more time. I knew this was coming; they told me it was coming. I just didn't think it was coming so soon. I thought I had till the end of next month to win Sophie over and convince her to move with me…now I have till the end of the week.

"Things are progressing at a worrisome pace in the Rome office. We need someone to take control now, and none of the Italian candidates we interviewed have the experience or the desired drive we're looking for to run that location. There is a lot of failing business in Italy due to the economy, and a lot of potential for claiming those businesses and remaking them in a way that can benefit more than just a bottom line. We want to save those institutions and those jobs. We need you there."

This is what I've been working toward. For years I imagined a big, fancy firm sending me overseas to some exotic location, somewhere I can invite my family and treat my parents to the lifestyle they deserve after decades of supporting my brothers and me. A place I can flaunt my wealth and revel in the number of rungs on the ladder I've climbed.

I imagined the moment in finite detail.

I'd find a beautiful white sand beach in Sicily, or a vineyard in Tuscany, grapevines stretching far into the horizon. It didn't matter where, just the most picturesque and indulgent loca-tion. I'd ask a local to take my picture, maybe before sharing a drink with them. In the image I'd hold a glass of wine or a beer, and look out over a sunset so freaking glorious it would become the top-rated filterless Instagram image. I'd smile care-lessly, looking away from the camera, not concerned with whoever is taking the picture. I'd project contentedness, wanting for nothing, and drenched in obvious wealth and privilege.

Then I'd send the photo to Natalie and wait for her to beg to take me back.

I wanted to hurt her, make her jealous, make her see I wasn't useless. I came to her, in a moment of uncontrolled desperation, and I proposed on her doorstep. She rejected me flat out.

"Get off your knee, Tony. You're embarrassing yourself. I thought you got that we can't be together." She tried to look contrite, uncomfortable by what she had to say to me because I was too in love to listen to her before she moved out there. "I didn't want things to end like this, but you need to hear me when I say I want more. You're not enough. I'm sorry, but I need more than you and your love of art…as romantic as it is.

You're a good man; you'll find a woman who is okay with being a professor's wife."

It crushed me. She called me romantic, like it was cute. Corny. Unnecessary. I thought our lives were planned out, but she had bigger and better things to achieve. She placed value on her life by adding dollar signs, so that's what I did. I kept accruing wealth with the intention of throwing it back in her face one day.

It was an asinine, awful fantasy. Things weren't right with us that last year, and I was too blind to see it. I ignored her when she would try to tell me we were over. She hurt me, but I placed the concept of our love higher than what she needed to be happy.

I soon learned after graduating with my MBA and entering the workforce that my idea of earning money fast enough to shame her was a faraway dream. I forgot the fantasy, put the pain of Natalie's words aside, and focused on improving myself, being the best at everything. It consumed me. I disregarded who I used to be, became someone new.

I didn't intend to start on this path, but I've embraced it, and I accept who I am now. There are days I have doubts because I know I didn't do this for the right reasons, which makes the doubt so much harder to face, but I don't regret the choices I made.

If I hadn't made them, I wouldn't have Sophie.

Sophie. The beautiful, enticing, aggravating, brilliant, witty, sensual Sophie. My Sophie. Our would-be relationship is far from perfect. I sit at my table and can almost see her naked, eating pasta in the seat across from me. It will forever be one of my favorite memories, but I refuse to let it be one of the few I have with Sophie. I need to suck it up, sit her down, and talk to her.

Fuck talking, I'm going to kiss her, tell her I love her, and ask her to move with me.

That stops me in my tracks. It's only been a few weeks. Am I so in love with this woman that I can spend the rest of my life with her? The answer is so fucking simple it makes me laugh. Because that's just it—I do want to spend the rest of my life with Sophie. I love Sophie, and I love us, and our fucking crazy mess of a relationship we've had so far.

I'll lay out the pros of coming to Italy, talk about the stories she can write, how I'll make sure she's eating well and tending to her ulcer. I'm still pissed she never told me about that. She deserves better than a fridge full of leftovers and white bread with almond butter.

She deserves espresso in a café in Rome…decaf and in moderation. Long weekend trips to Nice or Croatia…shit, I'll even go to Switzerland if she wants to. She should be writing her articles on a balcony overlooking a skyline that is centuries older than any in America's.

I love Sophie. The thought fills me with purpose, determination.

I am in love with Sophie, and I'm gonna ask her to move with me. I text this phrase to my entire family the second I think it, then I put the Italy job offer packet away in case she comes up. I don't want to spoil the surprise. My phone buzzes with a barrage of messages. Okay, maybe I didn't think that text through. But I was caught in the moment.

The first is from Nicky.

Why? You'll be missing out on all the sexy Italians. J/K bro. Don't kill me. I like Sophie. Seriously, you can't kill me. I'm ma's favorite

The next from Pa.

Go get your girl, mijo. *She is a lovely woman. Do you think Italy sells fresh* guasca? *I'll ask your mother.*

And Santiago.

I'm happy that you've found someone, Tony. Make sure you do everything to deserve her.

Ma's text stops me in my tracks, makes my gut curdle. The thought never even occurred to me.

What if she doesn't want to move to Italy?

Of course she'll want to go to Italy. We crossed the indestructible barrier last night. I stayed at her place. It's the green light I've been waiting for since taking her to brunch. I've been listening this time, not like with Natalie, and I've heard her, even without having to hear the words.

I open the door to my apartment, intending to run down and tell her about all the amazing things I've just come up with, somewhat proud of myself, but she's right there, her hand raised to knock on my door.

"Hi," she squeals, then jumps into my arms, her legs wrapping around my waist.

"What's going on?" I laugh because she's still squealing.

"I did a thing, and now they want my thing. And it's all over the thing." She pushes out of my arms to start jumping up and down. "I'm so excited I'm forgetting words. Forgetting words is not a great quality for journalist."

"I can see that. C'mere and sit down." I tug her toward the couch, and because I'm still going crazy from my realization I pull her into my lap, not wanting to be an inch farther from her. She doesn't fight me, just does a little dance in my lap, which does not help the arousal I feel upon seeing her in a tiny tank top and tiny shorts. Why is everything she wears around the apartment building so tiny?

"Tell me what's going on?" I smack her bottom. "Stop moving like that or I'm gonna bend you over the couch and fuck you before you can get a word out."

She kisses me, all hot and excited like we've been fighting. "Oh, I want that. Me want."

"You're devolving into a caveman. Speak English, woman."

"Wait for it."

"Waiting."

"You ready?"

"Pretty damn sure."

"I got a new job!"

My excitement drains like tanking stocks. A new job. Writing jobs can sometimes be remote. Maybe that's what this one is. I grip her thigh, she's wriggling so much she's about to fall off.

"What? That's amazing. Where?"

"This new branch of *The New Yorker*. It's mainly focused on online publications but there is a lot of investigative journalism. They're seeking locals with stories to tell and a unique perspective on our city."

"So, you're gonna be writing about New York?"

"Yes, mostly about Staten Island. Show my hometown's true colors."

"Good luck with that."

She rolls her eyes but hugs me a second later, and I'm fucking glad she can't see my face because I'm so crestfallen. It's not the whole, getting a new job thing, that doesn't matter. I'm proud. She'll be able to work somewhere her talent can be fully utilized. But she can't write about the inner workings of her hometown from across the ocean.

She starts talking about her new editor and the ideas she has for the first edition. I listen, I try to listen. I nod and smile, laugh when she jokes. Encourage her when she has doubts.

This is her dream job. She'll never leave New York now. Even after everything we shared, the bridges we crossed, she'll always be a New Yorker living in New York. I won't call her out for it or make her feel shame or guilt. She belongs here.

I belong in Italy.

This mess between us was always going to be a fling. I did it again. I should have listened to her from the beginning. We were never going to be anything more than this. Kisses and sex and long looks.

I kiss her neck one more time, she giggles thinking I'm being playful, where really, I just need to compose my expression before looking at her. I breathe her in, a lotion scented with citrus absorbed in her skin. I'll never forget the smell, or the way she moves on me, or how she feels in my arms.

She isn't Natalie. She isn't doing this to hurt me. She has a life and she deserves to live it as she sees fit. I pull the pain in, blockade it behind a brick wall filled with waffles and articles of cat memes. Things will be lighthearted from here on out. No forbidden promises, no hoping we'll ever be more than two

261

strangers who had a connection and enjoyed it for a month. I'll always hold her close to my heart.

I pull back, a big smile on my face I can feel is fake but I'm hoping she won't notice because I'm such a goofball most of the time anyway.

"We need to celebrate. Champagne and pizza."

"Oh, can we go to the good place for pizza, not the fast place?"

"The good place doesn't deliver."

"We can take a cab."

"And drink champagne in the car on the way over."

"Yes! I've always wanted to do that. Let me go get changed." She heads toward my door then turns on her heels and runs back to me, flinging her arms around my neck before giving me a big, exuberant kiss.

She starts to run out.

"Sophie, wait. I—"

I'm moving to Italy. I love you. Come with me. Travel the world with me. Grow old with me.

"What?" she asks.

"I'm so proud of you, baby."

"Thanks, Tony. Thank you for being awesome." She hesitates, looks like she wants to say more, but turns to run to her place instead.

Being without Sophie is going to be agony.

I close the door to my apartment and lean on it, massaging my heart. This hurts so much more than when I broke up with

Natalie, thinking I might have to face a near future without my Sophie.

I text my pop, needing him now.

I was wrong. She won't come with me.

Giving up so soon, mijo?

The words sting. He doesn't understand.

What's the point of fighting? She'll never give up her life to move with me.

Would you give up yours to be with her?

I pause, thinking of everything we've said and done and fought over this past month. I think of the art opening at the Met. The way she embraced my family, even Santiago, how she supports me and cares for me. The other day she shielded me from a dog, for Christ's sake.

Could I give up everything I've worked for to be with Sophie? I created a false dream then personified it. It consumed me. What would I be without it?

I don't know.

That young lady deserves more than I don't know.

She does. She really does.

But I can't give it to her.

She was right—this whole time, I've pushed for something more than a fling, I tricked and schemed, I made her care for me.

And after everything, I'm gonna leave her, just like she thought I would.

How am I gonna tell her? How can I? It's impossible.

So I make the worst decision I've ever made in my life.

I don't say a fucking word.

17

SOPHIE

AND GOD IT HURTS.

I knock on Tony's door, a blueberry crumble I baked from scratch in my hands. I feel elated after the other night. We're moving forward in a life together, as a team. And it's all going to be okay. This month has been rough, hell our whole relation-ship—and I'm totally cool with calling it that now—has been one weird roller coaster ride through hell, purgatory, and heaven.

Mostly heaven, with lots of orgasms.

But we're even now. He met my sister. Helped Gemma with the Murray situation. I suggested he meet some of my friends, and he didn't tease me how my introverted self can't keep more than a couple at a time. I know he wanted to tell me he loves me the other night. I felt it. It was on the tip of his tongue, just as it's been on the tip of mine.

I'm saying it to him tonight. He'll open the door, and I'll give him pie, and tell him I love him. I'll tell him that a long-distance relationship can work. We can make this work. It will be perfect, like nothing else has been perfect in my life before. This one thing I'm going to do right.

I knock again when he doesn't answer and press the small door-bell that sounds like an oven timer going off. He's home, there's music playing.

The door opens, and he smiles when he sees me, but he closes the door, just enough so I can't see what's inside, and leans against the doorjamb. He tries to act casual, but his grin is a little off. A little fake. It reminds me of how Gemma looks when she's trying to deflect attention.

I ignore it, his place is probably a mess because he's trying a new recipe and he's ashamed to show me. He won't be thinking of messes or cooking once I give him pie.

"Pie."

Christ, I had a fucking speech planned, and now I'm just standing in the hallway, expectantly holding out the pie to him, like he's supposed to know what it means.

"Sorry, I mean…what I want to say is." I sigh, not wanting to do this in the hallway. "Can you let me in? I need to talk to you for a bit."

"How about we go to your place? Let me turn the music off and grab my keys."

"No, we're right here, I already lugged the pie up the stairs. Let's go inside and sit."

"Nah, you don't wanna go in there. I'll carry the pie down for you."

Now I'm suspicious. "Why don't you want me to see your apartment?"

"My A/C isn't working."

"I can feel the cool breeze coming through the door."

"I got a dog, and I know you hate dogs."

"Animals aren't allowed in this building, and I don't fucking hate dogs. *You* hate dogs."

"I was trying to cook something, and it went wrong and now everything smells—"

I can't take it anymore. This isn't some light and funny banter; he's hiding something from me. He's nervous, he does this head-scratching thing when he's nervous, and right now he's basically digging a hole in his scalp.

"Let me in, Tony."

His expression turns hard, challenging me in a way I haven't seen since we first argued on the street.

"No, Sophie. Now isn't a good time."

Fuck that noise.

I shove the pie into his hands, so he's forced to take it then push the door open and walk past him. I don't know what I expect to see: a naked woman lying on his couch, a bunch of cocaine sorted into neat little lines on his coffee table, all the possibilities more ridiculous than the last. What I do see might be worse than everything I imagined combined.

His apartment is empty. The couch is gone. His TV stand, the pictures, and paintings have been wrapped in bubble wrap. There are boxes everywhere—*moving* boxes. In my shock, I glance at his kitchen counter and see a stack of papers. I walk over to read what it is, almost in a daze. It's a partially completed lease termination form from the building office. He's going through the checklist, making sure the apartment is in order before handing over the keys. There are little inked-in check marks on the paper.

The move out date is this week.

He's been up here checking shit off his moving to-do list while I was downstairs baking him a fucking pie and planning to tell him I loved him and wanted to give this relationship a chance.

I scan the form for the little box that says, 'break Sophie's heart,' but either it isn't there, or I don't rate a box. I rest my hand over the form and feel it fisting involuntarily, crumpling the paper.

"So, you got the job?" I stare at the shelf where all his cookbooks used to be. They're gone now, stuffed into some box.

"They offered it to me." He puts the pie on the counter, watching me.

"I thought you wouldn't have to leave until the end of next month." The acid reflux I suffered from all the meals he cooked me seems to be returning with a vengeance.

"They need me there sooner. I'm supposed to head over to the corporate apartment in Rome in a few days."

"*A few days?*" I say it more to myself than him, stunned and hurt.

Acid churns in my gut; it's rising and poisoning my heart. I know this feeling, this corroding, toxic mess tainting my blood. Heartbreak. Betrayal. All things I never thought I'd feel with Tony. I was so sure. So fucking sure he loved me.

"Were you even going to tell me?"

"Sophie—"

"Did it never occur to you that this is something you should tell the woman you're fucking on a regular basis?"

"Don't say it like that. You're more than that."

"I can't possibly be anything to you, Tony. If I mattered to you, you would have told me the second you knew. That's what people in relationships do; they don't hide things this massive from each other."

"Oh, we're in a relationship now? When it's convenient for you to become self-righteous, you get to decide what we are to each other? Give me a break."

"I thought the other night made things clear. You said you were all in. You said you would wait for me. How is this all in? This feels like fucking wham, bam, nice to know ya."

"You made it painfully clear you didn't want more than a fling."

"I tried that, Tony. I tried telling you that all fucking month, and you refused to listen. You've lied and tricked me, made me want you more and more, and now you throw me to the side like a piece of trash? I thought we were going to give this a go." I grab his arm, make him look at me. "Something else is happening here. I refuse to believe after everything you've done to fight for us, you'd give this up like it's nothing."

"You want to talk about fighting for us? You said you were with me too, or did you conveniently forget that in your haste to turn me into a villain?"

"What are you talking about—"

"I was going to ask you to come with me, Sophie. I want you to be with me in Italy, and I thought you understood that."

"Yeah, there were moments I thought you might be leaning in that direction."

"Then how could you take this new job? You have to be here for it. You took it, knowing it would put another fucking barrier between us. You knew this would prevent you from saying yes to me. You did it on purpose."

"Tony, me living here and you being in Rome is not the end of the world. Long-distance relationships can work. They don't all end up the way you and Natalie—"

"Don't throw that in my face."

"Why not? You're throwing my baggage into mine. I've dreamed of working for this publication my whole damn life. I can't turn it down now. Why won't you even consider long distance?"

"You know why."

He tries to turn away, but I grab his hand.

"Tell me. Say it."

"Because they don't fucking work. God, Sophie, do you want me to write it in blood? I loved Natalie, and the second I was out of her sight she fucked anything with something dangling between its legs."

"Don't be disgusting, Tony. You're better than this. Don't do this."

Why is he giving up so easily?

"I can't do long distance. I can't. I think about you being over here without me, and I go nuts. One day over there, knowing you're mine, and that I'll only see you, what, once or twice a year? That would kill me. Tell me you could do that."

"It doesn't matter. At least I would try." I take the lease termination forms, crumple them up and throw them at him. "You're not even willing to try, you goddamn coward."

I can't look at him. I walk away but he chases me, stands in front of his door so I can't leave. Acid burns in my eyes, streaks down my cheeks.

"You've introduced me as your *friend*. You didn't tell me when you were first offered the job. Yeah. I heard that damn phone conversation, and you didn't trust me enough or think me worthy of that piece of your life." He grabs my arms, forces me to look at him. "I am not the other men in your life. I am not your father or the one shit boyfriend you've had."

I pound on his chest. "And I'm not Natalie."

"No, you're worse."

His words are a slap, putting me in my place.

"Why?"

"Because I didn't love her like I love you."

His confession hangs in the air between us. It's the first time he's used that word, said it out loud, but all I can see are the boxes lying around the apartment. There's probably a plane ticket for one snugly tucked into his passport.

"Don't. Don't say that. Not now, when I'm standing in the middle of all these boxes. It sounds like a fucking lie." I cover my face with my hands, shame making me feel two inches tall. "Oh God. You have been one floor above me, packing. Packing! I might have even heard the packing tape roll as you closed up the boxes, if I listened hard enough. But I was so blind, I lost myself in you, and I refused to see what was right in front of me."

Tony cups my face, his hold gentling.

"I'm right in front of you. Me. I love you, and I want you to——"

I shove him away.

"Don't fucking say that to me. You don't love me. Someone who loves me would have told me about this. They would have asked for my help to pack, so we could at least make the most of the time we had left. You didn't even…" I can't say it now. It would sound so pathetic.

271

"What?" he pushes into my space, his forehead nearly on mine. "I didn't even what? Didn't ask you to go with me? Would you have said yes, Sophie? You love New York. You love being near your sister. You have this new job. You'd never have gone with me if I asked."

I glare up at this imposter, this stranger I thought I knew.

"I guess we'll never know now."

Both my hands clutch my shirt, directly over my heart. The pathetic organ has shriveled to nothing in a matter minutes. I turn to leave, unable to stay in this place a second longer. All that's left for me here is corroded memories. He did this to me: dissolved my will and made me depend on him, to count on him when I knew better.

It was supposed to be a fling, and he made me love him.

"You know what, Tony?" I say, anger churning like a defense mechanism, keeping the agony at bay. "I don't know what my answer would have been had you asked me to move, but at least I would have known that there is a man who wants me in his life, not one makes that me feel five inches tall."

I stride toward the door, intending to never look back. My heart buckles in on itself, a misshapen gadget made of sharp metal, crushed by a trash compactor.

I feel his hand on my arm but wrench away from him.

"Don't you fucking touch me."

"Sophie, would you have said yes—"

My phone rings. It's my sister's tone. "Just shut up and leave me alone," I say to him, pulling the phone from my back pocket and answering. She's exactly who I want to talk to right now. I need her more than anything, but when I hear her hollow voice as I answer the call I realize it's Gemma that needs me more.

"Sophie."

The dead tone sends a spark of fear into my heart, waking it up from its pain.

"Gemma what's wrong?"

"Murray cheated. It's over. He's at the door. I won't let him in. He keeps yelling."

That's all I hear before the phone on her end crashes into something, and we get disconnected.

"That fucking asshole," Tony says, having overheard.

I can't look at him. Don't want him to commiserate with me on Murray's despicableness.

"Yeah, there are a lot of those around these days."

"I'll drive you to her."

Oh, hell no. His hand is burning a hole through my skin right now. If I sit in an enclosed space with him after enduring his thorough heart-stomping I will implode. I can't think of anything more humiliating.

"I don't want to be in a car with you right now. I don't want to be anywhere near you."

"Tough shit." He crowds me, but I'm not scared of his hulking presence. He'd never physically hurt me. But he doesn't have to. He's already destroyed any faith I ever had in sustaining a relationship. Standing in his apartment filled with moving boxes is utter agony, a constant reminder how he's cared so little for me.

"I care about your sister like family," he says angrily. "I'm not letting her deal with that asshole alone. Get your stuff; I'll meet you in the lobby."

If we take his truck, we'll get to her place faster than the subway, and I don't want to chance hailing a cab or ride share. I hate him right now, but I need to use him, so I can get to Gemma. Gemma is what matters. Not my feelings. Not the pain erupting inside me.

This is a test. The powers that be are testing my strength, and goddamn it, I will come out on top. I will not let this moment, no matter how small and humiliated I feel, destroy me. I won't let this be like how I was after Brian. Ruined, a wisp of nothingness. No substance left, just yearning to be back with him no matter how horrible I knew he was. Addicted.

But I'm not addicted to Tony—I'm in love with him. It's a million times worse.

As I leave I hear him call out, "And don't think this conversation is over."

"It's over," I yell back. "Everything about us is over."

"Hey."

I look up, halfway down the stairs. He's leaning over the railing, a beautifully stubborn and determined expression on his face. I know what he's going to say, so I cut him off. If I hear those words, I'll collapse, and right now my sister needs me to be strong.

"Just shut up. You're a fucking liar, Tony." I scream, running back down to my apartment with my hands over my ears. I'm tugging at the short hair on the side of my head, the pain in my temples keeping me distracted from the pain in my heart. But it's never going to stop hurting, and Tony will always be the man packing a floor above me, preparing to leave me.

I hate Italy. I hate him. For the first time in my life, I hate this damn city.

I change into jeans and sneakers and wait for Tony on the sidewalk. He comes out, sparing only a glance for me as he gestures toward the truck, parked in its usual spot. I don't think I'll ever be able to look at that spot again. I know I'll never be able to look at this building the same way…especially after he's gone.

The emotion I'm trying to tamp down boils over, the stress and agony of the past ten minutes threatening to pull me under. Why did he lie? Why won't he give us a chance? Why does it have to be all or nothing?

A sound comes out of me as we reach the car. A sob, but I cover it with a cough, not wanting him to see how devastated I am.

Pack it in, Sophie. This won't help Gemma.

But of course he notices.

"Sophie"

"If you say one word to me, *one*, I will jump out of the car. I don't care how fast it's moving, or if all that's on my side is the bridge rail. I will jump."

He stares at me for a second. His shoulders a wooden board, and his fists knotted balls of iron. I can almost see the words, itching to spill out, scream at me, telling me all the reasons why he did what he did. Why I should move with him. None of them would matter. I cannot possibly justify why he wouldn't have told me he was leaving in *three fucking days*. Why he won't even try long distance.

He's a coward, I remind myself. A liar.

Another minute goes by and I say, "I need to get to Gemma. If you don't want to take me—"

He opens the passenger door for me but doesn't help me into the truck. The absence of his hands on my waist stings, but I clamber in anyway.

275

Gemma. I'll get through being in this car with him by focusing on Gemma.

"Where?" he asks.

I give him her Upper East Side address, and we go. It's the most agonizing, awkward, miserable car ride of my life. He takes the Brooklyn Bridge to FDR Drive, and of course there's traffic, there's always traffic. I think I remember him saying how he never takes FDR Drive because of the assholes that frequent this road. Why is he taking it now?

I glance at him without actually looking. He's still stiff, his usually plump lips are thin and his eyes...they look like a stranger's eyes, cold and dark, unfeeling. He's bottling himself up too, but it's not working. I can feel his anger, as palpable as the humidity outside. The stink of it hovers in the truck, bounces back and forth between us like a tennis ball on fire. I wish I could catch that fucking ball and throw it out the window. I want to rip him apart. I want to destroy this car.

I want him to hold me and promise me he'll love me forever.

I squeeze my eyes shut, willing the tears pooling in the corners not to fall. Not now. Please hold on for a little longer.

He hurt me. He's a bad person. Keep thinking that. He's like Brian.

I almost wish that were the case; it would be easier to hate him now. Instead he's driving like a modern-day knight in a pickup truck to help me rescue my sister. God, my head is spinning. He called her family. What does that make me?

A cab cuts us off as we're turning onto East Seventy-First Street. He puts his hand out in front of me, protecting me, like a mom would if she needs to stop the car short. Someone who doesn't care about me wouldn't do that. Someone who doesn't care about me wouldn't drive me to help my sister after I've just called him a fucking liar. Someone who didn't care about me would have let me run off and take a cab. Fend for myself.

Tony, my Tony, would do all those things in his kindly, gruff and brutish way. Just like he's doing now, and keeping quiet as I demanded earlier. His compassion only makes what he's done more baffling.

"This is her place," I say when he passes it.

"There's a spot big enough for me over there."

"You can just drop me off; I don't want you coming up."

He hits the dashboard in a violent burst of energy, his anger filling up the truck, finally breaking free of whatever cage he's tried to wrought. "Just let me fucking help you. Murray might be up there, and he might be angry or drunk or whatever. I don't know what situation you'll be walking into, but I'm not letting you go in alone when you could get hurt. You can hate me all you want, but I can't do it."

I don't argue, mostly because I'm grateful, which is so fucking confusing because now I'm grateful in addition to angry, hurt, heartbroken, confused, and in love. I might be all those things, but the love I feel for him is still swarming my body like a fucking beehive, making the other emotions that much more excruciating.

He parks, and after the truck is locked we both run to the building. I use the key Gemma gave me in case of emergencies and let us both in. The lobby is cavernous, made of marble, like a temple to some ancient god. The guard at the desk recognizes me and waves as we reach the elevators. I thought riding in the car was bad, getting into an elevator with him is even worse. And now he's talking.

"When we get up there, give me your key and let me go first."

His expression is hard, unwavering. I disagree with him out of spite.

"No, the second I know where Gemma is I'm going to her."

"Sophie, we should be careful."

Hearing my name on his lips is crushed glass tearing up my heart. The song lyrics to N'SYNC's "Tearing up my Heart" begin to filter through my mind, and I've never hated my crazy, all-over-the-place brain more, especially because I want to share the inappropriate thought with Tony, but I can't now. It's his fault I can't, right? I didn't do this to us.

I didn't take that job knowing he'd ask me to move with him. He never told me he wanted me there. Not in words…but that's the magic between us. We never really need to say it, do we?

"She's my sister." I can't say anything else, but I know he gets it. He wouldn't wait if it were one of his brothers in pain.

We get to Gemma's floor, and we don't have to wait at all to see what's going on, but it does make my panic subside a little when I see Murray banging on the door to get in. He's not in there with her, which means she's all right, at least physically.

"Gemma, open this goddamn door, you cunt."

The word sends a shiver down my spine, and I go to rush at him. Tony beats me to it. He barrels down the short hallway like a fucking linebacker and digs his shoulder right into Murray, tackling him to the ground. Punches are thrown. Murray's no match for Tony's size, though, or his muscles.

I watch for a little, making sure Tony doesn't kill Murray. Eventually he gets Murray on his stomach, with his hands behind his back, and Tony's knee at the base of Murray's spine. He's muttering to him, threatening him.

"Don't kill him, Tony. That's my job."

I let myself into the apartment and freeze when I see drops of blood on the floor near a broken vase at the entryway.

"Gemma? Gemma, honey, it's Sophie."

"Sophie?" I hear, coming from the direction of the balcony.

My heart seizes, fearing I'll find her standing on a ledge. I run past the lavish living room and breathe a sigh of relief when I find her not on the balcony, but sitting on the floor, her head resting against the glass sliding door. The door hasn't even been opened. She looks deflated. She's wearing one of her kick-ass power suits—she must have come home from the office when she found Murray—but her hair is a disheveled mess, hanging in a limp braid over one shoulder. She has one shoe on but no mascara tracks running down her cheeks. No tears.

"Honey, you're bleeding." I squat down and take the hand she's cradling. I can see glass in the jagged mark along her palm.

"I pushed the vase off the table. It broke, then I tripped and landed in the pieces."

Her voice sounds numb, so quiet, like all the life has drained out of her. After the death of first husband, and now this, I don't know if she'll ever be the same.

No, I can't let the vibrancy of my sister's soul wither and die over a man. Two men. She's stronger than this, just like I have to be. We'll be stronger together.

I pull off her one heel and say, "We need to clean this."

"I don't care about the shoe."

"Not the shoe, dummy," I say affectionately.

She lets me pull her up, and we walk to the guest bathroom. I don't want to take her near her bedroom in case that's where she found Murray.

279

"You know the first aid kit is in the master bath." She knows what I'm trying to do. "We can go in there. I found him at the office then stole his keys and came back here. He chased me. I don't know what he would have done if he got in. Probably try to blame me for the whole mess. Fucking coward." She turns her head toward the entrance. "The banging stopped."

"Tony's out there with him."

"Did Tony hurt him?"

"Yes."

Gemma nods, then lets me use tweezers on the cut to get the rest of the glass out. She doesn't twitch, doesn't so much as flinch as I mess around in the wound, it's like she's lost all sense of feeling. I wash and bandage the cut, then help clean her face, taking all her makeup off. She looks a little better when we're done, more like herself, unable to hide her apathy.

"We should check on Tony," Gemma says, pulling me into a hug.

I clutch her close to me, happy to give her any affection she needs, until she says, "Sophie what's wrong? You're squeezing me like a car crusher."

"I'm so sorry this happened, Gemma."

She pulls away, scrutinizing. "Something *is* wrong."

"Yeah, Murray is a douchebag who needs to be castrated."

"Stop. You look like you're walking on glass, and it isn't for me."

I can't talk about it. Don't make me. I'll fall to pieces.

"Gemma, let me be here for you. You don't need to take care of me. We're gonna be fine." I pull her into a hug again, this one for me, and she comes with ease. We stand there, supporting each other, loving each other. And that's all I need.

There's a gentle knock on the door, it's gotta be Tony.

"You go change clothes, and I'll deal with it."

She shakes her head. "I want to thank Tony."

"I've got this. Go."

Gemma takes a few steps before turning back to me. "Something happened between you and Tony, didn't it?"

"It's not important. I'll tell you later." After he's left me. After he's a thousand miles away and on what might as well be another planet.

"Don't lie to me, Sophie. Not now."

Only her plaintive tone could make me say what I do.

"He's moving to Italy in three days. I'm staying here." It comes out like lava. "That's what's happening. It's all over. Now go change. I'll order us Chinese food and ice cream."

Emotion peaks through her detachment and I hate that I've added to her troubles. I should have kept my mouth shut.

"We're talking about this when you come back."

"Whatever," I yell back, bracing myself for what might be on the other side of the door. I creep past the broken shards, try to sweep them to one side with my foot, stalling, then take a deep breath before opening.

It's only Tony, just Tony. Soft black hair streaked with copper, brown eyes speckled with gold and secret caches of hazel. Sensuous mouth. A jaw made for stroking. A body made for holding me. Lips made for my kisses.

I grip the doorframe. Hard. Steel myself. Look toward the hallway.

"No dead body."

281

"It was hard not to kill him, but I told him to leave and not come back for a few days." He hesitates before answering, probably wanted to say something funny, like his mob friends already took care of the body for him and now he owes them his first born. Any other day it would have been a great moment. I would have laughed, probably rolled my eyes then kissed him.

But he doesn't joke. I don't laugh. The conversation is stilted and painful.

"That's good, it will give me time to help Gemma move out." I take a deep breath, knowing I need to say it. "Thanks." Not exactly profound, but it's all I can manage.

"Can't you look at me?" His voice breaks, and that above all else makes me glance. There are tears in his eyes, and it's the final swing of the ax chopping down the damn holding my emotions back.

Hot tears spill onto my cheeks.

"I can't, Tony. I can't look at you or touch you. I can't think about you. Because you're leaving me, and you won't even give a long-distance relationship a chance."

"I can't, Sophie. It feels like acid in my gut every time I think of being apart from you. Please understand."

"I don't. I can't understand how it's gotta be all or nothing with you."

"Because I know we're meant for all. I know we're supposed to be together. I love you."

If he loved me, he wouldn't give me an ultimatum.

"Don't contact me. I can't bear to see you again before you leave."

He wants to speak but I hold my hand up. "I need to be here for

Gemma. Let me do that. I can't focus on what's happening between us."

He pauses for a second, stares me down, begs me with his eyes to reconsider. After enduring a moment of silent he nods, resolute.

"I love you, Sophie. Just know that I'll always love you."

I don't have the energy to be angry anymore. The car ride stole it away. So did his kindness in coming here. His words, his actions, they just keep taking away my will. It's better that we're ending this misbegotten fling.

"Goodbye."

I close the door and make it three steps before collapsing onto a decorative chair by the entrance. Gemma finds me a few minutes later, sitting quietly with shocked tears running down my cheeks. I was running on anger and pain, but now I barely have the strength to sob away the stinging ache. It hurts so much I think the damn ulcer is about to burst. Gemma grasps my hand and leads me toward the couch where we both crumple in on ourselves.

We're a hot mess, but it's okay. We can be a mess together. I'll never be truly alone. I'll always have my sister.

But the heartbroken, insidious voice in my head disagrees. Tony is leaving, like I always knew he would. And I'll be here, with my sister and a job I love.

That's what I wanted.

Isn't it?

18

TONY

LETS SOPHIE DECIDE.

Two days of misery later.

My pen scratches across the paper, dotting the I's and crossing the T's as I finish up the early lease termination form. In twenty-four hours I will no longer reside in this apartment. In forty-eight hours I'll be in Italy, living a new life.

A life I always wanted. Surrounded by the painters I kept company with as a kid, working hard at my new job and exulting in my favorite city in my free time.

But I don't know if I want it anymore.

"Is that all, boss?" The lead guy from the moving company asks me as his men cart the last of the boxes out of my apartment.

"Let me take a look around. One last time."

"You got it, we'll be out in the hall." The big guy stops before turning to me with a little smirk. "You might want to have your bedroom cleaned or something before calling your landlord for the final check. There is something fancy that spilled in there, stinks like crazy."

An image of Sophie hurling my cologne across the room shocks me from my melancholy state. Makes me smile. She always made me smile. "Yeah, thanks."

"No problem." The worker leaves with a nod.

"He's right; what happened in there?" Nicky asks, scratching his beard as he leans against the kitchen counter.

"Sophie."

"You seriously need to give us all the dirt on how you guys got together," Santiago says from the other side of the counter, flipping through the details of my new job and the apartment they've set up for me.

"I don't want to talk about her."

"*Mijo*, you can't give up so easily," Pop says, exiting from the bathroom, toilet paper roll in hand. "You love her. She loves you. What is the complication?"

"Dad…"

"Don't even try to get him to talk to us about this, Diego." Mom comes out of the bedroom, her hair pushed back by a colorful handkerchief. She'll fit right in when she visits me in Italy, a trip they're already planning. "*It's complicated. It will never work. She has this new job. You wouldn't understand.* I never thought you were one to have this many excuses, Tony."

Why did I invite my family over? Because I want to be tortured. Because the second they heard Sophie and I broke up, they came swarming. At least one of the Rodriguez clan has kept me company the past couple days. Helped me pack. Made sure I was eating.

They knew it was bad when I ordered chain-brand pizza.

I love my family. But right now, I want them all to shut up. The

Sophie-sized hole in my chest too large to talk about. All that's left is anger and bitterness and complete fucking misery.

I rest my elbows on the counter, and cradle my face, groaning as her crushed expression flashes before my eyes.

Why does it have to be all or nothing?

Because the thought of a long-distance relationship scares the hell out of me. Because I'm scared she'll hurt me like Natalie. She'll grow tired of me. She'll see through me to the imposter I am. Years spent working to achieve a goal wrought from a fucked-up fantasy originating in spite and revenge.

That's who I am. Sophie deserves better. She deserves to work her dream job. She deserves a man who isn't a hypocrite.

"I accused her of being too scared to move with me. But I'm the one who's scared. I'm the one who can't trust in a long-distance relationship."

"Sweetheart, you're not built for long distance. Even if Natalie had loved you the way you wanted, it wouldn't have worked. You thrive on taking care of your loved ones. How could you feed that part of your soul thousands of miles away?" Ma gets a hard look. "But you not telling her you were leaving this week is a stupid not even I can cure."

Of course I told them everything. They're my family.

"I know. I know. I fucked up."

The hole gapes wider, swallowing me up. Consuming my every fucking breath. How am I going to function over there with this pain and no family to lean on?

"Language."

"Yeah, you did."

"Not helping, Nicky."

"Tony," Santi says, coming around the counter and gripping my shoulder. "Do you love her?"

"Yes." No doubt in my mind. No hesitation. She's a permanent fixture in my heart. She brightens my day. Shows me the man I can truly be. No rules. No lies. She makes me want to be better.

"You going to do nothing and hang around here moping *o qué?*" Pop claps me on my shoulder. "Show her. Tell her. *Do* something."

Santi nudges my shoulder. "Don't let this chance go."

Even Nicky gives his two cents. "You'll be a major asshole if you do."

"Nicky." Ma taps the back of his head in her usual chastisement. She turns to me. "What do you want, Tony?"

The answer is simple.

"Sophie."

"And what are you going to do about it?"

Long distance is out of the question...but it's not the only option. There's something else I can do to keep her. And I will keep her. I'm listening this time. I hear what she wants. I know what I want.

The hole fills in a bit as a plan forms. It's like a business plan. I've accomplished this much. I'm not giving up now. I have forty-eight hours to do everything I can to win Sophie back and I will pull out all the stops.

I spot the other form from the building management mistakenly dropped off. It's a crazy idea, and it might make her flight instincts kick in, but at this point, what the hell do I have to lose?

I dash to the counter and turn the form over, relieved that the other side is blank. I grab a pen and spill my heart out, put every ounce of unbridled truth and love into the words. It takes a minute, maybe less, to write. The sentences come easy, from my heart, always on the tip of my tongue.

"Nicky, can you go to that place you buy bouquets? Order one of each kind and send it to Gemma's apartment? Have them deliver this with it."

"You got it, *parce*," Nicky says, heading out the door with one of the few Colombian slang phrases he knows. Nick can come off self-obsessed and uncaring, but he's always there for me.

"You going to win her back, *mijo*?" Pop asks.

"I'm going to show her what I'm willing to be for her. What really matters. Then it's up to Sophie. I won't make this choice for her. I won't assume. I won't chase. I need to respect her enough to let her decide."

"You sure you don't want to sit outside her window with some grand romantic gesture?" Ma asks.

"Ma, how would you have liked it if Pop did that?"

"He did do that."

"And she married me."

"I love you guys. But this is Sophie and me. We've gotta do things our way."

Sophie's intelligence, her creativity, sparks the flame of passion in others. She's my inspiration. I refuse to be the one to put the flame out. I'll help foster it, I'll shelter it, but I'll never try to take it away.

Never again.

The ball's in your court, Sophie. What's it gonna be?

19

SOPHIE

LOVES TONY BUT IS IN DENIAL.

"Hey, should we go out for sangria once we're done?" I ask, stuffing my sister's stuff into boxes.

I'm pretty impressed with us. We had our breakdowns—or I did—slept together in the guest bedroom, then woke with renewed purpose. Get Gemma the hell out of this fancy schmancy apartment. She and Murray moved in together in January and since he was footing most of the bill for the place, she hadn't really had a say in where they went. In fact, she seems kind of relieved to be leaving, keeps pointing at things and solemnly stating how she hates the item and is so glad to never have to look at them again. I'm still concerned by her pseudo calm state, but I figure this is part of her grieving process now.

"No sangria for me." Gemma sits on the floor next to me and begins assembling a box to stuff with clothes.

"Why? Do you think the alcohol will turn you into a crazy person, and you'll hunt Murray the dick down and cut his balls off? If that is what happens, you know I'm a loyal sister. I will look the other way, and provide the box to put the dick in."

"No." Gemma snorts. It's not really a laugh, and I don't blame her. I might joke around, but inside I feel my pores begin to leak blood as I turn into a grief monster from the sea of sorrow and poor judgment.

"No sangria for you either." She throws some shoes into the box, not really caring about placement.

"Hey, be careful with those pumps; you probably spent half a paycheck on them."

"You want the uncomfortable things? You need them more than I do, and we're the same shoe size."

"What? I'm a hermit...I don't need gorgeous, overpriced designer shoes. And I won't be able to wear them on my new job."

New job. Dream job. I want it. Why aren't I happy about it?

You took the job because you knew I might ask you to move with me.

I didn't know that. When did I know that?

"I quit my job this morning while you were in the shower," Gemma says, dropping a bombshell as easily as talking about traffic. "And you're moving to Italy, and everyone is fancy there, so you should have designer stuff. Also, all this was purchased with Murray's money, so I don't have any qualms in giving it away."

I basically go deaf after she so crisply states I'm moving to Italy. I don't know where she gets this notion. I told her everything that happened between Tony and I while we were curled up in bed eating ice cream and cookies, gleefully getting crumbs in Murray's bed with no intention of cleaning the sheets, and I made it very clear that it wasn't happening.

"What—what are you talking about? I'm not going anywhere. I have an amazing new job. I can't leave when my life is just starting." I'm stuttering and having a little freakout. My stomach is rumbling with tension and sweat is pooling on my neck and chest. "I'm n—not going anywhere. New York is my home. Tony is—he's leaving. It—it—it's over."

"Honey, honey, stop. It's okay, come here." My big sister pulls me into a hug, and I rest my head on her shoulder. "Sweetheart, you're in love. You're so in love with Tony that when you think of staying here and him leaving you start to have a panic attack. I won't let you live a life built on regrets, Sophie. Not like me."

She's petting my hair and rubbing my back. It calms me, but not enough to stop the tears starting to fall. I thought I was okay this morning, at least stable enough to stop crying like a madwoman every time I think of Tony flying away from me and never coming back.

Oh. Oh, it hurts so bad. It's worse than the most hostile pains I get from my ulcer, or when my appendix burst, or all the cramps from past periods wrapped into one. It's beyond the physical now, tormenting me from some sixth dimension. Aliens have taken over my body and decided to squeeze my heart until it turns to ash.

And yet I can't give in. I'm a stubborn New Yorker, after all.

"Give me one good reason why you shouldn't move with him," Gemma demands when I shake my head no.

"My job. I'm supposed to submit my first proposal next Monday."

"I may have done something in addition to quitting my job while you were in the shower."

Gemma pulls over the laptop we've been playing music on and opens her email. She clicks on a message and it's only until I read the "from" line that I realize it's not her email account, but mine.

"What did you do?"

"Just read."

"If you messaged Tony I'll kill you."

"Read the damn email, Sophie."

> Hi Sophie,
>
> Got your email. I have to admit I was a little surprised when you said you're moving. You were so excited to be working on *The New Yorker* native piece. But after reading your article on rape culture in the schoolyard, I know you're meant for bigger things then what we'd planned. The interviews were concise yet poignant. I felt those women's fears and pains, and throughout it all your voice rang true. You have a gift for this, and it's something I think you can do remotely. If you do end up moving, I would be willing to put you on some pieces overseas. I'd have to pay you as a freelancer, but we can come up with steady articles for you to write. I'll have legal and HR write a draft work agreement. Still glad I found you for our team.
>
> -Gina Lee

"How did you do this? What would have happened if they said no?"

"The way I see it, they sought you out. They want you, no matter what you're writing. You need to have more confidence in yourself, Sophie. Forget about the imposter syndrome and embrace the fact that you're a damn good writer. Demand some shit. Be happy."

"I can't leave you."

"I won't be alone. I've decided to move to California and hang with Mom for a bit."

I sit back on my heels, a little surprised at that. "You hate San Francisco. It's the most expensive city in the country."

"I don't hate it; I'm not accustomed to the west coast pace. Maybe that's what I need. All this." She waves around at the very fancy, contemporary life she and Murray inhabited. "It's not me. I know it's not." Gemma points in my direction. "And I will not be your excuse to run away from love. Give me another reason."

"He didn't tell me he was leaving this week. I thought we had till the end of the summer. Something must have changed, and he didn't think it was important to tell me."

At that she nods. "That was shitty. But, I gotta be honest, Sophie, I think it came from a place of fear rather than not wanting you to go with him." She taps her bottom lip, thinking. "You told me he said he loves you."

"That doesn't matter. The things he accused me of...you should have heard him."

"What did he say?"

"He said I took the job because I knew he was going to ask me to move with him. How would I have known that? Am I a mind reader?"

"No, but you read people. You're good at it, too, good enough to use it to your advantage." She grabs hold of my wrists, pulling them down and forcing me to look at her. "Tell me the truth. Me. Did you know he was going to ask you?"

"No."

I'm all in.

Be with me.

Stay with me.

"Maybe. Maybe there was something in the back of my mind telling me he wanted me to go with him. Maybe I thought of him potentially asking me, and I froze inside, not knowing what answer I'd give."

I did not do what his ex did. I did not use the excuse of a more permanent relationship to run away. I am not that person.

Or am I?

God, I might be that person. I might have let my fear fuck this up.

"But he only confessed he was going to ask me to move with him after he fucked up. Any guy would say that if they were trying to prove a point."

"No, honey. All men aren't like that; all men aren't Murray or our dad. Don't generalize, you're better than that." Gemma's expression is a little pitying, her mouth bunched into a teeny spot on her face, like she's desperately holding back everything she wants to say, but trying to be delicate about it.

"Just say it. You're so annoying when you're trying to be nice."

"You keep a barrier around your heart. You always have. But you can't do that with a relationship, Sophie. You need to be brave enough to talk. Even a simple conversation requires bravery, especially the bravery to admit your mistakes. It's the little things that make a relationship, the things that might not mean anything at the time. Those minute details are your foundations—the secrets and jokes and hopes that you build a life on. You talk and share pieces of you, and he shares pieces of him, and it forms this rope, this connection that grows stronger with every teeny, seemingly insignificant detail. But you'll never take hold of that rope if you keep yourself distant."

I did exactly what his ex did. I might not see Tony as unworthy or as less than the man I imagined for myself—in fact he's more than I ever thought I deserved— but I still turned from him when I saw him coming to me. I left him hanging. I hurt him. No wonder he can't trust me to have a long-distance relationship. No wonder the idea of leaving me here alone to my second thoughts and seeds of doubt reminds him of a woman who spit in his face.

My eyes have turned into a leaky faucet. Not for me and how I contributed to fucking up my relationship—it wasn't all Tony— no, these tears are for Gemma, too. She isn't talking about her bond with Murray, which always seemed superficial. She's talking about her first husband—a man Mom and I never mention by name, because every time we do Gemma crumples, her soul chipping away piece by piece. I thought being with Murray would mitigate that pain, but I can see she's as much in love with and hurt by her first husband as when he passed away.

"Go to Italy, Sophie. Be with Tony. Be with a man who loves you, and who will do anything for you."

"He wouldn't do a long-distance relationship."

"Would you want to do that? Really? Would that make you happy?"

No, it would be miserable. Just like Tony said.

"If anything, I need you to be with the man who punched out your sister's cheating wretch of a fiancé."

I snort through my steady tears. "It was more of a tackle than a punch."

"Semantics. Either way, he—"

The doorbell rings.

"I'll get it," I say. If it's Murray, I'll tell the guy to fuck off. If it's Tony…I might stand there and stutter and babble like a crazy person until I either close the door in his face or jump into his arms. That's what I'm feeling inside—less heartbroken and more uncertain about my future than I've ever been.

But I am certain about my feelings for Tony. It's time to make a choice.

I wipe my tears and snot away on my sleeve before opening the door, not sparing a thought for how I look. Luckily, it's neither Tony nor Murray, but a deliveryman with two bouquets. One is edible, with different kinds of fruit and exotic-looking chocolate, and the other is paper, rolled up to look like flowers. They're both addressed to Gemma, not me.

"Who are these from?"

The guy shrugs. "Don't know. But there's a card with the paper flower one."

As he leaves, I realize it's not a card, but a handwritten letter. This doesn't seem like Murray's style. The paper flowers are stunning, little origami tulips and roses in about fifty colors.

"Gemma, someone sent you fruit and chocolate."

She meets me in the entryway, confused. I give her the letter to read as I rip open the plastic on the edible bouquet and start munching on a coconut-and-chocolate-covered pineapple.

The best part of a breakup is all the shameless eating.

"Who's it from?" I ask, watching her face as she reads it, a smile twisting her lips. She looks sad and happy all at once. "I swear, if that's from Murray and you're smiling like that, I'm gonna kick you off the balcony."

"Here." She holds it out. "It's not really for me."

I grab the letter and stuff another fruit in my mouth. Gemma sits next to me on the floor and puts her arm around me, reaching for the chocolate.

Dear Gemma,

You are awesome. That jerk is a Class-A douchebag. I can't imagine how any man could do something so idiotic to a woman so kick-ass and kind. And I know you're kind, because you deftly handled my dumb brothers teasing you all night long at the batting cages without smacking them once. That is saint-like behavior.

Tony, it's from Tony. I try to hand the letter back to Gemma, but she forces me to keep reading. Soon I'm devouring his words, wishing he were saying them to me here instead of so far away.

My only explanation is men are idiots. They do things for stupid reasons. Reasons that don't make sense, in hindsight. Society dictates men to be strong, when really, they're as scared as everyone else. Scared they fucked up the best thing that ever happened to them. Scared that the woman they love might never trust them again. And if you're thinking I'm writing this letter for my own purposes, to prove to you that I AM MADLY IN LOVE WITH YOUR SISTER AND WOULD DO ANYTHING TO KEEP HER, then you would be correct. And that right there proves how selfish and dickish men are.

But I really do think you're cool, and I know you're more than strong enough to move past this, because you're Sophie's big sister. You're her hero, and by extension you're mine. I would really like to call you my sister one day, maybe one day soon, if that gorgeously freckled and stubborn woman with you will let me into her life and accept my apology for being an idiot. But can she really blame me? I'm a man, after all. A man sweetly, and disastrously, in love.

Sincerely,

The man with a million names who loves your sister

Antonio Miguel Luis Rodriguez

At the bottom of the page there's a small note.

Turn the letter over, Sophie.

I flip the letter like a crazy person, hoping to see something else there, some other words I can consume and brand into my mind.

"What's that?" Gemma asks, seeing he's written the letter on the back of some form.

"It's got my building management name on it, I think—holy shit." I see the title of the document—it's an application for an apartment in our building. It's for the top floor, in the super nice apartment they recently finished renovating. It's got a balcony and a massive kitchen and is crazy expensive. But the crazier thing is, it's not only Tony's name on this application, it's mine too.

"But—but he's moving to Italy. He took that job."

Gemma is beaming at me and tears are forming in my eyes again. I seriously have trouble believing I have any left to cry. I'm like a busted pipe with all the shit I've been leaking since last night.

"Sophie, he's trying to tell you something."

"I know. I know what it is, I'm just freaking out."

It's a backup plan. A Sophie backup plan. One that gives credence to the words on the opposite side of this simple piece of paper.

I am madly in love with your sister and would do anything to keep her.

Even give up a job in Italy if I decide I don't want to move. So, we wouldn't have to do long distance. Keeping me is more important than getting the job he's worked toward for years.

"Oh God, I love him."

"Yup," Gemma nods, laughing at my ridiculous outburst.

"I'm gonna spend the rest of my life with him."

"You fucking better."

"No." I stand up, clutching the form to my chest. "I need to think. Can I borrow some clothes? I'm gonna go think."

"What? Sophie, you should go to him."

"No. No, I need to think. I need to do something."

"If you talk yourself out of this, I'm gonna kick your ass."

"No. No, I—I'm gonna take a walk. No. Where's my phone? I need to make a call."

My heart is racing. Running back into the bedroom, I spot my phone on the nightstand then tear it out of the charger. I search through my contacts, find who I'm looking for, and dial.

"Hello?"

"Hi. It's Sophie. I'm sorry for everything. I've changed my mind. I know what to do now."

Gemma leans against the doorframe, her arms crossed and her eyes narrowed.

I speak to Gemma and the voice on my phone. "I've got a plan. It's crazy. But I've got a plan."

"How can I help?" Gemma asks.

"We need to go to every dollar store in the city and buy all their candles."

"Please don't tell me you want to set fire to something."

"What? No. Do you think I'm a pyromaniac?" She's laughing at me, but I can also tell she's wary. "Can I borrow some clothes?"

"Of course."

"Can you keep him away for a few hours?" I direct my question to the phone.

"You bet," my willing accomplice replies.

I lay out my plan. They're laughing and giddy by the end of it, but I don't care. It's ridiculous, and so am I. Tony and I thrive on being silly and outlandish. We're only able to be that way with one another.

It's time to wave my freak flag high and proud.

It's time to get my man.

20

TONY

GETS A ROSE.

The time to say goodbye to New York is over. The new chapter is starting, and even though I wait on a precipice to hear from Sophie, my heart balancing on a knife's edge, I keep my hopes tempered. Keep praying in my mind for her to see how much I love and accept her.

"My boy, I'm so proud of you," Ma says for the fiftieth time. She demanded my attention this afternoon, taking me for *affogato*, indulging on the High Line.

We're sitting on two wooden lounge chairs overlooking the Hudson, New Yorkers and tourists alike enjoying the old railway turned park. It's a peaceful place, one Ma likes to take me whenever she's got something to say. But today, she's not talking. I'm suspicious.

"Ma, what is it?" I take her hand. "You only bring me here to lecture me."

"I have nothing to lecture you on. You're a grown man."

What a load of bull.

"That's never stopped you before."

"You're leaving in a day," she says in a huff, her brown eyes giving the patented Mom look. "You think I don't want to spend time with my son? You always worried me, Tony. The middle child, striving so hard to be perfect and achieve goals that were never really yours. But I see this new life suits you, and—well—I'm not worried about you anymore. This'll be a grand adventure for you. Your greatest one yet."

"Living in Italy will be quite a thing." I pull her close. "You and Pop are welcome. Any time. You know that, right? This is as much for you as it is for me."

She smiles, but I don't think it's in agreement.

"What? Just say it."

She frames my face and kisses my cheek. "Promise me one thing, Tony. No matter what happens, you'll be selfish in Italy. Gorge on food, take in the art. Be happy and do something for yourself."

"I promise," I say, confounded and amused. Where is this coming from?

"Come on," she says after we finish our snacks, checking an incoming text on her phone. "Your father has made you something special."

"Please tell me its *arequipe con oblea*. Please. Please."

"Something even sweeter."

We drive home to Brooklyn, to my parent's place. It's dark by the time we get to the block and park the truck in the nearby lot. I walk with Ma's arm hooked around my elbow. After I'm gone, I don't know when I'll see this place again. I try to memorize every detail as we approach our building.

I count the cracks in the pavement. I scratch the ears of the bodega cat, asleep on a white plastic chair still warm from the day's sun. It growls at me like always.

The block has transformed a million times since I was a kid, but it will never lose its heart. Brooklyn will always be Brooklyn at heart—ain't nothin' gonna change it.

A text comes in on Ma's phone again.

"Go on up to the roof," she says.

I look at her suspiciously. "What's going on?"

"Nothing. Just go. Don't you want your treat?"

"You can't dangle dessert in front of my face like a bribe, Ma."

She smiles gleefully. "It's working though, isn't it?"

"Only for *arequipe con oblea.*"

She kisses me on my cheek, misty-eyed, then sends me on my way. My whole family has been so touchy lately. I knew it would be rough, the days leading up to my departure, but the added heartbreak has them treating me with kid gloves.

Thinking of my heart makes it crack a little. I check my phone as I trudge up the stairs. No messages. No missed calls. I even go on social media in the hopes she's written some cryptic post hinting that she's at least thinking about me.

Silence.

I reach for the door handle, gripping the warm metal. Not even *arequipe* can soothe this pain.

"Choose me, Sophie." I whisper to myself, shutting my eyes and resting my head against the worn, red door to the roof.

I'll send her a text. Maybe she didn't get the letter or the bouquet? That's why she hasn't messaged. Sophie never keeps her opinion to herself, at least not with me.

Just another reason I love her so much.

No. I put my phone away. I promised I'd let her make this decision for herself. No grand gesture, no standing outside her window with a boom box over my head. No pressure.

I pull the door open and step into the most massive, grandest gesture I've ever seen.

The canopies have been removed, my brothers' little tables with their personal items stored in the shed we use when it rains or snows, all replaced by a sea of candles. And fucking rose petals. There are Christmas lights lining the edge of the roof, lighting the space up like the middle of Times Square. It's magical and brilliant, and not just in luminosity.

In front of me lies the thickest path of roses and little origami flowers I've ever seen. I don't move, just let my gaze follow the trail before my feet, and there she is at the end of my path, as she's always been meant to be.

My Sophie. Radiant like a shamrock bathed in fire in a short green dress that shows off her freckle-covered skin. Candlelight reflects and wavers in the pools of her eyes, so bright and shining, ethereal in the glow.

She's holding a single red rose. And I know she wants to give it to me. Like the final contestant on *The Bachelorette*.

I laugh. What else can I do? I laugh, and she laughs with me, knowing this spectacle was created to bring me mirth and joy.

Her smile fades, but she holds her hand out to me. I go to her, tripping over paper flowers as I walk. She snorts at me.

I love her snorts.

"As part-owner of this building, I have to tell you, this is a fire hazard."

"Only if you keep kicking the paper flowers into the candles."

I reach her, and instead of taking her outstretched hand I grasp her hips and pull her close for a kiss. I push my tongue past her lips, needing to be connected beyond the surface.

"Tell me you're mine," I say against her mouth, one hand gripping her waist, the other combing through her hair.

"I'm yours. I love you."

The words are warmer than the million candles covering the roof. They wrap me up, rest against my skin, like freckles I'll live with forever.

My body starts to shake, and I kiss her again, the rose in her hand falling to the floor as she clutches my T-shirt.

"I'm so sorry, baby," I say as we pull away. "I should have told you the second I knew. I never should have expected you to forget your life and move with me. I promise we'll be happy here. You can decorate the apartment however you want—except the kitchen, that space is mine—and we will eat right, and we'll make sure Gary isn't getting any bigger."

"It's still weird you're okay with me naming my ulcer."

"I love you so much you could name every part of your body, and I would not care. Your large intestine can be George, and your liver can be Jose, as long as your heart is mine. I want to be with you, and if the past few days have shown me anything, it's that not having your vibrant, gorgeous, brilliant spirit in my life is living through the worst nightmare."

"Sheesh," she says as a tear tracks down her cheek. I kiss it away. "I was supposed to be making the speeches and declarations."

"You don't need to say a thing, just knowing I get to keep you is enough."

Somehow, we've ended up on the ground, covered in petals. Wax drips onto my sandals.

None of it matters.

Sophie wants me. She's mine.

My girl comes to her knees and cradles my head. Her thumb brushes my cheek, and I feel wetness spread across my skin. Of course I'm crying, my European and South American sentimental state combining to turn me into a waterfall of emotion.

"I called your boss. Told him you needed another couple weeks before moving, so I could move out there with you. He said okay."

"Wait. What?" I ask. Michelangelo's got nothing on me today.

"You deserve to live in Italy, not because you worked hard for that position, but because you'll be closer to your heart's desire. Surrounded by centuries of art and architecture I know your soul craves. I can't take that away from you."

"But your job—"

"Gemma pulled a trick out of her hat, and they said they're willing to work with me on a freelance basis. Remotely."

"Shuddup." I swear I've lost my brain. Words escape me.

"I'm serious."

"You're moving to Italy with me?" I wrap my arms around her, the position putting her slightly above me, my hands on her ass.

"I'm moving to Italy with you."

"Together?"

"That's what *with you* means."

I laugh full out now, and it's so good. I tumble her down to the ground, cover her with kisses. I hold her so tight she has to tap me, letting me know she needs to breathe.

Our lips meet, and the kiss is so frantic and needy our teeth clash. We laugh at each other and the next kiss is better, smoother. We find our rhythm, the one I've only ever experienced with Sophie, where our lips and tongues and hands, every part of our bodies, feed off the other.

When we pull away she asks, "Would you have really stayed for me?"

"Damn straight." I stroke her cheeks, her lips, the fuzzy flyaway of her curly hair. I drink her in. "I would do a lot more to earn back your trust. Your love. To be with you."

Her expression softens, her forehead rests against mine.

"There's nothing you need to do to earn my love or trust, Tony. I love you so much it hurts every goddamned second, but I love the pain. When I think of you out of this country, without me, all I can see is a future filled with clouds and gross brown snow."

"Brown snow?"

"Yeah, like everything is perfect and smooth after the snow falls, and then it turns muddy and gross once the cabs start driving over it and spraying it everywhere. That's what my life would be like without you."

"Gross brown snow. No worse fate. Tell me again."

I don't need to explain what I mean.

"I love you."

She kisses the outside corner of my eye.

"Again."

My nose.

"I love you."

"Once more for good luck."

"I love you. I love you. I fucking love you."

I kiss her beautiful, dirty mouth with every phrase. Basking in the words as she says it over and over again, burning it into my mind and my heart. When she's done, we lay down together on the petals, holding each other as the candles burn down.

A very loud, very obvious shutter click echoes behind us.

"Really?" I call looking back to see my family and Gemma standing in the doorway, watching us.

"You didn't think we weren't going to record this," my Ma says, an actual video camera in her hand.

"What if we'd started having sex?"

"Then I would have taken over," Nicky claims.

Gemma smacks him upside the head, making Ma and Santiago laugh.

"Welcome to the family, Sophie," Pop calls, holding out a tray of something. "Would you like an *arequipe con oblea*?"

"Go away," I grumble, burying my face in Sophie's neck.

She snorts then shoos the nosy parkers out. The roof door closes behind them.

"When are we leaving?" I ask.

"Two weeks."

I look at her, so thankful to have this gracious and beautiful woman in my life.

"Thank you for letting me be me."

She puts a hand over her stomach and contritely says "Gary and I are also very grateful to have you in our lives."

I laugh, the bark echoing across the roof. "C'mere, you weirdo."

We laugh and kiss under a blanket of candlelight, our hands clasped, and the hole in my heart full again.

EPILOGUE

Tony is clutching my hand, and his leg is shaking up and down. It's a good thing Tony's office sprung for first-class tickets or the passenger next to us would be having a fit, he's shaking so hard. My man is a nervous wreck.

Aside from Tony flying out to Italy for a few days to prep the office and get our new apartment set up, we've barely spent the last couple weeks apart. I know him inside and out, and yet I still keep learning and discovering new facets of what makes Tony, Tony.

"Baby, you're gonna crash the plane if you keep shaking like that." I put my hand on his thigh to calm him. He's as tense as a steel rod, and not in the good way.

"Don't say that." He flicks my arm, but as the plane lands at Leonardo da Vinci airport he clings to me like a puppy afraid of a thunderstorm. "Oh, fuck, this sucks."

"It's almost over." I never would have figured him for someone who hates flying. I'd usually tease him about his fear, given how often he has to fly, if it weren't for the sweaty terror dripping off his skin. Instead I hold his hand and kiss him when he looks like he's about to lose it.

We debark, go through customs, grab our bags—most of our stuff already shipped and waiting for us to unpack at the apartment. Tony said he could have hired a service to set the apartment up, but I wanted to do that together.

"I want to set up our home," I'd said.

"You're right," he agreed with a smiling kiss. "We need to make it ours."

His desire to start our life together in such a perfectly simple yet profound way had me pushing him up against my apartment wall. There were boxes all around, just like when we'd first met, except this time I was packing to leave, with my Tony.

The driver, Guiseppe, greets us, who Tony has used the past few times he's visited Rome. His English is great, and he has all the insider knowledge of the city, having lived in Rome his whole life. Our apartment is in Monti, where a decent amount of expatriates reside. It's pricey, but Tony was provided a great moving package and raise along with his promotion.

The windows of the cab are down, and my hair is fluttering around my head like a thatch of butterflies. I can't help but stare at all the sights, wide-eyed, pointing at things I've only ever seen in textbooks or travel shows. There's so much to explore and discover, the ideas for articles filling my mind like books in a library.

We stumble into the apartment, exhausted from the nine-hour flight and the emotional ups and downs of moving away from home. It's like going to college all over again. Mom even flew out to New York a few days before we left, wanting to say goodbye. Gemma and I spent a full day with her in our pajamas eating take-out. Dad didn't show, even though Gemma confessed to inviting him. It doesn't hurt when she tells me. I have so much love in my life, I find the strength to forgive and move on, accepting that he isn't capable of being there.

Tony spent a day with his family too. They went to a Mets game, then cooked him his favorite dishes for dinner. Afterward Nick and Santi took Tony to their local bar, where they drank till three in the morning. I had to send them rude texts for the hangover Tony suffered in the morning.

The whole Flanagan and Rodriguez clan drove us to the airport to see us off, they even parked in the exorbitantly overpriced temporary lot to walk us to security and help get our bags checked. It was hard, leaving them. Despite Tony's fear of flying, he held me as I cried, missing my family. Saying goodbye to Gemma felt like ripping my heart out.

"I'll be okay, Sophie. I'll be with Mom in California."

The move will be good for Gemma. She'll come visit me, and I'll visit her, and we'll have video chat to keep in touch. She's only a call away. But no matter how much I rationalize, I'll always miss her.

Tony and I held hands walking through the airport, both of us wrung out emotionally. We took comfort from each other.

"Our families aren't gone," Tony said, cradling me against his shoulder as I cried in the airport. "Distance doesn't matter, that bond is strong. And we'll have each other. I'll always be with you, Sophie. You'll never be alone."

I sigh into a kiss, comforted by that truth.

When we enter our new apartment building, a cloud of fur erupts from the door at the end of the hall and comes flying at us. I step in front of Tony instinctually. The owner comes to collect the little yippy puppy, apologizing in Italian for the disruption.

"Thanks for saving me from the vicious ball of fluff."

Tony's thanks is filled with sarcasm, but he takes my hands and kisses the back anyway.

When we reach our apartment, I walk straight into the bedroom—our bedroom—and collapse on the bed.

"There are sheets on the bed."

"Yeah." Tony lay down beside me on his stomach. "Don't be mad, but I knew you'd be really out of it after the flight, so I had the movers at least set the bedroom up a little. There should be towels in the bathroom too."

I scooch over and nuzzle into his shoulder before looking up at him.

"I have to tell you something."

"You love me?"

I grin, excited to finally get this off my chest. "Yes, but something else."

"You can't wait to spend the rest of your life with me?"

"Yes, but not that."

"If it weren't for our families wanting a big wedding, you'd elope with me tomorrow?"

I don't know how to broach this subject without it sounding like it's coming from left field, so I spit it out.

"I knew you were home, so I turned my music on really loud."

"What?"

I roll my sexy man onto his back and rest against his chest, giving him a piece of me, just like Gemma said. "You wanted to know why I was blasting my music after Gemma's engagement party. When you came back from Italy after that first trip, after the week apart, and it was super late? I came home late too, and I bumped into a neighbor. He mentioned it was a night for late arrivals, and when I asked him what he was talking about, he said you'd come home from a trip a few hours earlier. I marched straight to my place and blasted my music…knowing it would probably wake you."

He doesn't speak for a second, then shock melts into mischievous joy. He wraps his arms around me and tumbles me beneath him, settling his hips into the cradle of my legs. His erection rubs against my center.

How can he be hard after all those hours of travel?

"You little minx. You lured me down to you."

"That wasn't my intention." He licks where I bite my lip, stirring my pot to boiling. "Okay, maybe it was a little."

His cock presses harder into me, making me moan. He is definitely not tired anymore.

"I think—" I groan when he reaches into my stretchy airplane pants to stroke my pussy. All thoughts of naps vanish from my mind.

"What is it, baby?" He kisses my skin, licking the meeting of neck and shoulder. My brain has turned to Jell-O, words ripped away like torn pages from a book.

I grip his hips and push my pussy up into him, squishing his hand between us. He thrusts his fingers inside me, coating himself in my wetness.

"I think we should christen the apartment."

"Where?" He sits back on his heels, undoes his zipper and lets his beautifully hard, straining cock go free. His movements are graceful and powerful. I'm a frantic mess as I shove my underwear down, kicking them away. I yank him back by his shirt and grab his shaft, lining him up with my sex. He holds himself up as I slide onto him, letting me do the work, watching where we're joined.

I'm greedy for him, needy to the point I'm panting to get him inside me. I'm impatient as we wait for his cock to break through, to stretch me to the point it burns so good.

Once he's all the way in—no barriers between us, as we made sure to get all those details squared away before traveling—we both take a second to feel it, the fucking crazy sensation of being joined like this.

I pull him down until he's lying on top of me with all his weight. I love having him pressed against me, crushing me with his considerable strength, feeling taken over.

"Everywhere."

I kiss him, long and lingering. We tumble along the bed, his cock remaining inside as I try to get on top, and he pushes me back underneath him.

Suddenly we roll too far, and he's about to career off the bed. I grab him, pull him on top of me until he's back where he belongs.

"Don't worry, baby," I say against his lips. "I got you."

———

Thank you for reading book 1 of the Stupid Awesome Love Series. If you enjoyed it, please take the time to leave a review on Goodreads or one of your favorite online retailers. Thank you!

Keep reading for an excerpt from book 2, *Waking Wild.*

waking wild

BOOK 2 IN THE STUPID AWESOME LOVE SERIES

Chapter One
Gemma
is fine.

The first time I see him, my eyes recoil as if the sight is too over-whelming for my addlepated mind to comprehend. He's unloading massive bags of soil from the back of a well-used pickup truck. A dirty, dark blue tank hugs his chest. Khaki shorts —also covered in grime and soil—frame his bulging thighs, straining against the fabric like an Olympic swimmer's against those stretchy things they wear now. Oh, if he were soaking wet that would make this so much better. But the only moisture on his body comes from the sweat beading on his beautiful, dark skin.

It's a strange sensation, admiring this beautiful man while not feeling it anywhere in my body. There was a time I'd have been eager to run over and introduce myself, indulge in some harm-less flirting to get up close and personal with those muscles.

Now I can't even force my body to blush at how absolutely stun-ning he is. I just stare at him. A marbled work of art. A sculp-ture I don't understand the significance of. What was the artist's purpose in creating him? To taunt me? To wave in my face, screaming, *Hey, Gemma! Hey, look at this gorgeous man. Isn't he beauti-ful? Don't worry, he's probably exactly like the rest of them. Liars. Cheats. Buttmunches.*

"Gemma, this way," Mom calls to me from the small office. "Stop staring at nothing."

"I'm not staring."

I was totally staring.

Mom points her best Mom finger at me as I reach her.

"All you do is stare at shit these days. At the wall. At the ceiling. At the ground when you walk. I'm sick of it. You've been here a month; it's time to put your life back to together."

"Need I remind you I found my fiancé face deep in his boss's vagina last month?"

"No, sweetheart, you don't need to remind me. But you do need to get over it. I will not let this affect you like—"

I give her a hard look, daring her to even mention my first husband's name. It's a taboo subject in my family, and I want it to stay that way.

"Anyway," Mom goes on. "You need to get out of the house. This will be good for you."

We're at the San Francisco Botanical Gardens, and my dear mother Lillian Flanagan is forcing me back into society before I'm ready. All I want in life is to stay in bed, in my Star Wars pajamas, and never get out again. Is that too much to ask?

"I don't know anything about plants."

"You don't need to; you'll be the kids' counselor, herding them to their activities around the garden."

"I don't know anything about kids, either."

"You practically raised your sister."

"Yeah, and the experience scarred me. Sophie was a nightmare."

"You love your sister."

A woman with pin-straight black hair, amber skin, and a long, straight nose greets us at the entrance of the office. Her khaki shorts and green staff T-shirt suit her. She blends well with her surroundings, looks like she belongs. I, in my black jeans and boots, stick out like a sore thumb.

"Opal!" Lillian hugs the woman, embraces her warmly.

I paste a smile on my face as Mom introduces me.

"Opal, this is my eldest daughter, Gemma. She just moved to California."

Opal extends her hand and I take it, brightening my smile until my teeth hurt. Step one: don't squeeze too hard. Step two: act like a normal human.

"Nice to meet you. Lillian says you're willing to step in as our day camp volunteer?"

"Well"

"Of course she is," Mom interjects. "I can't do it this year because the origami class I'm taking forced me to change my volunteer hours, and our regular summer counselor moved to Pennsylvania to influence the swing vote. Gemma would be happy to volunteer."

"Mom"

"And by volunteer, I mean get paid minimum wage. She doesn't have a job yet. Been sitting on my couch watching Lifetime movies and yelling at the heroines for a month."

"Mom, if you don't shut up I'm gonna throw you off the Golden Gate Bridge," I say, sweet as pie, still smiling.

"She was always dramatic."

"I'm not like that anymore."

"More's the pity."

Opal winks at me, seeing the embarrassment my mother excels at causing, and waves us into the office.

"Well, come on in and let's get your paperwork in order. I've got some pizza if you're hungry."

"Don't get Gemma started on the pizza here."

"Not a fan?" Opal asks, handing over a tax form to fill out.

"The pizza here is not pizza," I point out. "If anything, it's a hybrid of bread and cheese and some mush Californians think is tomato sauce."

Lillian's laugh bounces off the walls of the office like the tinkle of fairy wings. It's been so long since I've visited her that I've almost forgotten it does that—suffuses you with a sense of wonder. Hearing it reminds me of when she was still in New York— how she used to laugh so freely with my sister, Sophie, and me, and how the laughter snuffed out once she discovered Dad with his paramours, again and again.

But it's all okay. Lillian Flanagan got her laughter back. She only needed to move across the country to get it.

Maybe this is where I'll find mine.

Unlikely, with a point five percent chance of go screw yourself.

Mom's frizzy gray hair bobs as she chuckles. Her untamed locks are what mine will be when I'm her age, the red in my frustratingly outlandish curls coming from her side of the family. She's wearing a thin cardigan with a pashmina, leggings, and a flowing floral dress, appropriate for the cool Bay Area weather. There's a rolled up scarf around her hair that doesn't match the rest of her outfit, but she doesn't care. She's her own lady, and she does what she wants. I've always loved that about Mom. Like Opal, she fits right in with the other San Franciscans.

Me?

I'm so New York that I might as well have a massive neon sign pointing at me, blinking 'Sarcastic Bitch' at everyone.

"Sweetheart, the pizza is California pizza. You can't keep comparing everything to New York. If you miss it so much, go back."

"You know that's not an option."

I glance out the open window, a sweetly scented breeze filtering through the screen.

"It's nice out, right?" Opal asks, unlatching the screen and removing that barrier as well.

I take the pen she hands me and angle my head down to the paper, but my gaze won't turn away from the view out the window.

The man from earlier is closer now. He looks my way, and I should pretend I was simply glancing in his direction, but I can't spare the energy to turn. Mr. Marble Statue spots me and smiles. His eyes shine like glass pots of dark amber honey sitting in the sunlight. I've never seen that color before, and it's almost…refreshing, finding something new. I moved to California for a change of scene, but I didn't think I would get it from the male corner of the world.

He may be shockingly beautiful, but I doubt he's any different from the men back home. Even so, it takes all the willpower I have left to look away and focus on the paperwork.

The pen freezes just before writing my last name. It would have been Shaw by the end of next year. I should get used to Flanagan. It's a good name. I like it. It's my mom's name. Sophie and

I changed our surnames to Mom's maiden name when she and Dad divorced, a pledge of solidarity to the woman who raised us, even though it was Dad we lived with after Mom moved to California. The name change only erected another barrier between my father and his children.

I've tried, repeatedly, to break that barrier down. But there's only so much you can do to convince a man who doesn't care about anything but himself to love you.

My wandering mind is drawn back to the window. The man is gone, leaving the lovely vista of the gardens in his place. Somehow, it seems a little less vibrant without him.

I hand Opal my driver's license to photocopy. Mom pats my hand when we're alone, smiling at me kindly, her pushy nature replaced with tender understanding. I squeeze it quickly before letting go, simultaneously needing and hating her pity.

I appreciate her care, but it's too much right now. I can barely process getting dressed in the morning, let alone full hugs and emotional support. Her softness feels like a million bee stings.

"Thank you for doing this," Mom says quietly. "We were in a real bind trying to find someone at the last minute."

"You know I'd do anything for you."

"I want you to do this for you, sweetheart."

"I was fine where I was."

"On my couch?"

"Yes, on the fucking couch."

Opal walks back in at that, her eyebrows raised, no doubt judging my language.

"Sorry," I say quietly.

"I don't care how much you curse as long as it's not in front of the kids."

"I won't."

Opals eyes me fastidiously, her hands folded carefully on the table, before nodding shortly. A decision made. Good for her.

I hope she judges me incompetent and banishes me back to life in bed. I was good there.

"We'll get all this processed. In the meantime, why don't I have someone take you on a tour of the garden?"

"I'll do it!"

"Actually, Lillian, can we chat about your schedule for the next month? I have a few questions."

Opal and Lillian exchange glances, sweetly trying to be subtle. Mom doesn't do subtle. She just hits you over the head with a brick. She may have been born in California, but she spent the majority of her years on the East Coast making her nothing but brash and adorably abrasive.

"Sure. Of course. How about Jack? He knows the place better than anyone."

"Great idea." Opal grabs a map of the garden and draws a line on the paths. "We're here. Follow this and you'll come to a small bench right off the trail. Take a walk, take in the sights. The garden is a fantastically peaceful place."

"Oh, I love that bench." Mom nods so enthusiastically I worry her head will fall off. "It's a great bench for thinking."

"Jack will meet you there and then take you on a tour."

The last thing I want is social interaction, especially with a man, but Mom looks so hopeful, so endearing, that I've got to get off my ass and do this for her. If I need to convince anyone in the world that I'm managing, it's her.

"Great," I say, taking the map. "I love a good thinking bench."

"Gemma" Mom's tone is cautioning. "Try to be open minded."

I grin brightly at both of them, giving them my pearly whites.

"I'm nothing but open minded."

As I leave the office Mom calls out, "That's a crock of shit, Gemma Flanagan."

Flanagan. What did I think would happen when I changed my name? I didn't do it the first time around, why was I so determined to do it this time? It would have been the final nail in my makeover coffin. I would have become the person Murray fashioned me into. I fit that mold at work, but at home it never suited, no matter how hard I denied our incompatibility.

At least I was comfortable back home. Here? I'm the fish out of water. The ugly duckling. I've never stuck out more.

I pass an old couple strolling hand-in-hand on the path. They nod at me, bid me good morning. I smile back.

Is it me, or does the woman look scared when I show my teeth? Nice. If all else fails, I can take up a career in scaring old ladies into dropping their purses.

I find the small trail leading to the bench. Opal was right, it's perfectly peaceful here. I can barely hear the foot traffic from the main path. Even the sounds of cars are muffled by thick crops of trees and plant life. I'm completely alone, immersed in nature and tranquility.

I fucking hate it.

I groan, resting my face in my hands. What is wrong with me? Where am I? What planet did I move to? Where are the honking cab drivers and the women running like Olympic sprinters in seven-inch heels to make their trains?

The trains. I never thought I'd miss the MTA. But I do. What the hell is BART and MUNI, and why can't San Francisco have one shared form of transportation instead of ten? And why do I need ten different forms of payment for every single one of them? San Franciscans have no idea how to commute.

Oh, and the passive aggressiveness is killing me. Before I moved out of New York I thought I'd cry if someone so much as said 'excuse me.' Now I'm dying slowly from politeness poisoning, and the unwillingness to fight or argue.

Nobody argues here. No one is loud and aggressive, screaming at pedestrians for walking into the street. They wait patiently as the unaware idiots step into the crosswalk with their faces pressed to their phones.

I look up at the tree canopy, praying to the nature gods or whatever hippy, tree-hugging force makes all this plant life thrive through California's drought.

"I just want someone to be a jerk to me. Is that so much to ask? I want a bagel boiled in the good water. I want real pizza. I want to go home."

Nobody answers. There's only silence and branches blowing in the wind. It's so serene I might go crazy. I stand, closing my eyes and covering my ears, the sound of gently rustling leaves building louder and louder in my head until it could combat rush hour traffic in Times Square.

"I don't want to be here. Why does this bullshit keep happening to me? What did I do to deserve this?"

I clench my fist against my stomach, holding back the nausea and fear; chills race down my spine. The trees answer me with tranquil rustling. To anyone else it would be calming, but to me it's the lock clicking closed on my prison cell. I'm not supposed to be here. I should be back in New York, engaged, living the perfect life I worked so hard to craft. The perfect, fake life that kept me from going fucking crazy like right—this—second.

The pressure builds until I'm panting and I can't take it anymore, and I kick the bench with all my might.

As my foot hits the wooden planks something cracks, and I'm only fifty percent sure it isn't my heart. I open my eyes. The bench leg I booted is now lying on the ground, the bench itself lopsided and tilted. The wooden slats are accusatory: *Why? Why have you done this? I was just an innocent bench, you crazy bitch.*

Oh God, what is wrong with me? I broke the quiet and thought-provoking bench that was probably donated by an old couple trying to get a tax break.

I go down on my knees, observing the damage, seeing if it can be fixed. Why does everything around me break?

Because I'm the one doing the breaking.

I feel burning behind my eyes. No. Not now. It cannot be a fucking broken old bench that makes me cry after years of tear drought. I see the bench, lying so stupidly on its side, and I want to bawl.

""I'm sorry. Oh, shit. I'm sorry," I sniffle, reining the tears in, forcing them back into the box I absolutely need to keep locked tight in order to stay sane.

"What the fuck is wrong with me?" I dig my fingers into my now-ruined tailored jeans, the knees covered in dirt. "What did this bench ever do to me? I am such a crazy bitch."

"I would never call a woman a bitch, but crazy? Yeah, that seems to fit here."

I don't need to look over my shoulder to see who it is, because who the hell else would it be? Life hates me and deems it neces-sary to humiliate me at every turn.

Sweaty sculpture man looks down at me with pity in his honey-pot eyes. His voice matches his expressive gaze, mellow and warm and smooth as syrup.

I pat beneath my lashes, relieved to find them dry, then stand to face him.

Yup, he's still sexy as sin, and with this new perspective I can appreciate it all up close. He's not only muscular, he's tall as well. He could be a linebacker with all those rippling divots and curves covering his body. He's added a tool belt to his dirt-covered ensemble, and it only serves to highlight the cut of his waist and hips.

"You wouldn't call a woman a bitch?" I ask, plastering a smile on my face, trying to divert his attention from how I was whim-pering on the ground...about a bench.

"Never."

He's so adamant that I have to challenge him.

"Not even if she cut you off on the road?"

He crosses his arms over his abundantly muscular chest and says matter-of-factly, "Road rage is for the repressed, and she most likely was late for her kid's recital or soccer game."

"Not even if she stole something out of your grocery cart, after you bought it?"

"She's probably hungry. I can't let someone go hungry. Maybe she's got low blood sugar."

"Not even if she hurt your mother?"

I think I've got him now, but he waves that one away, like it's the easiest come back he has. "My mama can take care of herself. Nobody messes with her."

He's won. I've got nothing left. The pretense is over. I have to confess I kicked state property. Maybe something in the useful-looking belt can fix the catastrophe I've caused.

"You wouldn't call a woman a bitch?" I ask again, stalling. "Ever?"

"Miss, not ever." He tilts his head, the closely shorn curls against his head shining as they dip into a beam of light. "Why is that so shocking to you?"

"Not even if she kicked a really old, probably important bench in a city park and broke it?"

I step aside to reveal the damaged bench. He observes it, his expression somber. I can tell he's concerned and focused because his obtrusively masculine jawline is so tight his chiseled features look like they might pop off his face.

He steps forward, and I skedaddle out of his way as quick as I can, not wanting to be within a certain distance of him. I don't know why, but I have this awful feeling if he comes near me, the carefully erected, fragile wall I've built around my heart might disintegrate. His presence is abrasive, unruly.

He glances at me as I move, but I can't decipher what's running through his mind. The jaw is still tense. He's probably thinking I'm nuts.

I was in the dirt apologizing to a bench.

He kneels and bends over, starting his inspection. I bite my bottom lip. Hard. I'm going to hell, but even the devil itself couldn't divert my gaze from his well-rounded ass. And still, nothing stirs in me. My appreciation is objective.

He pulls a wrench from the back of his tool belt and a screw from a side pouch, then sets to work. Barely a minute passes before he stands and says, "Done!" His smile is so bright and jarring I think I might go blind from the effervescent force.

"You fixed the bench." I point at it like an idiot. "How did you do that?"

"It was wobbling yesterday so I knew I'd need to work on it today. The screws come loose every now and then." He leans toward me, as if to whisper, and my body jerks back. When he sees my reaction he lifts his hands, placating. I'm acting ridiculous, like an abuse victim would react to a man coming near her. No. I'm not this person. I am not some wacko afraid of being near men for no damn reason.

He didn't marry me with a big lie hanging over my head. He didn't cheat on me. He's a nice guy, fixing a bench.

Stop being so weird, Gemma.

I ignore the wary feeling in my gut. We're about two feet away from each other now, and he's staring down at me with that grim expression again.

"What were you going to say?" I ask, smiling up at him openly.

See? I'm fine. I'm not some peculiar person who's developed a psychosis with men I find attractive. Nope.

He considers me for a moment, most likely trying to parse out what exactly my damage is. Kneeling next to me, he points at the bench's leg joints with a screwdriver. "Just that the bench is old, and I have to tighten the screws every now and then. Lillian told me she sent you here for contemplation, and I thought I should fix it before it crashed under you." He lowers his voice in a mock whisper. "She does this to all the new volunteers. Thinks she's playing a prank on them in hopes the bench will tip over while they're sitting on it."

My mother would have no shame in doing that.

"That can cause a lawsuit."

He smacks the screwdriver down on his palm. "Nobody would sue the garden."

"That's adorably naive of you."

He amends his statement with a searching glance. "Nobody with a heart would sue us."

I'm tempted to launch into a speech about how most people suck, and I've assisted on a million legal suits to prove it. But that might make me seem crazier than I already am. I don't want him to think I'm crazy.

Not that it matters what he thinks. He doesn't matter. Nothing matters.

He shifts on his heels and comes within less than a foot of my skin. Shouldn't I be feeling something? Should my skin be tingling at his proximity, and my body shifting with the awareness of his?

There's nothing. I'm completely numb.

"I'm glad the bench didn't break while I was sitting on it. I might have developed a complex about my weight."

He sits back on his heels, his tone flat and disbelieving. "Yeah, because kneeling on the ground and apologizing to an old bench is a much better outcome than a weight complex." He points at my dirty knees. "And you ruined your pants."

"You're a man; you wouldn't understand." I fruitlessly try to brush the dirt off.

He tilts his head again like an adorable, inquisitive puppy, and I don't know how it's possible because he's so rugged, and cute isn't a word I'd ever use to describe him.

"I wouldn't understand about weight problems?"

"Look at you." I gesture to the large amount of person next to me. "You probably eat like an elephant, run for an hour, then step out of the shower with another row of abs."

I stand, offering him a hand up. He takes it with a gracious nod. His hand is almost twice the size of mine. Dirt cakes the lines on his fingers, the granules scrape against my palm.

His grin grips my previously comatose libido and slaps it awake. The shock of it nearly shoves me onto my ass.

Whoa. That was definitely a feeling. One I want to avoid from now on.

For updates on Waking Wild's release, sign up for my newsletter

ACKNOWLEDGMENTS

Thank you to my amazing developmental editor Stacy Jerger, and my copy editor, Kiezha Ferrell. You both saved my bacon countless times and this book would not be what it is without you. A big thank you to Sofie Hartley for the epic cover as well.

Thank you to my first time betas, Deborah and Jurae, your critiques were invaluable.

This was my first self-published book and I could not have done it without my mom, who is also a writer, and who took my endless questions with endless patience. Thank you.

ABOUT THE AUTHOR

Ceri is the author of quirky and sexy contemporary romance novels. She has a major weakness for sappy cuddle moments as well as hot and steamy sex scenes, and a penchant for writing sarcastic dialogue. She loves romance that isn't afraid to be awkward and uncouth, and thrives on flawed characters with big hearts.

A New York native, Ceri now lives in California with her two cats, Mercy and Eugene Fitzherbert, who should be very thankful she didn't name him frying pan. She is a proud functioning introvert and lover of all things geeky. You can find her haunting the Twitter machine or posting pictures of her ridiculous cats on Instagram.

Want exclusive content, bonus scenes, and more?
Sign up for my newsletter.

I can't stop fantasizing about my neighbor.

Ben is tall—like, *really* tall. His beautiful eyes and lickable skin have me hypnotized. And don't even get me started on his dimple. It's as if he was made to drive me crazy.

The walls are thin. Paper-thin. Accidentally-on-purpose-overhearing-him-having-great-sex thin.

I've got it bad enough on a regular day, but this heat has me crawling out of my skin, restless and desperate. My hormone-fueled, vibrator-assisted fantasies aren't exactly helping me cope.

And now he's at my door.

Things are about to get sticky.

A Different Kind of Perfect

Colton Evans loves both men and women but never thought his family would approve of his long kept secret. After falling head over heels in love with Bleu Leroux and Alexis Mirskii, he's finally forced to confront his fear of coming out to his police officer father.

Alexis Mirskii overcame years of abuse at his father's hands, eventually becoming a successful chef. It wasn't until meeting Colton and Bleu that he found something was missing. Even if that something meant falling in love with a woman and a man after considering himself straight his entire life.

Bleu Leroux, a former troubled teen and drug addict, has always struggled with her past and never thought it possible to find someone who could accept her, let alone two someones.

A night of tragedy began the trio's journey toward love ten years before ever meeting. But can they put aside the complications of their pasts to create a future together?

COPYRIGHT

Sweet Disaster

Stupid Awesome Love Book 1

ISBN-13: 978-0-9998441-1-3

Published by Ceri Grenelle

www.cerigrenelle.com

Cover Design by Hart & Bailey Design Co.